ABANDONED

ABANDONED

An Anthology of Vacant Spaces

Legion of Dorks presents

Edited by

L.R. BRIDGWATER

Edited by

KELLY LYNN COLBY

Cursed Dragon Ship
PUBLISHING

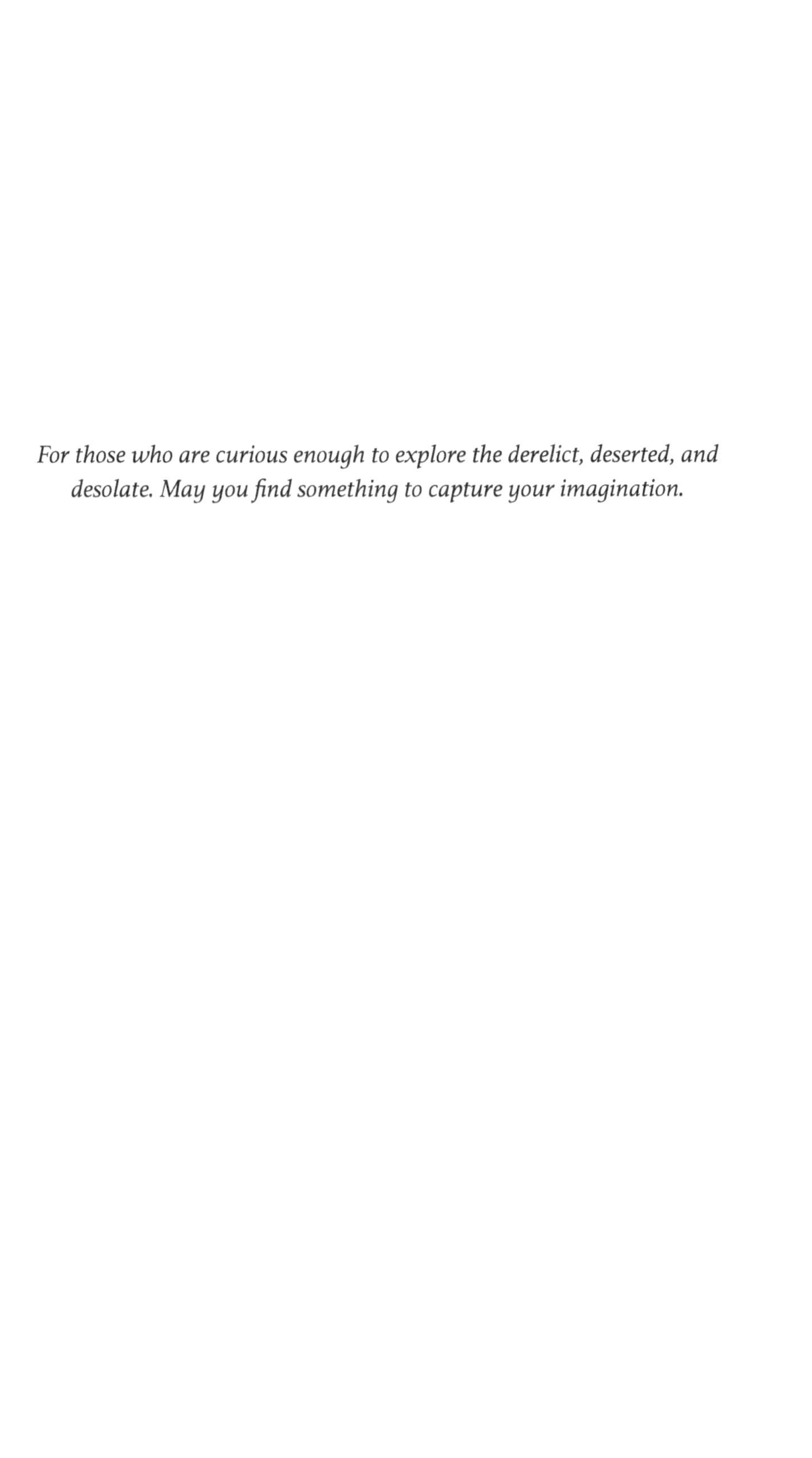

For those who are curious enough to explore the derelict, deserted, and desolate. May you find something to capture your imagination.

Contents

Hall of Abandoned Things

JEN BAIR

Lavella found the Shop of Trinkets and Oddities easily enough, though the glass in the shop front window didn't look promising. Grime gummed up the corners and a crack spider-webbed from one side.

She had walked halfway across the city. The hanging sign said it was open. She would at least try the door. She took a steadying breath and pushed in through the heavy wooden door, its emerald-green paint in far better condition than the window.

The smell of musty books and oiled cloth put a taste in her mouth like degraded leather. If she'd wanted to chew on a saddle, she would have visited a farm, but instead she had taken her heavy heart and even heavier coin purse to this one last hope.

A slender bookshelf stood waist high in the entryway with a blue, leather-bound book propped open on top. *The Azure Pot* was written in gold lettering above an embossed drawing of a lidded pitcher covered in intricate glyphs. The book was askew and dusty streak marks showed it had been moved long after the last good cleaning the shelves had seen.

Someone had been in here. It likely wasn't the shopkeeper, since he would have cleaned his shelves. Perhaps a customer who no doubt went away empty-handed?

Lavella closed the door harder than necessary, hoping to catch the attention of anyone within earshot, but she got no response. It didn't take long to search the entire ground floor and confirm the shop was empty of personnel, though it was full of strange objects: an array of hair tufts neatly bundled in a row, a painting of an infant's head with hairy spider legs sprouting from its many misplaced eyes, and a set of scales that were out of balance.

None of that would help her. She needed the shopkeeper. As a last resort, she took to the stairs at the back of the shop, calling out "Hello" as the stairs protested her passing.

The upstairs floor held two rooms. One had a desk and a floor-to-ceiling bookshelf, full to bursting with stacks of books laid on their sides in front of those lined neatly on the shelves. The second door was locked.

She knocked, hoping the shop owner hadn't died in his sleep some time ago. She received no answer. She hadn't expected one.

Thoroughly disappointed, she rested her forehead on the door, stared down at her shoes, and considered her next step. Her arm itched where she had last put the needle to her skin. The pain it brought echoed the pain in her heart. It somehow made her feel less alone, made the pain more bearable. Her father had said time would heal her broken heart. It had been nearly a month since Jonathan, her light in the darkness, had died. Her suffering only seemed to grow worse. Every day in a million ways she was reminded of him.

She needed something to forget. The shopkeeper was the only person who could possibly help her. Well, short of the permanent cure a sharp blade would offer.

She swallowed hard. Jonathan wouldn't want her to hurt herself. The needle was the best compromise she could come up with, unless the shopkeeper could help.

It seemed he was long gone, though, the shop abandoned. She kicked the door with her foot and heard a small scrape at its base. She bent to see a glint of metal poking out from under the lip of the door. A brass key. Had someone slid it there just now or had it been there before she arrived? She wasn't sure.

It was a bad idea to use the key, she knew. Walking through an open store was one thing, but unlocking doors was another. Still, she couldn't just leave. Before she could second-guess herself, she inserted the key and turned it.

There wasn't a snick of the lock opening, no turning of the door handle or opening of the door. At least, not that she remembered. The door was simply open and a man stood a few feet away, tall and devilish in a dark suit. He must have heard the door because he turned to smile at her, all blinding white teeth, smooth skin, and thick, dark hair. He was ageless and dashing with charm oozing out of him like juice from a grape. For a brief moment, Lavella forgot why she was there.

"I'm glad you made it," he said in a voice so compelling, so distractingly absorptive that she grew dizzy before she realized she'd forgotten to breathe. He steepled his fingers, propping his chin at their tip, and his face looked like an angel atop a church.

"I'm...you're...what?" she mumbled, her words falling from her mouth like half-eaten oatmeal.

His smile widened and some deep, primal part of her brain kicked up a distant, drunken ruckus, telling her to run to him and to run *from* him at the same time. That last part was far too easy to ignore with her attention captivated by his presence as it was.

His words were casual. "I have something I need from you quite desperately." She imagined desperate needs were discussed quite frequently in his presence. "And I have a feeling you are just the one to fulfill this particular task."

The urge to run away stumbled its way forward. Her primal ape brain finally caught her attention, or perhaps it was the oily feeling that seeped through her when she spotted the predatory gleam in his eye. She stepped back, seeking to retreat through the doorway, only it wasn't there.

When her hand passed through the air, a glance told her there was no door. No doorway. No key. In fact, there wasn't anything there at all. No empty space, no swirling black vortex. Simply nothing.

Terror surged through her at the disconcerting detour from reality. Instinctively, she widened her stance and held her arms out as if she could catch herself from falling, though catch herself on what, she wasn't sure. Was she falling? She had no means to orient herself, so she couldn't tell and that was more terrifying than anything else.

The man was her only point of reference, so she turned back to him, her breath quick. Staring at the point where his polished black shoes hovered in the air, a faded vision of a floor was visible. A ghost floor, made of wood or marble or sand, she couldn't tell. It only existed where his shoes met the ground and a finger's width in each direction besides.

The man spoke. Lavella was focused on not falling over in the nowhere and it was all she could do to listen to his words.

"There is an item I need. An artifact. You will retrieve it for me, and I will set you free. Simple, yes?"

Her head bobbled in a gesture he must have taken for refusal.

"Come, now." He took a step forward, the ghost floor moving with him. "I'll tell you what. I'll throw in the shopkeeper. You can keep him if you find the artifact before the third bell."

With a sound like a bullfrog being trod on, Lavella found her voice. "I don't want him anymore. And I don't want to help you." She wanted to say more, but her throat clinched up tight in fear and her words failed her.

"That's unfortunate for you, then, Lav," he said and it sounded like "Love," the endearment like a caress coming from those sweet, treacherous lips, "because I don't want him either. It's against the rules to kill him, and so he has become an unwanted pet who fails to amuse me." Even talk of murder sounded like a symphony in that voice.

"Who are you?" she croaked. "*What* are you?" It was plain he wasn't human, though he looked the part well enough.

"Djinn. Genie. Granter of wishes," he said with a wave of his hand, "though I've been called demon. And angel. God, even. But genie is close enough."

"If you're a genie, then I wish to be out of here, back to my life." The wobble in her words turned her demand into something less than intimidating.

The genie heaved a theatrical sigh. "Alas, dear Lav, you did not rub my lamp." The words were stated plainly, yet they felt lascivious to her.

Rub my lamp. Was there a lamp? Had she missed it? Lavella knew better than to look around, searching the nothingness. It wasn't as if the lamp would simply be floating next to her. If it had existed in the room before everything disappeared, it was there no longer.

"Where is your lamp?"

"Gone. I have left it behind, battered as it was. I seek a new home. Find me one and you may get your wish."

"And if I don't?"

He laughed, the sound like butter sizzling in a pan, all caramel warmth and sinful goodness. "Then you remain my pet, just as the shopkeeper has."

Closing her eyes in thought brought out near-instant hysteria. The world swirled dizzily and she let out a squawk, her eyes flying open, her breath coming in ragged pants. "Fine. I'll do it. I'll find your artifact. Where do I look?"

"You're a human from the mortal realm. You'll know when you see it. Search the Hall of Abandoned Things. Don't fail me, Lav." As he spoke his warning, the genie faded while the ghost ground solidified, spreading out from his shoes to form a stone floor of swirled red. In a moment, the man was gone and a room had materialized.

She stood in a vast, pillared chamber, like a throne room of some ancient god. The room was a mess, piles of treasure alongside shelves of junk: tattered cloth, sparkling jewels, rusty pots, and towering jade statues. There was no rhyme or reason to the layout, just piles and piles of infinite wonder and worthless refuse and everything in between.

Somewhere in the chaos was an artifact and she had to find it. The thought was overwhelming.

A distant *thunk* drew her attention. The room echoed terribly, but she thought she heard muttering. She followed the sound, though no matter which way she circled the various piles of items, she couldn't find the source of the noise. Eventually, it died down and all was silent.

"Hello?" she called out. Several heartbeats passed and she was about to call out again when she heard the distinct sound of chair legs scraping along the stone floor. A moment later, an elderly man long overdue for a haircut poked his head out from behind a distant pile.

"Oh!" he gasped, in delight or alarm, Lavella wasn't sure. "Don't!" he yelled, covering half the distance to her, arms flailing madly, before making the slightest semblance of sense. "Don't agree to anything! Not a thing. You mustn't agree to anything he says."

When he reached her, she couldn't help but step back in alarm at his wide-eyed look of distress. He grabbed her arm as if to keep her from running off.

"You didn't agree to anything, did you? He's a devil, I tell you. Don't make any deals with him."

"With who?" she said, though the genie was the only man he could have been speaking of. She thought it best not to upset the old man further and gathered her thoughts for a proper conversation. "You're the shopkeeper, aren't you?" she said, hoping to derail the conversation and calm him.

He was having none of it. "Did you make a deal with him? With the djinn?" He shook her arm.

"I..." Her mouth worked silently for a moment before admitting, "I did."

"You *fool*. How could you do something so idiotic? Don't you know that's the way to certain doom?"

Lavella had her own doubts about finding the artifact and getting back home, but she was clear on one thing. "I didn't have any choice. It was agree to his terms or stay in that place of nothingness forever." A shudder ran through her so violently it wrenched her arm free of his grasp.

The old man threw his hands up. "Well, now we're both stuck here. Does *that* make you happy, fool girl? Much better off, eh?"

She was willing to bet the only reason he was here was because he had made a similar deal with the genie, but it wouldn't help to point that out, so she chose the diplomatic route. "As I said, I didn't see any other choice. Would you like to continue scolding me or shall we put our heads together and see if we can find a way out of this mess?"

Her words came out tart, but they seemed to do the trick because after a moment of gawking at her, the old man closed his mouth and gave one final harrumph. They stood there in silence, both of them breathing hard after the confrontation.

"You are the shopkeeper, aren't you?" she asked once they had calmed themselves.

"Of course I'm the shopkeeper. That blasted djinn has taken up residence in my bedroom, which means *you* were at the shop when he caught you." He turned to give her a squinty-eyed glare. "That means you were in my bedroom, yes?"

A flush worked its way up from Lavella's neckline. "Never mind that. You've been looking for the artifact the genie wants?"

He continued his glare for a moment before relenting. "Yes. I've been working through the books on the far shelf. This room is a maze. Took most of a day just to find my way around." He turned and headed back in the direction he had come from and she dutifully followed on his heels. "Mothballs, torn pages," he muttered. "What a disaster. An earthquake might do this place a favor. Can you read?"

The question came abruptly and Lavella stammered out her reply. "Yes, of course."

"You never know with young folk these days." He circled around a pile of items mounded up against the back of a bookshelf and she stepped over a rusty goblet as she followed him. "The whole lot needs dropped in a sinkhole if you ask me."

The lot of young folk or the lot of items? She wasn't sure.

Around the next pile sat a wooden desk longer than she was tall and covered in a stack of books nearly as tall as her head. "What can you tell me about the artifact? Do you know what we're searching for?"

"Let's see here," he said, grabbing a book on one end of the desk and passing it to her. The title was too worn to read. "It's been called Culcotta's Palace. Seems to be only one of many names, but I haven't found anything to confirm that." The old man gestured at the book towers scattered around the desk. "I started out searching for anything castle-shaped, but nothing turned up, so I started reading these. What'd you say your name was?" He had a habit of throwing questions out like punctuation marks.

"Lavella."

"I'm Burnith."

"That's an interesting name."

"As my wife always said, my rage Burnith within me." He barked out a laugh before stretching his back and sitting in his chair.

She pictured him with a wife, the two of them laughing together in their old age. It reminded her of Jonathan and the blissful future that had been snatched from her, along with her happiness.

She yearned for a needle.

Burnith scooted his chair to the desk. The legs screeched as they slid across the stone, drawing her from her thoughts. "Pull up a seat if you can find a chair light enough to heave over here."

She pushed down her pain and cast her eyes around, but didn't see any chairs in the immediate vicinity, so she wandered off a ways, making sure to track where Burnith's desk was so she didn't get lost.

The room was a wonder of interesting and disturbing things. She saw a hideously desiccated corpse lying on its side, limbs huddled in on itself, skin-like covering pulled waxy and tight. A locket lay near its neck, as if it had fallen off, but it was far too shiny to be so old and it was coated in far less dust than the mummified remains. They weren't the only remains she stumbled across. Three more bodies were sprawled on the ground, though more skeletal and less mummified than the first.

The hall was a wonder of curiosities and wealth: chaise lounge chairs covered in tatters of green or blue silk, books with gilded edges with titles written in languages she'd never seen, jewel-encrusted eggs, the jawbone of an animal coated in a reddish-amber substance, tiny figures made of gold, scepters, rocks with intricate carvings, and things she couldn't identify.

Any piles devoid of rotting corpses had her picking through them out of curiosity. Eventually, a chiming pealed through the chamber from a far distant corner, reminding her of the genie's condition: find the artifact before the third bell. She headed back to where Burnith sat squinting at his book. He looked up at her approach.

"Find a chair yet?"

"I seem to be finding everything but a chair. Why are there so many bodies in here?"

He shrugged, still squinting at his text. "Genie's previous artifact hunters?"

"I should hope not," she said. Some of those bodies had been around for a very long time. "Burnith, the genie said if I could find the artifact before the third bell, you would be released with me. I just heard—"

"With you? What happens if we find it after that? He told me the same thing, but I figured if he wants it and I find it, he'd be willing to wager my release over it." His voice grew quiet and only the echo of the room allowed her to hear his next words. "That's the only thing that's kept me going."

Lavella stood silently for an awkward moment, not sure of what to say. "Well," she said hesitantly, "we've still got a chance, so don't give up yet. That bell I just heard must have been the first ring, so we still have—"

"Second," he said.

"What?"

"That was the second bell. First one was not too long after you wandered off. You went to find a chair near four hours ago if my watch is still working right."

"No, you must be wrong. Surely I haven't been wandering for that long."

"Time does funny things here."

She had only just arrived, so she wasn't confident enough to argue with him. Instead, she said, "I didn't hear a bell ring until just now."

"You not hearing it doesn't unring it."

She supposed that was true. The odd nature of the items filling the room must have distracted her enough she hadn't heard it. That meant they didn't have long before the next bell rang. "How long between chimes?"

"About three hours."

Three hours. That was all she had before she was stuck in here, possibly until long after she died and her body became a dried out husk or a pile of loose bones. How horrid.

Or was it?

The needle had done a poor job of masking her pain. She had considered ending her torment. But, then, that was why she had come in search of the shopkeeper. She hadn't been willing to give up just yet. "Don't you have anything to go off of? You've been here for a while now, haven't you?"

"Nearly a month, I think."

"There, see? You probably know right where it is, you just didn't realize what it was. Think hard now. What clues have you come across so far."

He looked at her with dazed, owlish eyes, blinking slowly as he thought.

Lavella's own thoughts pondered how he had survived in the hall for a full month. There were no signs of food. Had he slept? Perhaps time was different here, after all.

Burnith replied, "Not much of anything in the way of clues, really. The djinn wasn't exactly forthcoming. I know some names it goes by, though. Culcotta's Palace, the Emperor's Mansion, the Blue Boat—"

"The Blue Boat," she said. "What kind of name is that? It doesn't match the others. Did you look for a boat?" Mention of the genie made her stomach do a flip. If she stayed here, how long would she last, waiting for that wretched, beautiful man to return? Ending the pain was one thing, but replacing it with terror at the thought of visiting that place that was not a place was no option at all.

"I looked at every blue object in this entire room, or just about. None of them look anything like a boat or a palace or even a little bit house-like. I'm telling you, I don't think it's in here at all."

It was a strange dual feeling to both want to die and want to live. Currently, the desire to live long enough to get out from under the genie's reach was almost overwhelming. She wrung her hands, wanting for all the world to wave her arms in the air and yell at Burnith to *think,* but she would look just as crazy as he had when she first saw him.

Her emotions were all over the place. She sat on the floor and wrapped her arms around her legs, pulling them in tight to her chest, trying to contain the flood of warring feelings. A laugh escaped her. "If I came in your shop and you told me you had a genie, I would have begged you to let me meet him. He would have sounded like the answer to everything."

Burnith let out a long sigh. "I get a lot of people coming in the shop looking for miracles. Most of them leave disappointed. I don't have anything to make a person rich or beautiful or make someone fall in love with them. If I had that sort of thing, I wouldn't be running a trinket shop." He leaned back and scratched at his frazzled gray hair. "People don't think of that, though. Not when they're desperate for something."

They sat in silence for a moment and Lavella's overwhelming feelings calmed a bit.

"What is it you were hoping I could do for you?" Burnith asked, his voice taking on a compassionate tone.

She gave him a rueful smile. "It won't matter unless we get out of here. And if we don't, I suppose I'll have my miracle either way." She had been too worried about finding the artifact and what would happen if her time ran out to feel the ache in her heart. "I suppose 'Be careful what you wish for' is a lesson I won't soon forget."

She pushed her way to her feet. "Let's keep looking. Our time isn't up yet."

Burnith closed his book. "I suppose it won't hurt to wander the room until the next bell. The books are slow going." He arched his back, pressing in on it with his knuckles. "If I recall correctly, I stopped digging through the piles back that way," he said, pointing at the nearest pillar. She followed him through the room until he reached a big pile next to a smaller one.

"I figured the fastest way to get through all the items was to move everything from one pile to the next." He climbed onto the bigger pile and started tossing things one by one into the smaller pile, pausing to inspect anything blue.

Lavella worked on the next pile over and soon the small pile was heaped with items, growing until it rivaled their bigger piles. It was long, slow work, even with her throwing anything that didn't fit the name off as quickly as she could. Some of the items were heavy and she had to push or drag them off the pile. Soon she was sweating profusely and had to pause to catch her breath.

As the hours passed, she noticed her weariness didn't seem to grow with the passing of time. If she took a minute to rest, then as soon as her heart rate slowed, she felt like she hadn't worked all day. It was a strange, incongruous feeling. She hadn't eaten in hours, and her labor didn't make her hungry or weary. It was easier to estimate time by tracking the quantity of items moved rather than an ache in her back, like she often did when she was gardening. Not that she had gardened since she had lost the person she loved to share its beauty with.

"How long before the next bell?" she asked.

Burnith looked at his watch, tapped the face of it a few times, then announced, "Twenty minutes? Maybe thirty?"

She looked around in despair. Together, they had sifted through almost four piles, but there were hundreds of them remaining. Burnith had gone through almost half the hall in his first few weeks, but he admitted he had been lax about looking at every object as the time wore on, so there was every chance he may have missed it and there was still half the room that hadn't been searched. They weren't going to find it in time.

"How many references did you find in the books?" she asked.

Burnith picked up a long, curved stick made of wood, sanded smooth and decorated with colored stripes at one end. He tossed it onto the discard pile. "Four in total," he said.

"How did you know those were references to the artifact we're looking for?"

He paused to stretch his back, something he'd been doing more often as they dug. "Well, he said he's looking for a new home, a mansion fit for an emperor. First reference I found called it the Emperor's Mansion and said it was also known as Culcotta's Palace."

"What else did it say about it?"

"Not much. Just that it was priceless and timeless. Something about being a miraculous creation, beyond mortal comprehension," he waved his hand dismissively, "that sort of thing. Nothing useful."

"And the Blue Boat? Where did you see it called that?"

He climbed down from his pile and she climbed down to meet him. "That was in an old book, falling apart at the seams. The page was worn and faded. Could barely read it." He scratched absently at his side. "I'll show you."

She followed him back to the desk. He passed it and located a book on a shelf two piles away. He flipped through it gently before holding it out to her, pointing to a word that looked like Culcotta, though it was written by hand in faded ink with a swirling font that was hard to decipher. Blue Boat. She saw the title in capital letters a few words farther down the line.

"I'm not sure this says Blue Boat. It looks more like Blue Bot."

Burnith snorted. "I thought that, too, but Blue Bot doesn't make any sense at all. That extra swirl makes me think it says boat."

But Lavella wasn't listening to him. She was staring hard at the letters, following the swirls to see if they could be deciphered to read 'pot' instead of 'boat.' If the swirl at the bottom was decorative instead of part of a letter…

"Blue Pot," she said. "Does it say 'Blue Pot'?" She shoved the book at him, pointing at the word. "Does it?"

"Well, give me a minute to look at it," he said, shooing her hand away. He stared at it for an interminably long time. "That's a possibility." He nodded. "At least as likely as a Blue Boat, though I haven't seen a blue pot, either."

Unable to contain her excitement, she let out a squeal that startled him enough to drop the book. "It might not be a blue pot."

He stared at her like she'd grown a second head. "You just told me the book said Blue Pot. Now you're saying it's not a pot?"

She shook her head, holding her hands up to stave off his objections. "It's a blue jug. A pitcher, really. With a lid on it. Have you seen anything like it? Covered in strange writing and with a long skinny handle that's kind of swirly?"

He got that far off look in his eyes again and she wanted to slap him to hurry him along. "I might have seen something like that," he said slowly.

She flapped her hands. "We don't have much time. Where? Where did you see it?"

"If it's what I'm thinking, it's over this way." She followed so close on his heels that he started taking shorter steps, almost jogging by the time they arrived at the far corner of the hall. "It was somewhere around here," he said, pointing at a general batch of three piles.

It would take an hour to go through everything, but now that they both knew what they were looking for, sorting would go much faster. She clambered onto the nearest pile, throwing things left and right.

Burnith started in on the pile next to hers. "How do you know what we're looking for all of a sudden?"

"*The Azure Pot*," she said simply.

"Well, I know we're looking for an azure pot, but how do you know what it looks like?"

"No, *The Azure Pot*," she said, putting emphasis on the title.

"Is there an echo in here?"

"It's the book just inside your front door. It's on display there with a picture of the pitcher drawn on the front."

"Really?"

"Yes. Didn't you put it there?" She was breathing hard, but didn't slow. She was too scared to ask how much time they had left. He didn't seem to know the minute the bell was supposed to go off, anyway.

"No, that would be Mackille. He would come in once a week and unbox anything new that came in and figure out where to shelve it. He must have put that one up after I disappeared. I half expected him to show up in here one of these days when he came looking for me."

"Your bedroom door was locked. He probably did come looking for you."

"I haven't paid him for a while. I hope he's found a good, stable job somewhere else."

"I think he has. Your shop was pretty dusty when I came in."

"I hate dusting that place. Moving everything to wipe off shelves takes forever. My wife used to do the dusting, bless her heart. She knew how much I hated it."

"Where's your wife now?"

Burnith paused. "Local cemetery."

Lavella's motions slowed, the pain squeezing her heart so intensely she couldn't breathe. But it passed and she blinked her eyes. "I'm sorry."

He nodded, using his feet to nudge a statue until it tumbled down the pile. They worked in silence.

The next time she slowed to catch her breath, she asked, "How long ago?"

He answered as if they had never paused their conversation. "Six years. Sickness. Doctors couldn't do anything for her."

"I'm sorry," she said again. Then, "Does it get any easier?"

"Missing her?"

Lavella nodded.

"No. There's no getting over it when someone you love dies. There's a hole there, and it doesn't grow back. Not ever."

Lavella tried to pick up a stone shaped like a knee-high cow, but it was too heavy and she ended up half-sprawled on it, her elbow knocking into the cow's head on her way down. She waited for the pain to fade. "How do you deal with it? How do you keep going when your soul is bleeding?" Her voice was raw.

He gave her a small smile. "You find any way you can to slow the bleeding. Clot the wound until it scabs. Some days that scab gets ripped clean off, and the pain comes fresh and hot. Other days it just aches and aches until you can't stand it."

Lavella inhaled a ragged breath, unable to hold back the tears. "I feel like I've been abandoned. Maybe this should be my home." She gestured to the hall around them. "A place for abandoned things." It felt like nothing could be so symbolically accurate for her.

"Oh, come now," Burnith soothed. "You deserve better than this place, no matter how you're feeling at the moment. I don't know who you lost, but I'll bet they'd feel the same way."

"My dearest friend. The knower of my soul. He was my lighthouse in the darkness. And now he's gone." Her words failed her.

Burnith was quiet, leaving her to her grief. When her tears quieted, he said, "It pains me to think like that. My wife and I shared the best years of our lives together. She knew me like nobody else on this Earth. Even though she's gone, she's still here in ways. She lives on in my memory. In the ways I've changed by knowing her."

Lavella nodded. He was right. She still had her memories, though holding each one of them was like holding a knife by the blade. They hurt too much to feel like a blessing. "I can't." It was all she could say, the only words to express how she was feeling. She couldn't stand to think of him, to know she would never see him again—or talk to him. She couldn't bear to face the world without his comforting presence.

"I know." And it sounded like he did. Something in the way he said those words told her he felt the same. Life was too much for him to bear, yet he kept on living. She didn't think she was that brave, that she could fight that hard to keep her broken heart beating.

"How do you keep going?" She had already asked him in a philosophical way, but this time it was for him alone.

He stood, kicking gently at a few trinkets. "It helps to stay busy."

That was true. She'd been plenty busy since arriving in this godsforsaken room, but she'd been distracted enough not to want to search for a needle. It was better than she'd been since he died.

"And it helps to have someone who understands." He made his way down his pile, coins and rocks sliding on cloth and skittering to the bottom. She was closer to the bottom of her own pile and made her way over to steady him.

She put her hand on his arm. For being old and gray, his arms were lean with muscle from weeks of digging through piles. "I'm glad I met you, Burnith."

He smiled. "I hired Mackille partly because I needed company. The shop gets lonely in between customers." He looked around, his eyes panning across the vast expanse of the room.

It must have been lonely in here all these weeks. She could see the bags under his eyes and the stoop of his shoulders. She had chalked it up to old age, but now she wondered how much of it was the burden of his loss weighing him down.

"It turns out company is a pretty good balm for a wounded soul," he said. Their eyes met and she could see the depth of his loss in them. He must have seen the depth of hers, as well, because they both cast their eyes down at the floor. She spotted the lip of a long, skinny handle peeking out from under a sage cloth.

It was blue.

Lavella felt his shoulder stiffen when she let out a gasp of wonder. She dared not uncover the item because she feared she was wrong. That it would be some other object.

Burnith must have felt the same because he asked, "What's wro —" then paused. They stared at it until they were interrupted by the peal of a bell echoing through the room.

She moved before she was aware of what she was doing and bent to move the cloth. "Genie, I have your artifact!"

Her fingers closed around the handle of the azure pot. It looked just like the image on the cover of the book.

As the sound of the bell faded, echoing into the distance, the room disappeared.

For a terrifying moment, the world ceased to exist. Burnith was gone, the artifact was gone, her hands were empty, and she was utterly alone.

Was she dead? Staying in that infinite emptiness sent panic coursing through her and she opened her mouth to scream, but the sound echoed endlessly into oblivion, swallowed by the nothingness that made her feel more alone than ever. When the echo faded, she heard a low, sultry chuckle from behind her.

She tried to spin around to face the sound, but she had no leverage. Instead, she was forced to wait as the genie stalked into her line of sight, his polished black shoes once again hinting at an invisible floor. He held the blue jug in his hands and wore a triumphant, almost crazed grin.

"You found it, Lav. I'm impressed." His voice, still velvety smooth, had a coarseness to it, like burnt bacon being scraped from a pan.

"Where's Burnith?" she demanded, surprised by her forceful tone.

"My lamp has known your touch," he said, the words suggestive, though they felt oily to her. "What is your wish?"

Though she had a wish, she knew better than to waste it on the likes of him. "I wish nothing of you," she said, "but I demand payment as it was offered to me. Where is the shopkeeper?"

The genie's eyes hardened, a contrast to the smile stretching his lips. "I thought you said you didn't want him?"

"And you made it clear that what I wanted didn't matter. Without him, I wouldn't have found your lamp. Set us free." She stared him down, refusing to flinch before the anger she saw brewing there. "Both of us."

His greasy smile slid from his face, replaced with a sour look that further sullied his dashing appearance. She found his false presentation transparent now that she was no longer blinded by reckless hope.

"You're no fun at all," he said. She flinched when he snapped his fingers angrily at her. He disappeared and she was left in the emptiness. She stayed very still to avoid the feeling of vertigo that movement brought.

Had she angered the genie with her boldness? No doubt. Would he leave her here to go mad? Just as she was about to call out, the world winked into existence, and she found herself back in the Shop of Trinkets and Oddities.

Burnith stood a few feet away, farther than they had been in the hall. He was half-crouched with a wild-eyed look that told her he had returned through the nothingness, as well.

He clutched at his chest, pressing on it as if trying to keep his heart inside his body. The panic that was still coursing through her had her leaping to action, latching onto him as he wobbled, stumbling back a step.

One bony hand clutched her shoulder, shaking with pain or panic, she wasn't sure.

"Burnith? Are you okay?"

He took several shallow breaths before nodding slowly. His breath evened and he eventually stood upright, no longer clutching at his chest. "I'm getting too old to run this shop. I've seen some weird times in my days, but I am definitely too old for this crap."

She chuckled, almost manic with relief. Burnith scowled at her, but that only made her laugh harder. He ignored her.

"You're right about the state of the shelves," he said, shaking his head. "You aren't looking for a job, are you?"

Her laughter abated as she looked around the store. "Not really. I came here looking for a miracle." She thought of the pain she'd seen in his eyes. The pain that mirrored her own. "But I think a little company might be a good substitute."

Jen Bair is an Air Force brat, Army veteran, and military wife. She loves traveling with her family to foreign places, real or imaginary, whenever she can. Her family is her life. Her writing is her passion. You can find her published works at http://jenbair.com.

A Silent Sphinx

MIKE ADAMSON

The mineral rights to Tamiko-7462 were almost as attractive as the prospect of terraforming, but the Colonial Surveyor-General was adamant no leases would be granted before the future of the planet, well out on the Orion Arm frontier, was better understood. Such an attitude, while ethically laudable, bred cowboy operations overnight, and the CSG had limited resources to police who had the right to be prospecting on Tamiko and who did not.

So, Jarred Chambers thought, it was just bad luck he had been picked up by CSG agents while extracting core samples from the Tamikan desert. He was an adventurer, ex-military, a skillset-for-hire, and he was here for the money: many would pay handsomely to know what was beneath the sands of Tamiko. The CSG's planet-side security were sick of fencing with the kind of cowboys who flew in to take quick readings, and had begun to play hardball—nobody wanted to fall into their hands out here, where the law was whatever they said it was.

And it was doubly bad luck, he thought, for the shuttle he had stolen to escape from them to go into engine failure thirty minutes into his flight.

If not for bad luck, you'd have none at all, he thought, as he gritted his teeth and fought the controls of the bucking craft, scanning the data displays for what could possibly be sucking the life from the ship. Instruments were wild, visibility fading as he plunged into fine silicate dust clouds, and crazy readings flashed up of mother-lodes, strange and exotic ores, gone again moments later as if the world about him were in radical flux. He caught a confused impression of passing through some off-the-charts electromagnetic anomaly, then the ship seemed to pick up a little, power returned to the engines and he regained longitudinal control. Too late—the slick hull sliced into the sands, slithered in a bone-jarring deceleration through stone and dust that slammed him forward in the straps, and the ship at last came to rest, nose buried in muck racing up over the canopy.

Godsdammit, Chambers cursed silently as he panted, running gloves up over his shoulders to examine his body for damage. Was anything dislocated? After a few moments he rested back, the straps retracting automatically, and checked his suit seals. He was okay, everything read in the green, which was more than he could say for the shuttle. Red lights scattered the boards and the holodisplays were out, screens down. He twisted in the pilot seat and checked the system status board, found engines dead, power failing, and knew he had a choice—send up a signal drone, which would vector CSG to him, to take him right back into their unamused custody, or trust to his suit's endurance for him to find something better before surrender became his only option.

The ship gave a lurch and he realized she was on unstable ground. Convulsively, he threw off the harness and switched the life support couples to his backpack, to climb out of the seat and feed himself to the hatch at the flank hull. The vision port was still clear and he saw the abrasive desert of Tamiko stretch on, dun, ochre and orange, into the flowing pinkish grit-haze, and shook his head.

Tamiko did not support life. The warm colors were deceptive, the temperature was almost low enough for ice to form, if there had been any water here. Gravity was 1.02 Earth-norm, atmospheric pressure presently 878mB, rotational period 23 hours 29 minutes, and it had a decent magnetosphere. These factors alone made the planet a prime target for terraforming—in every other way it was more like Mars.

Cowboys take cowboy chances, he thought grimly, knowing his promised payday from the Lodestar Mining Consortium was looking more remote by the minute. All he had to do was get in, perform a rapid survey to give them some idea of potential yields, and get out with the data, then they would know how hard to lobby in the face of the even-playing-field the CSG maintained. He was due a million credits for his services, and tax would never be payable on that sort of income, but his chances of recovering the data and finding a way off this hellhole were not looking good.

The ship could go under, submerging in some fine talc-like deposit, and probably never be found. He would die when life support expired. He could crack the hatch and step out, and, assuming he also did not disappear into the vampire-sands, he was back to the same equation. Air to breathe and *free* air may, in the end, be very different things. The shuttle shuddered again and settled, and he shook his head. *The hell with this, I'll take my chances*, he thought, braced himself, and disarmed the hatch for opening.

When the slab swung upward on its hydraulic arm, the wind swirled dust inside and tugged at his suit like a tormenting devil. He heaved out, felt his boots make contact with the grit, and sealed the ship behind him, to step away from its protective lee. This world was very primal, he admitted to himself, as he stood in the midst of the storm and felt its power.

With a locator fix between his suit CPU and the shuttle systems showing him the way back, should he wish it, Chambers strode into the storm, realizing the wind had begun to bury his feet in the minutes he had lingered. He had a slim idea of where he was going, what he was seeking—he could not be more than forty kilometers or so from his own ship, snugged down in the wastes and locked out by the CSG people. If he could somehow get to her, he could trick his way aboard, and then get off this dirt-ball. He may not collect his million, but he would be alive *and* at liberty.

But nothing could have prepared him for the sight that greeted him as he crested a dune rise a few hundred meters from the shuttle, and looked down on a valley in the rolling gravel and dirt, where the wind shifted dust in waves like froth across the sea. He fell to his knees in astonishment, raised a hand to protect his faceplate from the gale-driven grit, and stared at vast, curved ribs and spars emerging from the murk. Day was fading fast, the sun a golden ball among the haze, outlining the structural members and long-rotted internal machinery of a ship—one so vast it seemed to touch the sky, despite much of it clearly remaining buried.

Chambers licked suddenly dry lips and peered through the gathering red-brown gloom. He guessed it was maybe half a kilometer away, and he could reach it before full twilight. There may be nothing to help him among those sand-blasted members, but he was enough of a scientist and an explorer to know he had found something potentially more important than all the minerals on this planet combined.

Salvage rights were another matter, of course, the thought uppermost in Chambers' mind as he trudged through twilight toward the rearing skeleton of past glory. Let some raggedy-ass mob of Breakers in here and they'd have it smelted before you could turn round, shipped out and at market as pure metals. Who knew where half their goods came from anyway?

Yet, as he drew near, Chambers's brow creased. The wreck was so huge it could only be a colonizer ship. Nothing else built by humankind was so big. Yet none were unaccounted for. That only left alien origin, and suddenly the whole human race was on ground shakier than this slithering landscape. If it belonged to some people touchy about their lost artifacts, anyone trying to strip it may be inviting a shit-storm of a whole other kind. And then there were the diplomatic and scientific aspects to consider. Who lay claim to this? Was it implicitly a grave?

Immersed in glum thoughts about profit and the unfairness of laws which prevented one from accumulating it, Chambers was in the lee of the titanic ribs before the sun left him, striding down into the valley or crater around the wreck. He had already seen that this storm was excavating the ship, blowing the sand from around it in racing skeins, and that some other storm, maybe next week, would just as easily rebury it. No wonder orbital scans had not shown a hulk, merely concentrations of metallic ore in this region. But so huge a thing took time to uncover, and much was still down deep. Indeed, it must have been buried and uncovered many times, for the upperworks were the most eroded, worn away by perhaps a great many years of stinging gales, while the parts now coming into view seemed curiously untouched.

At last Chambers tripped his suit lights and cameras, swept the spars and rotten plates with twin pools of blue-edged white glare, and acknowledged to himself he had never seen engineering like it. It was not of human construction, and also unlike any alien tech he had ever seen.

"What the hell..." he murmured, as he strode among the ruined structure, looking up at what were likely some form of reactors or spacefolding drive, perched on great structural spars on the longitudinal axis of the more or less cylindrical body. And he had reason to shudder, as thoughts of an alien race went through his mind. Where he stood had once been a busy, living place in a vessel crossing vast reaches of interstellar space, and all that, all those beings, their business, their purpose, all that animated them as sentiences, active in their universe, was gone. It spoke softly to the fears of the human heart and mind, for if so sophisticated a people could encounter catastrophe, could humans ever be sure of tomorrow?

Now he was looking for any marker he recognized. He knew the glyphs of the major races of this sector of the galaxy, he read Belchasian script, Brandovalian, Marronite and Trikonian, but he found nothing. Not so much as a manufacturer's code was visible on girders, and in a fit of pique he drew his laser and burned in a symbol on many spars—a symbol commonly recognized to indicate that salvage had been claimed. It may not be respected if he could not somehow make a legal registration of the claim, but it gave him satisfaction to leave his mark. The metal, he noticed, was unusually resilient, taking a long time to yield to the beam.

Down here he was protected somewhat from the wind, and felt he could find shelter deep in the wreck that would tide him until daylight returned, when he could climb out of this depression and make for his ship. He abruptly remembered the CSG team and glanced back at the rim of the valley, half-expecting pursuit, but he was alone. They may come upon him here, that was a chance he must take, sure in the knowledge they were tightly bound by diplomatic protocols. Unknown alien wrecks were to be treated with the utmost respect until their identity was determined. Some peoples, Trikonians especially, despised any race that bounded up the ladder of technical evolution by back-engineering the science of others. If this was Trikonian hardware from some earlier age of spaceflight, to touch a single component would be to invite a hissy-fit diplomats would be smoothing over for years.

But as he penetrated the wreck, Chambers felt it less and less likely. He entered a section protected from the elements, leaving behind the gathering night of Tamiko, to wade through drifted sand as far as a bulkhead where a door was still sealed. He looked up at it in the glare of his lights and swallowed, for the portal was three times his own height. A Sendaaki vessel, perhaps? They were physical giants, and the shape of the door implied a species evolved to upright mobility.

He would never free the door, and settled against the base of the wall, figuring this was as far in as he was likely to get. His helmet deadened the endless drone of the worrying gale, and he could relax at last, draw on the fluid tube by his lips and eat pelletized food from a dispenser. His bodily needs were catered to by the suit's engineering, if not entirely comfortably, then effectively enough for a few days. He would be warm, dry, and under normal atmospheric pressure until the last liquid oxygen sphere in his rebreather was exhausted, then all his luck would be spent. He would gladly put out his hands for the cuffs if he found twelve hours O_2 remaining and was still nowhere near his ship.

How did I get into this? he thought sourly as he tried to sleep. *Cowboy risks... Cowboy risks.*

He woke with an odd, creepy feeling in the pitch blackness by the great door, with the most profound feeling of being watched. Perhaps it was the static charge the wind created in the ribs, but the wreck thrummed softly with electrical potential, and if systems existed which could still harvest that energy and put it to use, he realized the craft did indeed belong to a species beyond all knowledge. But when he flicked on a light and swept the vault, looking back toward the torn and jumbled metal leading to the outside, he found nothing.

"Damn," he muttered to himself. He adjusted his suit com pack and swept the normal frequency range, but could pick up no transmissions. Perhaps the CSG agents were nowhere near, or perhaps they were just outside, their coms masked by the storm and the wreckage's EM field.

But when the tall door hummed and ground slowly aside, he could not mistake the invitation, as if the craft were dimly aware that *someone* was there. It shuddered, moved about half its traverse, then jammed.

With thudding heart, Chambers came to his feet and stared at the open portal, at the inky darkness beyond. Perhaps the ship's surviving AI was expecting rescue or salvage, and was welcoming its discoverer.

Answers, if they existed, were on the other side of the door, and they could be worth a lot. Enough to perhaps mitigate his standing with the CSG, or give him something to bargain with. But he was practical, pragmatic, and went back to the torn sections, used his laser and laboriously cut away a piece of metal small enough to carry. This he jammed into the traverse of the door, to ensure it could not close behind him, then, with his heart in his mouth, stepped through.

Now the grit diminished underfoot until he walked on a nonslip surface, a coating of some sort over the metal. The chamber was merely a box, octagonal in section, though for what purpose he could not imagine. It ran back about twenty meters before he encountered another door, and this one hummed open softly, no dust having invaded its mechanism. Soft light came on, a string of what he took for emergency lamps, blue fireflies outlining the walkway of a T-junction.

The sound of the storm faded from his pickups and he moved in absolute silence on a tilted deck, his suit CPU building a return map for him based on orientation, turns and distances. His mouth was dry, for he had the shivery human terror of meeting the occupants of this vessel. Logic told him they were long since perished, but fear edged his mind as he crept deeper and deeper into the mystery of the great wreck.

Air composition was identical to the exterior, therefore the hull was open somewhere and gasses had mixed and diluted over a long, long time. Not much farther on, Chambers encountered a passage blocked with sand that had flowed in through some fracture, and took a different route, simply exploring. When he found a spiral ramp he peered up into the gloom overhead, but a few levels above he found sealing doors had closed off the well, which he assumed was around the limit of the still viable hull section. Beyond would be only corroding metal and the elements.

He set his boots on the ramp and followed it downward, knowing the spiral would stress his suit CPU's spatial perceptions. He disengaged the recording and began a new file each time he left the ramp to examine adjacent chambers, deeper and deeper in the craft. But for strings of blue fireflies in the gloom, he encountered nothing. Had the vessel carried no crew? That made no sense. Here and there he encountered what seemed to be alien workstations, arrays of displays and instruments, all dead, and whose function he could not guess. He had not seen a chair or anything he might interpret as being for the comfort of the crew, but the workstations themselves were elevated well above his own head, engendering images of giants standing to perform their work.

He could not have said what drew him on, if not for the chance of redeeming himself by the magnitude of his discovery. But some compulsion kept him moving, a dread fascination, as if the makers of this vessel were still here, hiding away, or at least some clue to their identity. He more than half expected anything he found to point to the Sendaaki, humankind's foes in the first, terrible colonial conflict, which had ended in armistice several years ago. They were the only race he knew which fit the stature he was seeing—other than perhaps the Mindrasti of Khlorifane, of which he had dimly heard: a distant world, a crossroads of culture; yet its exceptionally tall dominant species kept very much to themselves, and seemed to have no interest in exploration on the scale building such a craft suggested.

Mystery was thick as the dust of ages, in places where the hull had been invaded by the elements. Downward he went, aware he was well below current ground level, down in parts of the ship which had perhaps never been exposed to the atmosphere since the day it came to this world. Did it land or *crash*, he wondered. To be in such an advanced state of damage suggested the latter, yet what could bring down such a monstrous vessel? It was not unknown for malfunction to doom even the greatest ships, the specter of the *Magellan* disaster of AD 2338 had never left the human consciousness—perhaps Chambers had stumbled upon an alien equivalent.

The claustrophobia of the night-black vaults weighed upon him and he found he could not credit some mundane explanation. More was at work here, and he walked in a state of nervous anxiety, as if at any moment he may find the answer. From the spiral ramp, fore and aft ran corridors that branched through more turns and compartments than he could ever explore, and did not try; that was the province of the experts who would doubtless follow. All he wanted was one solid clue as to what happened.

Chambers expected the ramp to terminate at the lowest deck of the ship's habitable region, but a hundred meters below ground level it ended in the torn remnants of the lower hull. From smooth metal he abruptly found himself looking down at raw rock, heat-fused by intense energies. Now he knew the craft had not made a controlled landing, and the underside had been torn away in the final impact. Yet there remained a gap, and when he shone his lights into the space he found a stony gallery beneath the wreck, and an awesome darkness opened out beyond reach of his floods.

All good sense told him to turn back. He was now beneath hundreds of thousands of tons of alien derelict, yet compulsion drew him on—into the excavated crater beneath. He found he could drag a piece of twisted metalwork that hung by a thread, turned it, then severed its connection with a long laser discharge. The piece of wreckage must have weighed three hundred kilos, and fell with a resounding crash, to jam obliquely between ramp and bare rock. It gave him a precarious way down, and, more importantly, back up. With heart in his mouth, he scrambled down from handhold to handhold, until his boots took the slick magma-stone beneath, and he panted shallowly.

You're in the lion's mouth, now, you dumb cowboy, he thought to himself. *This really is one of the stupider things you've done. And yet...*

And yet, part of him would have willingly traded his life for the experience. Free or prisoner now made almost no difference. He was here, he was seeing this, perhaps a first contact situation, and very few human beings had ever experienced one.

Calming his heart with a deep draft of cool, oxygen-rich air, he closed his eyes a moment, then walked into the blackness.

He had no idea what he might have been expecting, but all preconceptions were swept aside, and he felt he may have blacked out for a while. Reality was more than he could understand or accept at first. When he had his senses back, he found he was sitting on the edge of a great precipice of fused rock that fell away into a secondary crater. His lights painted soft details hundreds of meters off, and he sensed this pit must have been a kilometer deep, maybe several, before erosion and landslides gradually filled it in, burying what it contained. The ship lay atop it, its weight pressing down, sending cascades of rock and sand into the abyss, yet enough open space remained, even after what must have been thousands of years, to reveal something incredible—terrible.

Chambers nodded silently, helmet bobbing a little in the reflected glare of his lights, now accepting what he saw. He could never have conceived of a ship being dragged out of space by deliberate intent, but the evidence was before him.

He could not estimate how vast the creature must have been in life, but if the desiccated husk was anything to go by, it was many times larger than the ship. All that remained were cartilaginous structures, or masses of fused mineral that must have performed the same function as cartilage in terrestrial biomes. They outlined what seemed to have been layers of body structure which gleamed faintly, far below, as if the creature had dried out utterly, shriveled and contracted, yet was still vast beyond ordinary measure. He could make out little of the morphology, the chaos remaining gave few clues—except when it came to the arms.

It may be wrong to call them tentacles, but they were clearly grasping members of some sort, and several ascended from the titanic crypt in arches of frozen stone, gleaming with calcite and a hundred other minerals. Ring-like structures here and there eerily suggested suckers, outlining the members. Their upper terminals were locked, hook-like into the starship's hull with what he could only interpret as a grip of Herculean tenacity, awakening visions of this veritable Typhon grappling with the vessel in its progress and overcoming all that science and technology might bring to bear. What spectacle had occurred here, unknown ages ago, waiting beneath the sands of Tamiko for human eyes to behold?

He was still wrapped in these thoughts when lights splashed the rock around him and he felt a hand on his shoulder, jerking him back to reality. Three suited figures knelt at the cliff edge and their combined lights played over the ghostly tableau. He turned to look into the faceplate nearest, and found the features of a young woman. The CSG crest over the forehead of each helmet told him his liberty was at an end, but he found he was unconcerned—grateful in fact, for human company of whatever kind.

"Quite a chase," the woman murmured, after they adjusted frequencies. He saw the name Kabila below the crest.

"How did you find me?" he asked with a faint smile.

She gestured to a companion who carried a hand-scanner, and an Australian accent floated in Chambers's ears. "I'd love to say we did something clever, but from the outer door inward it was mostly a case of following your filthy boot prints." The humor was as obvious as the fact the question did not rate a straight answer.

Kabila gave him a thin smile and nodded at the terrible vision before them. "But I think you just made the biggest discovery of all time."

"Part of me wishes I hadn't," he replied numbly. "But I had to know."

"You can't fight it," she added softly, her dark features as haunted as his own. "Curiosity killed more explorers than cats." They shared silence for a long while, as the Australian played the sensor over the remains in the pit. After a time, he showed the readings to his boss and she blinked. "That's odd. Thermal energy, EM field and an emission of photons, about a thousand times below visual threshold. Those things, taken together usually mean—"

"Life?" Chambers asked in a whisper. "That thing is *still alive?*" The agents and the fugitive stared down into the silent pit for long, difficult moments, then Chambers shrugged. "Why not? This is about as alien as anything I've ever seen, ever heard of. If human beings have learned anything in two hundred years out here, it's never to tell life what it can't do."

"We have to get better readings," the Australian voice came in their ears again. "That means getting closer."

The third agent gave a snorting laugh. He obviously had no intention of braving the pit. But Chambers, stone cold inside, still in the grip of his compulsion, spoke softly. "I'll do it."

Kabila spread her hands. "It's a commander's risk to take, and that means me. Now, I'd be happy to let someone else—someone qualified—go down there instead, but the rules forbid a prisoner being put to hazardous work."

He crooked her a smile. "You see some way around those regs?" He paused a moment. "If, just for instance, I wasn't a prisoner." The others glanced at him. "I mean, what's more important, here? Bringing in an industrial spy, or discovering life under an alien wreck?"

With a quiet *hmph* across her mic pickup, Kabila nodded. "We might just classify you as 'a civilian specialist assisting the CSG on Tamiko,' and leave it at that."

"I get my ship back?"

"Certainly. You *don't* get the data you worked for. That's the only condition."

"Free and alive? I can live with that." He craned to look down into the blackness again and was a long time speaking. "I want to go down there. I need to."

The agents were well-equipped, and had brought climbing gear from their ship in the expectation of having to work through ruined sections. A light winch and cable rig were available, and they had them set up in ten minutes. Chambers was tethered to the line and went over the edge with a sense of strange fulfillment, as if he walked a forbidden space, or was about to come face to face with a god. The fact he probably had his liberty returned was oddly unimportant to him, deep down, as he descended into the night, suit lights picking out the mineral glimmers of the nearest titanic arm, his cameras recording. Lights above blended into a background radiance, so as he neared the organism itself he saw, dimly lit, pitted fields of brittle structure, some kind of shell or carapace, utterly desiccated and drawn away from its proportions in life. With 320 meters of feather-light cable out, his boots met the creature and he stood on a vast, gently curved surface, wrinkled and ridged as if the tissues had contracted unevenly. He walked, feeling stony resilience, and looked up, the others' lights like stars in a black bowl.

Kabila's voice came to his ears. "What do you see?"

"Stone," he whispered, and moved on. The cable paid out a little to give him slack, as he crept carefully across the vast body. A hundred meters on, near the gargantuan rooting point of an arm, he found a fracture, deep and black, and his lights showed only a confusion of mineralized structures below. "This should be close enough," he added, and deployed the scanner they had given him.

Readings built slowly, transmitting back to the suit computers above, and he saw data he could not put sense to, other than to admit that life persisted. "Heat," he murmured. "Not much, just a few degrees above ambient. But there's definitely an EM field, and the wave dynamic suggests a focus about half a kilometer deeper. And, tremors. Just the faintest vibrations." He set the scanner down on the stony mantle by his feet and let it record for a while. "Yes. Ultra-low frequency, but rhythmic. Long and slow."

"My god," he heard from above. "A heartbeat?"

Before he could answer, the scanner registered a sharp spike in EM levels and his lights flickered. He felt giddy, a strange sense of force washing over him, and when radio static cleared he heard the voices from above talking about a massive surge, as if vast mechanisms had stirred momentarily. "The ship?" he asked tightly. "Is the AI waking?"

"No," Kabila whispered. "Maybe. But that spike came from *down there.*"

That's what knocked me out of the air, he thought, mouth dry. *Life, calling out to life.* The notion sent a strange thrill through him, and his thoughts raced uncomfortably to the crew of the craft above—those unknown giants gone without trace. What became of them, in the impact, in their struggle with this strange, strange lifeform? He grabbed up the scanner, to back away from the fissure. "Please tell me you have enough."

"Yes," Kabila whispered. "Come on up. You've earned your ticket out."

Yet compulsion was a strange thing. As the winch recovered cable and Chambers saw the unknown giant diminish beneath his boots, he was at once sorry to be going, and wanted to promise himself he would be back. Promise *the entity* here.

Where did that come from? He wondered sharply, yet could not fail to acknowledge it. He felt the life in this monstrous husk, and though he had no doubt it had torn the ship above from space itself, he perceived no malice.

Mystery piled atop mystery, but he knew an expedition would return to this remote and inhospitable world to begin to fill in the answers. And, in an inexplicable rush of empathy with the great and eternally patient intelligence, trapped in that pit, he knew he would be with them.

Mike Adamson holds a Doctoral degree from Flinders University of South Australia. After early aspirations in art and writing, Mike returned to study and secured qualifications in marine biology and archaeology. Mike has been a university educator since 2006, is a passionate photographer, master-level hobbyist and journalist for international magazines. Mike has placed some 190 stories to date, totaling well over 900, 000 words in print. You can catch up with his journey at his blog 'The View From the Keyboard,' http://mike-adam sor.blogspot.com

A Trip Down Memory Lane

ELLEN RIKHOF

The car slammed to a stop a few feet from the edge of the rocky cliff, close enough to send a pebble tumbling over into the rolling water. Alina wasn't paying attention to the unsettling stop though; she was too busy looking around at the tiny town through the window.

A sharp tang of salt overwhelmed her senses as she finally opened the taxi door. Insisting she would be fine, she thanked and paid the driver, shutting the door. Still, she couldn't help but look back until the car was out of sight, and she was alone on the grassy bluff overlooking the small village.

The wind lifted her dark hair, murmuring warnings into her ears as she walked. Teeth chattering in the November cold, she approached the base of the path and surveyed the ocean below. The waves tossed and churned underneath a bleak sky, almost devoid of color but oppressively dark. Over the water, a lone gull sent out a strangled cry as it was dragged back through the sky, struggling to break free from the wind's grasp.

She savored the salty flavor that filled the air for a moment, free to just observe the fury below. Then, adjusting the bag over her shoulder, she set off on a little gravel path, walking through the small town before her and up the winding hill.

The village was an unceremonious mashup of worn buildings. The battered general store with its fading paint, the closed movie theater, a few neon lights left blinking uncertainly. Turning left, she saw the few houses crammed onto the block, tall and narrow, with shutters pulled tightly and sturdy fences guarding their perimeters.

Alina shook her head slightly, breathing deeply. She thought back a few summers to when the store had just been repainted. The gleaming white walls with the dancing blue script of the label. She had walked into town with her grandpa that day, had laughed when they got a cone of ice cream to share. It made her cross her arms and stand up a little straighter to see it so dull now.

Far above her, at the top of the hill, Alina's grandparents' house sat at the edge of her view. Their house was a long walk from where she was now, and she resigned to the fact that it would take most of the day. The small beaten path at the edge of the seaside was the only way to their house, since no roads went farther than the small town. Why they had decided to live so far away from the rest of the people in the area, Alina could only guess.

It had been a while since she had last seen them—over a year. Now, she smiled into the cold at the thought of their reaction to her dropping by. She'd been in the area, visiting an old friend. Nostalgia was already thick on her mind, and so she'd made the trip here. True, this was her first time speaking to her grandparents since a long past August, but she already knew just how they would respond: Gram with warm hugs and endless questions and Gramps with twinkling smiles and firm handshakes.

The jagged pebbles crunched underneath her boots as she strode forward. The sky was darkening, a gray stain seeping through the overcast heavens. Weighed down, the clouds hung closely over the Earth, blotting out the sun. The swirling breeze seemed to grow in intensity with this change, cruelly whipping Alina's face as she bundled her sweater even tighter across her torso.

It wasn't far now, about a half mile. She could already see their small cottage in the distance. The new blue walls she and her cousins had painted the previous summer gleamed in the dark like a sea-colored beacon.

She stepped through the blowing grasses, bent over in the force of the wind, and then stopped, lips peeling down into a frown. The house was right before her, quaint and isolated. But all the shutters, all the doors, every last window was wide open. Banging against the walls in the howling gale. The door in front of her rattled at its hinges, shuddering in the wind.

In the dim, Alina almost didn't notice the little hand rake at her feet. She stumbled over it, turning around and looking out at the garden. She recalled the beautiful flowers from the summers of her past, bright pinks planted for her and deep purples for her cousin. She remembered dancing around the plants, singing and picking a blossom, the gentle scolding of her grandma that told her she wasn't really in trouble.

Her vision shifted slightly, dragging her from the memory with the shriveled black remains of the blooms. Now around her was a ghost garden, filled with brittle grasses and decaying flowers. Leaves were scattered in the little bed, and tall stalks had grown up untended. There were still gloves sitting primly on the edge of the short wall, a trowel not far behind.

Bewildered, Alina bit her lip. She reached out and folded the gloves, lingering with her hand on the wall, staring at the wild plants. Then she sighed and picked herself up, continuing to the house.

Standing on the front porch, Alina scanned around her, unease prickling inside. The door clattered, making her jump each time it smacked into the wall. No light seeped out from the house, and not a sound reached her.

In front of her rose the small cottage of her childhood summers. It had been cramped and full of love, bustling with adventure and excitement. Cousins ran about, playing in the garden, star gazing just from this little porch. But this house didn't resemble that one at all. It stood stately and ominously before her, long quiet and uncared for. It loomed against the shadowy backdrop, something out of place. Now, the house just seemed small, like it was hiding a secret deep within it didn't want anybody to discover. It felt rough, barbed, and gloomy.

She shivered once more, unsure whether it was from the cold or the anxiety that filled her. Slowly, she walked through the front door, calling out in a thin, breathy voice, "Gram? Gramps?"

There was no reply, only the methodic clang of the windows. Again, Alina shuttered, wary and unconfident. It did seem like they weren't home, but she hadn't seen them in town, and they never got out much anyway.

They're probably just upstairs, sleeping. Suddenly, she became acutely aware of how far away the other houses were.

Creeping inside the house, she decided to leave the door open. Even the unnerving noise of the wind was better than the feeling of suffocation that came with the exit blocked. Alina flicked on the light, sending a faint yellow glow throughout the interior.

She was only a little way in when she burst out coughing. Every surface in sight was covered in a thin film of dust. With each step, she spread the sparse white powder off the walnut planks, leaving a set of ghostly footprints uncovering the wood below.

The house was compact, the stairs just past the kitchen which combined with the sitting room to make up the first floor. Alina moved through the little collection of furniture over the thick rug congested with dust, pausing slightly at a photo framed on the coffee table.

It was one of her, holding her grandma and grandpa in a hug on the very couch she was facing. The white cushions weren't as frayed back then, weren't dripping in neglect. Alina stared at the picture a while longer, loneliness washing over her. All at once, she wanted to hold it tight and smash it into a thousand tiny shards of glass. Instead, she walked on, still hesitant, but now frightened of where her grandparents might be. She was most certainly the only soul inside, though Alina wasn't going to admit that until each room had been scoured.

The house was unbearably quiet around her, each footstep sending a booming echo reverberating through the room. Uncomfortably, Alina picked her way across the floors, wanting to hurry away from the entire house, but without knowing why.

In the kitchen, time was frozen to some long past dinner. There were plates in the sink, blackened and covered with a fuzzy mold.

Ants traversed up the counter, a steady stream of inky writhing bodies heading to the forgotten dishes.

This was the kitchen where her grandma had shown her how to cook, had baked cookies with her, laughing and sticking little globs of batter on her nose. Alina was reminded of the time they had first made snickerdoodles, Gram stirring the batter, Alina whisking the sugar mixture. The beautiful smell of fresh baked clumps of pure bliss. Only the cookies didn't smell of cinnamon, they smelled of rot and mildew. The sugar in her hands turned black.

Alina opened the eyes she hadn't known she'd closed.

Maybe she should clear up the house, wash the dishes after she'd looked through all the rooms. But Alina knew she wouldn't. That was too long to stay in this ghostly shrine to what had transpired and passed. What if she just asked a neighbor where her grandparents were? But inexplicably, she knew she had to search every corner. *Besides,* she thought, *they're sleeping upstairs. Right?*

The small glow from the light flickered, causing the somber yellow to flash off for a second before wavering back on. Alina hesitated for a moment, foot braced above the first step. Then she breathed, setting it down and walking up the creaking stairs.

At the top of the stairwell, she waited again, unable to put her thoughts into words as she gazed at the rooms below her. Finally, she turned away and walked into a bedroom. Swallowing down the bilge that filled her throat she looked at her old room. Like all the others, the disuse was apparent. Still organized as it had been, the room looked frozen in time. But it didn't feel like it. It felt like all the time in the world had passed, and this bed was there to haunt her, forcing her to stare at it and say, "That time is over."

But was it really? She only had one more room to search - it was a small house. Only a few seconds more to push back whatever ugly truth awaited her. *But nothing is wrong. Nothing.* She almost repeated the words aloud so she could cling to them, make them true. She had a hallway and a closet door left for her denial, that was all.

Alina sighed, feeling her body crush into itself, almost turning around and just leaving now. This wasn't exactly the visit she had imagined after all. But why not be thorough? It was only one more room, and she needed to know where her grandparents were. If she couldn't find them, it would take her ten seconds, tops, before she could sprint down the stairs, burst from the door, and race down into town to call a taxi home. Ten seconds was nothing. She could wait ten seconds.

Somehow though, she felt herself dragging her feet as she strode through the hallway. Felt her hand waver at the doorknob, before finally turning it and entering the master bedroom.

The room was just like her old one, coated in dust. Standing in the doorway though, she noticed the covers were ruffled, tangled about the bed. And she felt the temperature plummet. A decaying smell soaked the air, choking her. Alina gagged, losing her breath as her tongue became dry and her mouth filled with the emptiness of rot.

Suddenly, it was like she no longer controlled her limbs. Without meaning to, without even thinking about it, Alina had crossed the room in three quick strides. Past the bed, she now faced the open closet. Around the shadowy doorframe, she could just make out two figures slumped on the floor. She shrieked, seeing their cold, dead eyes, the purple ashen flesh, and the narrow trickle of blood that had dried onto their foreheads.

Then, from downstairs came a great crash. The front door banged shut, slamming hard into place. The windows followed, all at once. The sound of the bolt latching was the last thing Alina heard.

Ellen Rikhof has spent her life along the waters of the Puget Sound. A high school student, she dedicates her time to her friends and family, reading, and entertaining the fantasies inside her head. "A Trip Down Memory Lane" is her first published work. You can reach her at ellenwrites7@gmail.com.

Soul of a Beast

GREGORY D. LITTLE

Pieter's legs finally gave out as he staggered from the moonlit surf, just another piece of flotsam amid the debris of the ship he'd just sunk. He collapsed onto wet sand, fighting despair between coughing fits. After all his careful planning, some of them had survived.

Caught in the island's rising tide, Pieter had watched a handful of his shadowy financier's hired pirates bob to the ocean's surface on waterlogged crates and snapped hull beams. And if an old man like Pieter had reached the island alive, some of the hale buccaneers must have as well.

Hacking up the last of the sea, he allowed himself a brief thrill of triumph. *I made it here.* The island night blazed, crimson tendrils projecting a light like burning blood. *It's here. It's real.* "Found you," he wheezed. He just had to stay alive long enough for that to matter.

The wet sand was cool and soothing against his exhausted limbs. He let his eyes flutter closed. When he opened them again, it was daylight.

Foolish old man! Any of them might have come upon you in your sleep! Pieter's curses became complaints as he rose on tortured joints. The hiss and spray of waves filled the air with brine. Drying salt left his skin tacky.

The sky's piercing blue dominated the daytime palette. As expected, all sign of the previous night's fiery light had vanished. The immense fungal mass growing from the equally immense skeleton had faded from glowing crimson to dull rust in the sunlight. It was good to see it behaved the same way in nature as it had during his years of study.

Thick, feathered fronds soared above the skeleton wrapped around the island's low, brown mountain. The fungal forest was so dense Pieter couldn't make out individual bones. Had the fronds lain limp and been trimmed, the body would have resembled a shaggy highland pony curled upon itself in death. Instead, the fungus stretched up to the sunlight, and despite this conforming to his every prediction, Pieter gawked.

The sheer, vast *size* of it! And even now it gathered light like a plant, though not for growth. For it was tales of a nightly inferno upon the water that had ultimately led Pieter to this island. All that stored light would discharge again after the sun set, and he had no idea why. There were so many questions he wanted to answer.

Such thoughts brought a grimace. If he'd sunk the ship properly, he would be free to study. Pieter was weary of struggle with his prize so close. But he couldn't afford to trust the longing to simply assume he was safe.

Still, surely he'd earned a peek at his reward, and heading inland made sense. The open sand of the beach was too exposed to anyone watching.

The island was small, and the beast was large. Pieter soon reached a curving wall of fungus so thick it seemed a boundary between worlds. The hoof within was dozens of times wider than Pieter was tall.

Pieter's research had taken him all across the main continent. He'd seen the corpse of every known great beast, and they never failed to awe. The godkind's war with humankind had already been lost when the gods breathed life into the beasts as a final, bitter blow. Their titanic pets had eventually been defeated as well, with cataclysmic loss of life.

Discovery of a lost beast—Equus, it had been named—would be

the scientific find of the century all by itself. And that wasn't even counting this beast's uniqueness. Of all the beasts, the great horse was the only one to grow the fungus.

On the impulse of long habit, Pieter snapped off the tip of a frond and popped it into his mouth. The expected surge of energy arrived the moment he swallowed. Bouncing on his toes, Pieter instantly felt a decade younger than his sixty years.

Revitalized, he pondered how to find the surviving pirates and what to do when he did. The beach was too exposed, but if he moved aimlessly through the island's remaining jungle, he might stumble upon them unaware.

His gaze drifted up the massive corpse as he considered the problem. He'd only just realized the symmetrical depressions in the fungal blanket were enormous eye sockets when someone spoke.

"Hello," said a voice like a collapsing mountain.

"Who's that?" Pieter croaked in alarm.

"You can hear me! Oh, it's been so long since Mistress left. I've been so lonely."

"Who's speaking?" Pieter said, fighting panic. He didn't recognize the voice, but it had to be one of the surviving pirates.

"I'm right here!" The voice was childlike despite its deep resonance, and in horror, Pieter realized it was coming from *inside his head*. "Oh, at last! Someone to talk to! A little to the left. You were looking right at me, friend!"

A terrible understanding seized Pieter. Dread stilled his breath as he looked again into the skeleton's vast, empty sockets. "Hello," Equus said. "It's so nice to look you in the eyes."

"How is this possible?" Pieter asked after Equus's insisted-upon introductions. "You and your kind are dead!"

"It's true I'm not at my best," the corpse retorted primly. "But I'm hardly *dead*. When Mistress returns, she'll fix me."

"But your body—"

"I can't move, no. I can see, though. And hear. And talk! It's not so bad, though Mistress has been gone a long time. Did she send you? When is she coming back?"

The giddiness in that landslide of a voice made Pieter's head spin. "I'm sorry," he interrupted. "Mistress?"

"She and her family sleep beneath the ground," Equus said. "She said she would fix me. I miss her, but I know she will return."

The gods. He's talking about the gods. "Beneath the ground" was putting it mildly. The gods were imprisoned at the center of the planet after losing their war against humankind two centuries gone.

"But the others like you," Pieter began. Children everywhere learned the great beasts by rote. Crocodile and viper. Spider, lion, and bat. Owl, wasp, and wolf. Bear, hawk, and dragon. And now, horse. *How can this be happening?*

Equus cut him off with a whicker like a waterfall.

"Mistress said they are nothing like me," the beast said darkly.

"Which god is your mistress?" Pieter asked.

"A lonely little girl needed a friend," Equus said. "None of her family was like her. She made me and wasn't lonely anymore." As if that answered anything. Studying the gods wasn't something decent people did, so Pieter couldn't place the reference.

"What do you remember of the war?" he asked.

"Mistress and I kept away from that. Her family and the other animals did wicked things. The others were always so angry. I don't think they liked doing such horrible things to humans, but Mistress's family made them. I never did bad things, but humans found me and broke me anyway. I don't blame you. I suppose you just couldn't tell the difference."

"The other gods didn't make you fight?"

"They tried. I never listened. That made Mistress's family angry, so they wouldn't give the other animals a lovely mane like mine. Do you like my mane? I've never tried eating it before, but I feel connected to you now. Was it tasty?"

"Your *mane*?" Pieter asked, incredulous.

"Did you see it glow last night? Mistress used to tease me for being vain, but I never get tired of looking."

Something pricked at Pieter's mind. "Have you always had your mane?"

"Oh yes. My first memory is my mane sprouting between Mistress's fingers at her touch."

It's the fungus. It made him different from the other beasts. Not a slave, like they must have been. Equus's mistress had given him free choice.

"Friend Pieter," Equus said.

"Yes?" Pieter asked distractedly.

"Are you going to introduce me to *your* friends? They can't hear me speak."

Pieter's blood froze.

"Tell me where they are," he said.

The horse's reply was cheery. "Behind you."

Pieter struggled against his bonds, his feet and hands numb. He recognized all six of the surviving pirates. Lanky, weak-jawed Burlit, first mate of a sunken ship, squatted before a loose stack of wet driftwood, struggling to build a fire and growling more with each failed spray of sparks from dagger and flint.

At last Duendo, the pirates' stocky, hard-eyed captain, leaned over the pile, his back obscuring Pieter's view. When the captain rose, yellow-orange ribbons of flame licked upward. Duendo turned a blank stare upon Pieter.

"Keep staring at me, old man," Duendo said, "and I may kill you before I decide if we still need you." He tromped over, kicking sand into Pieter's eyes, adding burning tears to his list of woes.

Even through blurred vision, Pieter could make out the curled length of the surefire wrighting hooked like a gray, hand-sized talon over Duendo's belt. *That explains how he can make wet driftwood burn.*

All wrightings were forged into a shape specific to their purpose then charged with soul energy as a power source. A surefire could start fires even in things that didn't wish to burn. More, its wielder could will the fire to discriminate, burning only what they wished.

Pieter shuddered to think what someone with fine enough control over their thoughts could do to a person with one of those..

Duendo leaned down and whispered with fouled breath. "That was some stunt, old man. I give respect where respect is due. You nearly did for me and all my crew. I didn't think you had it in you." He laughed and shook his head. His laughter had an edge Pieter didn't like.

"Now, I've got a job to do. If you want to live a little longer, hope what I'm about to try doesn't work." With that, Duendo walked off.

"I don't think those men are your friends." Equus's voice crashed like surf into Pieter's head.

"They aren't," he tried to say, but his gag made it into a muffled, choking sound.

"You don't have to talk. You ate part of me. I can hear you think."

Pieter blinked. *You're right. Those men aren't my friends.*

"But they came with you on the boat that sank."

I needed their master's money to get here. He hired them to secure his investment.

A pause.

"You sank the boat." The shock behind the words left Pieter ashamed despite everything.

I did. I came here to find you. The man who paid our way wanted to find you too, but he frightens me. Pirates seldom worked for hire. That these particular pirates had made an exception to that rule only meant their patron must be extremely wealthy or extremely danger-ous. *I couldn't let his men actually arrive.*

"These are bad men?"

Yes.

"They brought a wicked thing with them, so I believe you."

At first, Pieter thought Equus meant the surefire. Then he remem-bered the wax-sealed crate stored in the back of the ship that had been guarded day and night. He'd stopped worrying about what it contained, certain in the knowledge that the ship and everything on it would wind up at the bottom of the sea.

But that same crate now sat on the beach, looking untouched.

What did they bring, Equus?

Equus's response was a whisper.

"Starsliver."

Impossible. Pieter's reaction was automatic. He had studied his entire life, and horrific weapons like the starsliver had all been used up in the war with the gods. *Those can't exist!*

"They used to. I remember the feel of them."

Iron Hell be strong, Pieter thought, wincing as he realized he was praying for Equus's mistress to remain locked up. *What did starslivers do?* Pieter thought. *I mean, before?*

"They ate."

Pieter brooded as the sun inched across the sky, searing his scholar's skin. He had never learned who exactly had financed his expedition, much less met them. Pieter had allowed his need to find the missing beast to blind him to the dangers of anyone who wanted to find and tamper with a great beast. *What a fool I've been.*

Any human smith of sufficient talent could forge a wrighting like a surefire. But not a starsliver. *Only one can forge them and he sleeps beneath the ground with the others.* Who had Pieter made his deal with, exactly?

"What's happening?" Equus asked in Pieter's head. "I can't see any of you, and I want to know what's happening! Can you still not speak out loud?" His voice had grown faint.

No, I can't.

"Friend Pieter, can you hear me?"

A surprising sense of loss descended. Pieter had eaten only a small amount of the fungus. There was nothing left now in his blood but the dregs. Like overused tea leaves, the fronds were spent, the link fading.

"Oh, if my Mistress was here, she would *punish* the wicked men! You could pray to her. She can still hear those who pray to her. But she won't be able to understand your words!"

Perhaps it was just as well Pieter was gagged. He wasn't sure he could bring himself to pray to one of the gods for help on the off chance that it might actually work. Not even his life was worth that.

The pirates appeared packed and ready, waiting on Duendo. He crouched on the balls of his feet in the sand, staring at a small pile of fungus cuttings. Their rusty hue had begun bleaching into a wan orange, withering quickly once severed from their source.

Pieter's sweating intensified as he stared. He yearned for another piece. With it, he could keep communicating with Equus. And though it shamed him to admit, his body craved the rush, something to blunt the pains of his bonds and age.

Pieter thought back to that fungus sample he'd traded a sailor for years ago. He'd managed to cultivate it with some difficulty, and had begun his search for its source.

Now, old and tired, he'd been perfectly content to arrive here and never return if necessary, leaving everything of his life behind on one final quest of discovery. He'd imagined living off food that didn't actually seem to grow on the island.

Have I sacrificed anything and come all this way for an addiction? The uncertainty left him nauseous.

Duendo pulled the surefire from his belt. The curved metal's faint sheen reflected the afternoon sunlight in dim parody. The pirate furrowed his brow in concentration as he grazed the wrighting's tip against the end of one of the fronds.

A thin stream of smoke curled upward, twisting playfully in the sea breeze. Soon a merry, white flame inched its way along the length of the frond, leaving a withered black husk and an achingly familiar, acrid stink in its wake.

Smiling in smug satisfaction, Duendo rose and approached a vaguely spherical shape of the same dark gray metal, covered in alternating protrusions and indentations and perched on a battered crate. He fiddled with the caller until it emitted squealing sounds that resolved into a voice.

"Report," the voice boomed in the air around the caller. Surprised, Pieter recognized it as that of his nameless benefactor, the expedition's financier. He'd never heard of a caller that could reach so far.

Somehow the caller made the voice sound otherworldly, like two voices layered atop one another. Pieter thought again of the starsliver waiting in that wax-sealed box. *Is the voice even human?*

"We narrowly avoided disaster," Duendo said. He gave an unvarnished account of his ship's sinking and Pieter's treachery. "I'll need a new ship, but matters are still in hand."

"Good," said the voice, not even commenting on the loss of the ship. "The rest of the expedition is still a day away."

Pieter squeezed his eyes shut. *Another ship. Of course.* His efforts had truly been in vain.

"By the time they arrive," the voice continued, "I want that creature to be an empty vessel or destroyed. Purge the infestation. Do I make myself clear?"

"Aye, sir," Duendo said.

"No more mishaps."

Duendo killed the connection then gathered up all but one of his men with a glance.

"Make sure the old man stays put," Duendo growled at the remaining pirate, Leven. "If this doesn't work, we'll bleed any last secrets out of him." He flashed a feral grin then made for the island's dry interior with the other four, their gaits rolling with memory of the sea.

Despair welled in Pieter, bringing with it an impotent rage. He'd come so close, and now he was going to die. And the growing hollow within him screamed to be filled with the fungus. *One final indignity.*

This ache foremost in his mind, Pieter's gaze drifted back to the smoldering pile of fronds. A surefire could produce an ordinary flame, but when constrained by its wielder, the fire behaved differently. It destroyed what it was permitted to destroy in the manner of fire, but drew no energy and gave off no heat from its fuel. In that manner, it could be tightly controlled, just as this flame had. Duendo had been testing his control of the tool with the fronds.

Pieter stared hungrily at the burning fungus. Enough of that smoke, and he would be insensate when Duendo finally returned and killed him. Ignoring the pain, Pieter strained against his bonds, his fevered gaze fixed upon the pearly smoke.

Such obvious need didn't go unnoticed. Leven smiled a crooked smile full of rotting teeth and swaggered over to the smoldering pile. He crouched down, his rat-face gloating.

"You want this, old man?" he said, his drawling accent making the words sound like mush. "Aye, we all saw you sneaking bites from that little stash aboard ship, how you'd get all twitchy if you went too long without." The words were a sneer, and Pieter felt a fresh barb of shame. He'd been forced to stretch out the small amount he'd had remaining. The long gaps between had left his skin crawling at times.

"And you won't get even a whiff," Leven went on. "Not after how many of ours you've done in. Still, seems a shame for it to go to waste."

Smiling mockingly, Leven leaned into the rising smoke and inhaled deeply. His eyes bulged wide, his jaw went slack and he collapsed in a heap atop the fronds. Spiteful with glee, Pieter remembered his first attempt to smoke the stuff. Or, rather, tried to remember. It was potent stuff when inhaled.

A spark of hope lit within him. His only guard was unconscious and starting to smolder. If he could wriggle free of his bonds he could do... nothing. He was on an island. He'd sunk his only transportation the previous night. Reinforcements were on their way. There wasn't any escape. There wasn't—

"Help!" Equus's voice was distant, the link almost gone. Even so faint, Pieter could distinguish the agony and terror. "Help! Friend Pieter, help me! They're *burning* me!"

The pain was tamped down by the fresh fungus in his blood, but Pieter could still feel the oozing lacerations on his wrists beginning to swell. But he'd managed to wriggle free.

The plaintive cries of poor Equus resonated loud and strong in his head. "Pieter! Pieter, *please!*" If a godly leviathan could whimper, Equus was doing so.

"Where?" Pieter left Leven drooling on the beach and dashed into the jungle as fast as his too-tired body would carry him.

"My back legs. But the pain is everywhere! It's *inside* me!"

Pieter had no idea where he was with respect to Equus's back legs. Fronds of fungus rose up in nearly every direction. Then a thick column of white flame twisted up into the sky between the fronds and above the blowing sand.

"Stop them," the poor creature sobbed. "Please, Pieter, stop them!" The silence that followed was worse than his wails of pain. But Pieter had no weapon. He was one old man.

His eyes fell on the wax-coated box, now quite unguarded. The thought of touching what lay within sent fear arcing through his nerves. But he didn't have to actually *use* it. The pirates would only need to believe he might. And after...

After was after.

Pieter cracked the wax seal with a sharp-edged stone. It peeled free in a great chunk and Pieter pried open the box's lid. Pillowed in a cup of black velvet was a slate-gray, metallic sphere about the size of a man's head and carrying the same faint sheen of the surefire. It looked so unremarkable that Pieter was certain Equus had been mistaken. But this flash of shameful relief withered when he examined more closely.

The sphere's edges blurred, seething before Pieter's eyes. He leaned in, forgetting to be afraid as he realized he couldn't actually discern the edge. Instead of ending sharply in a tiny, curved horizon, the edge grew fuzzier until it was no longer there.

That creature will be an empty vessel or destroyed, the voice on the caller had said. Surely the starsliver was here for that contingency.

His breath held, Pieter cradled shaking hands beneath the sphere and lifted it from its velvet bed. It was incredibly heavy for its size. Pieter's joints popped and shrieked as he rose, hefting the sphere before him.

Grunting with effort, Pieter followed that column of flame and the smoke it birthed, watching it grow nearer and thicker. This close he should have been able to feel the heat, but the surefire's flames were cold as well as cruel, the captain wisely starting only a fire he could control utterly.

Pieter burst through the last tangle of loose fronds to find Duendo and his crew standing before him, facing their handiwork.

The captain turned as he pulled his hand back from a swath of fungus freshly set alight with the cruel hook of the surefire. The flames burned, leaving only clean, perfectly untouched bone in their wake.

"Purge the infestation," the voice had said. *They're destroying only the fungus.*

Duendo's look of irritation went flat as he saw what lay cradled in Pieter's straining arms. One by one his crew turned and went still with shock and alarm.

"Knew I should have killed you," Duendo growled. His voice hummed with menace, but he made no move.

The fresh flames adding to the conflagration, Equus screamed again inside Pieter's head. It sounded like a world being ripped apart. A red haze of rage descended over Pieter's thoughts, and his sagging muscles woke to the call as though also set ablaze. He stood straighter.

"The surefire. Toss it to me. Gently."

"And how precisely would you pick it up?" Duendo said with a mocking smile. Already he was getting his confidence back. Pieter couldn't let that happen. He took one plodding step forward, and the pirate's face went tight again.

"Put out the flames. Now."

"I don't think I will, no," Duendo said. "I know I underestimated you once, old man. But I really don't think you're the sort to die for this thing."

"Mistress," Equus moaned, "is *he* here? His handiwork is close. His wickedness clouds the air like vapor. Closer now. Closer. Why does the world hurt, Mistress?"

"You said it yourself," Pieter snarled. "You've already underestimated me once." He took another step.

He saw it in Duendo's eyes. He had the man's attention.

"We can't stop, old man. What they'd do to us, I'd sooner take my chances with that thing you're holding. But if it's a swift death you want, give it over, and I'll make it quick."

The other pirates moved to surround Pieter as Duendo talked. The captain wasn't going to take "no" for an answer. Picturing the damage an enslaved Equus could do, Pieter knew he couldn't either. But he saw no way to save the beast if he couldn't put his hands on that surefire.

"Friend Pieter," Equus whispered, lucid again. "You must use it. It's too late for me."

No, Pieter said. *No, this is my fault! There must be a way I can make it right!*

"You guessed correctly. My mane is why I am different from the other beasts. But I am too far gone," Equus said. His words grew slurred. "When the last of it burns away, I will be just like the others. Please don't let them turn me into a mindless monster. Into a slave. It hurts so very much. Please, friend Pieter. Oh, Mistress, it hurts." The horse subsided into incoherent muttering.

That creature will be an empty vessel or destroyed. And even if Pieter could somehow stop the pirates, others would be here in less than a day.

He pictured an enslaved Equus swimming its way back across the sea to the continent and razing the fragile remains of human civilization. Pieter couldn't let that happen. All he could do was try to go out with a final, bitter victory over evil men.

"Last chance, old man," Duendo said, slowly approaching.

"All right," Pieter exhaled, hoping to sound defeated. He seized on a last, desperate hunch. "It's not as if," he said loudly, "I know how to activate this thing." *Please don't be too far gone.*

"Many times," Equus said vaguely, "hunger isn't felt until the first morsel is swallowed."

It ate, Equus had said of the starsliver. What would such a weapon need to whet its appetite? *Weapon.* Inspiration seized him, and as the ring closed, Pieter rubbed one of his raw wrists roughly against the sphere until the tortured skin broke open. He left a thin smear of blood along the sphere's seething surface.

"No," Duendo hissed, halting as Pieter's blood vanished into that blurred surface. The starsliver burst to life, blossoming with piercing light in the exact pattern of his smeared blood.

Duendo cursed, whirling to run. With a flash of hate and the fading strength of the fungus in his veins, Pieter hurled the sphere as hard as he could. The effort toppled him.

Light slithering greedily across its entire surface, the starsliver struck Duendo square in the back, and he sprawled on his belly, losing the surefire. Then he began to scream.

Alive and hungry, the starsliver pulled matter into itself, gobbling up everything in its vicinity. It started with Duendo. The mercenary's screams faded as if into a great distance.

Pieter rose to his feet, wondering if this was enough.

"Close enough, wicked thing," Equus hissed. "Close enough. Run away now."

The other pirates had already vanished. Pieter's withered strength threatened desertion with each step. He would never get answers to his many questions about Equus and the fungus, but he would witness something none had ever seen as he died. That had been what his life had been about, had it not? The study of things lost or things unknown.

The roaring of surefire flames was drowned out by the roaring of winds as the starsliver pulled all things to it in order to quench its hunger. Pieter fought the rising vortex in mounting horror. *Have I done something even worse than what I prevented?*

"Only life hungers endlessly," whispered Equus, and Pieter felt a measure of peace.

The flames cleaning the bones of fungus were pulled into the swirling gyre. Wider and stronger the vortex grew, the point of light at its center growing brighter as it consumed bones, fronds, stone, and sand.

Larger and larger pieces of debris took flight around Pieter, spiraling inward to their doom. He kept his stately pace as if in a trance, staying always just steps ahead of the vortex's edge.

Muscles aching, ears deafened by the howl of sucking winds, Pieter's retreat continued until the cool of an incoming wave slapped his heels. He could back no further, so he sank to his knees, tears in his eyes.

"I'm sorry," he whispered to Equus. "I'm sorry I brought this upon you."

"You stopped it in the end," said the great beast, briefly lucid, his fading whisper somehow audible over the din. "I will be with her soon. Pray to her with me, friend Pieter. She is no more like the others than I am. Pray to her, and perhaps only one of us need die."

And Pieter did. Arms shaking, he opened his palms to the sky in the manner he'd seen in historical drawings of prayer, making them ready to receive the bounty of the gods. Silently at first, then aloud, he prayed to the mistress of this magnificent creature where she slept beneath the ground, a god whose name he didn't even know.

His eyes stung, filling with burning tears as he finished speaking the words. The wind's howl reached a thundering crescendo. Just ahead of him, at the edge of the ruined jungle, a massive stone suffered to be eaten with a deep, thrumming crack that seemed to Pieter to be a word.

Done.

Then the vortex died.

It faded from whirlwind to turbulent breeze in the space between two heartbeats. In its last gasps, a heavy object like a talon dropped into Pieter's outstretched hand. His creaking fingers closed around its cruelly curved surface reflexively.

The surefire.

Inland, the last debris rained down into a great emptiness. Where the island had been sat an immense crater, an eerily smooth partial sphere scooped from the island as though from the flesh of a melon. Only the island's rim, a ragged crescent of sand and rock, remained unscarred. Already the sea poured in to fill the spherical depression along the southern side.

Pieter's gaze touched the surefire in his hand, and he felt a pleasant little jolt. It seemed to whisper to him.

Others come, he imagined it saying in a voice distant and feminine.

"I'll need this," Pieter said, finishing the thought. A presence filled the air around him. *Her* presence. Maybe it filled the whole world and he just hadn't felt it before. It nodded when he spoke.

And it smiled.

Powerless

JESSICA GUERNSEY

A loose flap waving on the temporary white tent was my only greeting as I stood outside it, the stench of dirt and manure permeating my hair. I should have worn a hat. At least I wore sensible hiking boots instead of my usual heels.

When my director said this place was in the middle of nowhere, she wasn't exaggerating. Nothing but fields and dilapidated buildings as far as I could see, the bright morning sun not helping. The coffee here was probably lousy, too. But she also made it pretty clear that this was not an optional trip. My career was already on thin ice.

The field just beyond the tent looked big enough to house a minor league baseball team, complete with surrounding lights. Though this team were all dark-suited agents that would take me down first and make accusations later. Why on Earth did they need an electrical engineer here on a farm, of all places?

I was stalling. I blew out a breath, trying not to taste the tang of manure in the air, then tugged the plastic flap aside and pushed forward.

If it hadn't been for the thin walls flapping with every breeze, this might have been a real conference room, right down to the plastic guards under the chair rollers and a table with a coffeepot. I made a beeline right for it.

The pot was cold, and empty. I should have noticed there was no power running to it before I even picked it up.

"Coffee is only available at meals," a voice boomed behind me. "And the occasional late night. Neither of which we are currently experiencing."

I glared at the pot a moment longer before turning.

The man taking up the entire entrance was just like the federal agents in the movies. On the younger side of middle-aged. Short-cropped dark hair. Tall. All shoulders. Even the squiggly cord hanging off the back of his ear. From his voice, I recognized him as the one that gave my flight and driver details, all on voicemail so I couldn't talk back or ask questions. This guy's heavy brow line said he didn't like being asked questions. Unless that question was "how high?"

I put on the smile I used for fundraisers, walked toward him, and extended my hand. "You must be Miles Becker."

"*Agent* Becker." He shook my hand as briefly as possible, barely enough to register a grasp. "And you must be Sunny Hardman."

"*Doctor* Hardman." I considered winking and decided against it. Thin ice.

"Of course." His tone was a touch patronizing. "Have a seat. We will start shortly."

He turned his back on me and pressed the earpiece, muttering something low and unintelligible as he departed the tent.

I eyed his back, letting my smile drop. No need to waste the wattage.

Four high-backed black chairs sat around the dark wood rectangular table. A cluster of water bottles sweated in the center. Since I wasn't here as a willing participant to whatever government agency my director owed a favor, I took the seat at the head of the table, leaning back and testing the springs on the chairs. *Nice.*

I reached for a water bottle. I was used to the dry air in higher climates and this humidity might kill me, if the smell of animal poo didn't do me in first. I preferred the city for a reason.

I chugged down the first half of the bottle, and had just wiped my mouth on the back of my hand, when Agent Becker reappeared with a new guy. Something about him was perhaps too *eager* to pin him as an agent.

"Dr. Sunny Hardman," I said as the man child jogged forward to grasp my hand.

"Dr. Thad Boward," he replied, then leaned in, "But call me Thad. Dr. Boward is my dad."

I raised my eyebrows at that, but nodded. He seemed like a good kid, but time frequently proved me to be an awful judge of character —had a former mentor to thank for that.

Agent Becker pulled out the chair at the other end and sat down —total power move—but Agent Becker didn't really know me. It was most likely in my top-secret government file or dossier that I didn't back down easily, even when it destroyed my career, and especially when I was right.

I resumed my seat.

Thad looked a touch uncomfortable as he weighed the remaining options. He took the chair right in front of him.

Agent Becker handed around slick-looking tablets, with "Sunny Hardman" on a yellow sticky note on mine. I crumpled the note and stuffed it in a pocket. Looking for the on switch, I instead found a biometric reader on the bottom. Interesting. I pressed my thumb to the space, and the device woke up, power buzzing happily in my hands, while I decided not to wonder how they'd gotten my finger-prints in order to set this up.

Agent Becker cleared his throat, but I waited a couple beats before looking up. Both he and Thad focused on me. I noticed Thad hadn't turned on his device, the sticky note with his name still visible in the middle of the screen.

"Before we begin," Agent Becker inclined his head slightly toward me. "You need to understand the seriousness of what you're about to see. We didn't bring either of you in lightly. We intend that you'll prove our decision to be correct."

I fought the urge to roll my eyes. Instead, I gave him the smile I reserved for the barista who never failed to spell my name wrong. "Do we need to raise our right hands?"

Thad blinked and looked at Becker. "Do we?"

Becker's left eye twitched just a little. One point for me. But my smile withered as I remembered the thin ice.

"Unnecessary." He looked back at Thad. "We have no official documents for you to sign. Know there is more at stake here than your honor should you choose to reveal why you're here."

"Absolutely." Thad nodded a touch too vigorously.

I took a moment longer before I said, "Fine."

Becker nodded. "Access your files."

"How do I?" Thad shifted his tablet toward Becker.

So maybe the reason he hadn't logged in yet was simply because he hadn't known how to use the tech, which was not that advanced. My lab used biometrics. Of course, that hadn't stopped my mentor from stealing from me and then accusing me of theft, but that wasn't worth thinking about right now.

The folder was labeled "Project: Potato Field."

"Potato?" Thad asked.

The look Becker gave him made me glad he'd been a fraction of a second faster than me at asking that same question.

"The more bland and irrelevant the name, the better." Becker returned to his device.

Well, I could make a battery out of a potato, so maybe it wasn't such a dumb name.

The first folder held a series of test results about soil and plants, percentages and numbers for things I could only vaguely identify. I was all about currents and electricity. Did I really need to understand how much of the underlying matter was wood chips?

The label on the next folder was "Photos." I tapped on that.

The first few photos were of a fairly empty field. I recognized the somewhat dilapidated house that squatted about 100 yards from the white tent. When I'd first arrived, the dark-suited driver instructed me not to approach the house. I was guessing the residents weren't entirely friendly.

Next were close ups of black metal showing through the dull brown dirt. Someone dug down nearly six feet before discovering it. More pictures showed a deep trench beginning on the edge of the disk, a few yards deep judging from the depth of the trench and the referential guides.

More photos showed the trench as it continued to stretch around the black metal shape.

Thad was shaking his head.

"These numbers," he started quietly, but got louder. "How is this even possible? The plants underneath this thing are hundreds of years old. That's so weird."

Thad must be some sort of biological expert who could translate that table into actual data. But not enough to make sense.

"I take it you haven't looked at the photos yet?" I said, still flicking through the images.

Sure enough, he went from confusion to abject horror.

"What is this thing?" he demanded from Becker.

Becker leveled the kid's demands with one laser look. Thad visibly deflated, but he didn't look away from the feed.

"It's a spaceship," I said. "Right, Becker?"

Becker shot me a look, but I had armor that had taken decades of belittlement to craft.

When I only cocked an eyebrow in response, Becker laced his fingers together. "That's one theory."

"One?" Thad flipped through the images, hunching closer to the device. "What are the others?"

"Cold War bunker that someone built out in the middle of nowhere just to abandon." I flipped back through the pictures. "Or it could be a hoax." I tilted my seat back. "Which is why they took so many soil samples. Gotta have some legitimacy."

Thad leaned back in his chair, causing it to skootch toward my end of the table.

Becker leveled me another look, but he'd have to try harder. Thin ice be damned. Didn't they come to me? Wasn't it my opinion and expertise they wanted? They had to want to turn the thing on. So they needed someone who knew about power, and my whole expertise was in theoretical electrical engineering.

"So are you a chemist, Thad? Biologist?" I asked.

"Biologist." He nodded, probably feeling back on safer ground. "Though my specialty is more anatomical anthropology."

My eyebrows went up at that. "Anthropology? So you're here to tell us just what was flying this ship when it hit Earth."

I think he went a little paler. Hard to tell, since he was so pale to begin with. The truth of why he was here must have hit him for the first time.

I leaned forward and pushed a water bottle toward him. He took it, twisted the top off, and started gulping down the water.

I was here to turn on the lights; he was here to pick through the bones.

I went back to my files as he wheezed.

One photo showed a dark spot on the side of the craft. Several were close ups of what may be a hole blown in the side. Hard to tell because there wasn't any warped metal I would have expected from this kind of damage. Maybe the hole brought the craft down.

I couldn't wait to get inside that thing.

Becker paused our first trip down to the ship as agents removed a trespasser. According to the files, the owner of the land was Jefferson Wilkes, but his Great Aunt Nellie lived with him and frequently hovered over the shoulders of the crew as they cleared dirt. From what agents holding her arms were saying, they had removed her several times from the site. This time, she was not having it.

"They're going inside," she said, her rough voice low. "I want to go inside."

No less than three agents tried to convince her to wait until it was "safe."

She huffed at them, tugged the sleeve of her shapeless brown dress from the hands of an agent, and stood her ground. She was all wrinkles, gray hair, and stubbornness.

I immediately liked her.

Becker's mouth hardened when he caught my glance. "Absolutely not. Bringing in two specialists is bad enough. I won't be responsible for someone's grandma getting herself pulverized."

That got Thad's attention, and he immediately stopped walking. "Has *anyone* gotten pulverized?"

Becker threw me a long-suffering look, like this was all my fault. "No, Doctor. Nothing inside is moving, which is why Hardman is here."

"Doctor Hardman," I said automatically, watching as the three agents took hold of the woman and brought her away from the site. They weren't rough, just determined. But so was the old lady. She resisted hard for someone of her age and petite stature. I added a few more levels of respect for the woman.

I made sure the agents were behaving before I turned back to take in the dig site.

Lights were everywhere, though not all were on just yet. Plenty of people were wearing various forms of protective gear. Lots of equipment was set up that looked strange and all science-y. I eyed their generator set up. Even without doing the math, I could feel the strain in the power grid's vibrations. They'd need at least another couple kilowatts if they were hoping to run all those lights without fluctuation. Many of my critics insisted one couldn't feel vibrations from power sources, but my research had proven that wrong. Sea turtles sensed the electrical currents of their prey. I could feel power vibrations and had always assumed what I did was just like the turtles.

The ship itself was mostly uncovered, easily half a city block wide, though they weren't finished removing all the dirt from the top. Rounded but not a circle. But the most striking detail was the material. In the pictures, the ship was a vague gray shape with no discernible features. Up close? It was one solid color. No shading or variety. No seams or crevices. No satellite dishes or ray gun turrets. Completely smooth and featureless, like a flattened silver egg.

Thad stood there with his mouth hanging open for a good chunk of time. I finally nudged him and we headed down into the trench that Becker's head was disappearing into. Stepping inside the trench brought the smell of fresh dirt and far less manure. Much better.

"It's bigger than I thought." Thad stumbled, not taking his eyes off the ship.

"Did you notice the material it's made from?" I asked.

"How could I not?" he said, stumbling again. "It's so smooth."

"And non-reflective." I grabbed his arm so he didn't fall with his next step. "All those lights shining on it? No reflection."

Thad stopped again, and I released his arm.

I kept walking and heard him scramble to catch up.

The blown-open hole in the spacecraft was nearly as high up as Becker was tall. A set of temporary stairs led up to it, with the big agent standing at the top, waiting, hands clasped in front of him. His stance made me want to slow my steps, inspect the outside of the craft more closely.

I pulled a voltmeter from my bag and touched it to the surface of the ship, just as Thad reached out, though he jerked back once he saw what I was doing.

I switched through the different settings, none registering. "No voltage. You're good."

"What did you say your specialty was?" he asked.

"I'm an electrical engineer." As we shuffled after Becker, I tucked the voltmeter back into its pocket. "I mostly work with theoretical systems."

"Theoretical?"

"Examining possibilities," I said, slipping back into the common explanations. "Like what Tesla was doing when he discovered alternating currents."

Thad made a sound like he understood. In reality, very few people understood what I did. Very similar to the number of people who also understood when my mentor—my *former* mentor—stole my work. But the stigma carried, and I looked like the one at fault to those who didn't understand. And really, who understands that different power sources have a specific vibration? Which is why the big boss felt this assignment was a grand opportunity to clear the dirt from my name. I was Becker's best option for finding an alien power source.

However, if they didn't use electricity, I went from valuable to a liability.

This time, when Thad extended his hand, so did I.

I thought it would be smooth, but it wasn't. The surface felt uneven, like an orange peel, though I couldn't see any bumps. Weird.

Thad must have thought the same because his eyebrows were all scrunched up and he'd brought up his other hand.

"Whenever you two are ready," Becker's tone was dry, and his face was the very picture of impatience.

So I ran my hand over the surface a few more times.

"Better get inside. Don't want Daddy to get angry," I whispered to Thad before heading up the stairs toward the opening.

He snickered a little and joined me.

I noticed Becker didn't have any protective gear or gloves. Not even a breathing apparatus.

"Are you sure it's safe to go in there?" I asked, peeking into the dark hallway.

"Perfectly," he said, reaching just inside the edge to remove battery-powered lanterns, handing one to each of us. "We've run extensive tests. Results are in your files."

I turned to Thad, raising an eyebrow.

Thad nodded. "Normal. Low humidity, but normal."

I joined Becker as he headed down the left side hallway.

Despite my previous precautions, I let my fingers trail along the walls here. Unlike the outside, this was perfectly smooth, like I had imagined. Mirror smooth. No cracks or seams. Light only came from the lanterns held by Becker in front and Thad in back. I kept mine off. No windows. Did the creatures that ran this ship have other ways to see outside? Or was looking outside not important to them?

I wasn't here to wax philosophically on the importance of visual stimulation. I was here to find the power button, and to get off thin ice.

At various points, I used my voltmeter and got absolutely nothing, not even the barest tick. I tried a magnet and it slid right off; the material wasn't conductive. So how was the thing powered?

Becker's frown deepened.

The air got heavier as we moved around what had to be the outside edge of the ship, no other entries to rooms or hallways, all just one long, curved hall.

Until there was an open door.

Was there only this one door or had we passed dozens of doors, hidden in the seamless walls?

Agent Becker nodded to an agent that stood in the doorway. "Dr. Boward?" Agent Becker said. "Come with me."

Thad looked at me as he shuffled past, eyes wider than I'd seen them.

I watched the two move further into the room, their lights shining on various objects. There was a divot in the floor, about as deep and wide as an office chair, that looked padded. Other things were in here, vague shapes in the dark and moving light that hadn't been on my tablet.

I tried asking the other agent. "Why aren't there photos of this room in my files?"

The agent had the whole "stoic federal man" vibe and didn't acknowledge me.

I sighed loudly.

I had plenty more to say, but Thad suddenly pushed past me, dropped his lantern at my feet, and headed for the hallway. I heard retching and wet splashes.

I turned back to the room, not so sure I wanted to see what sent Thad running.

The agent at the door had a smug set to his lips, and that's what decided me. I switched on my lantern and stepped into the room.

The floor looked identical to the hallway, smooth and seamless, but the metallic surface felt like a plush carpet.

Various shapes and things had been tossed around, like a toddler's room after a tantrum. For all I knew, they were highly advanced scientific equipment. Another divot in the floor revealed a padded surface. Something glistened in my lantern light. I moved closer.

I took a cautious sniff and then a deeper one. There was a sort of overripe citrus smell and maybe rust, but no decomposition or anything to send me scurrying.

I moved closer.

"Oh."

The divot was full of a sort of gelatinous goo that shifted colors under my lantern to varying shades of reds, oranges, and yellows.

There was an eyeball. Toward the edge. Focused right on me.

I might have held my breath.

It didn't move, just floated in the goo.

There were other chunks and bits. Maybe fingers? I shook my head. I was assuming it was a humanoid creature. Really, this could be a soup pot holding their midday meal. I wasn't the biologist; Thad was.

I went back to the corridor and found Thad still bent over and puffing.

He wasn't alone. A small hand patted his back.

"Nellie?" I asked.

Her small, wrinkled face peered at me over Thad's back, dark eyes glittering in the light.

"Have you been down here before?" I asked. I didn't talk to her like a child. The way she kept getting around the agents spoke of intelligence.

She came out from behind Thad and gave a small nod.

"Have you been in that room?" I pointed behind me.

Another small nod.

"Is there anything you want to show me in there?"

This time, her face split into a huge grin, and she dashed around me. I watched her easily evade the agent, who wore too much his surprise on his face. Even Becker inside the room didn't turn in time to catch her as she bolted past. I was right on her heels.

She stopped at the far wall, standing still for a moment until I stood behind her, lantern raised. Her thin lips pursed tight and her eyes squeezed closed. She rubbed her hands together for a moment. Hesitantly, she ran three fingers over the wall. Periodically, she would stop, splay her fingers forming a sort of wide triangle with the middle finger at the top and spreading the other two fingers out, and press them into the surface twice. She'd pause a beat, then would grunt and keep moving her hands. As she moved along the wall, her grunts became increasingly frustrated, her hands moving more frantically.

Agent Becker stood behind us, but after a few minutes of watching, when it was clear Nellie was repeating her searches and pressing, he murmured a few words in his earpiece. Presently, three agents entered the room. I watched them step carefully around the, uh, *filled* divot. It would seem that everyone on site knew about it.

"Nellie," Agent Becker's voice held a razor's edge. "I warned you about being down here without a proper escort."

Nellie froze. Then her hands dropped to her sides. Her head bowed. The three agents stepped forward, hands ready to catch her if she ran. But Nellie barely gave them a look as she turned and walked away from the wall.

Thad had reentered the room, looking breathless, his hair a mess. He stood next to the divot with the substance in it, casting a sidelong glance, like he knew he was supposed to take samples but couldn't quite bring himself to touch the stuff. Nellie paused ever so briefly next to him and I saw him look at her before she moved on, turning left in the hallway and toward the hole entrance, the three agents quickly following.

I turned back to Becker.

His eyes were squinty, and he leaned a little back from me, like he was expecting me to let him have it. I get why he did it. I did. But I didn't bother with a smile.

"Any idea when they'll finish clearing the dirt from the top of the ship? I'd like to go up there and see if there's any sort of receivers or other devices that might explain how to power it."

Becker blinked at me, then righted himself. "Supposed to be on track to have it cleared this afternoon."

I nodded. "Excellent. Any chance we can get a tour along the outside trench before then? I'd like to see the entire ship."

"You should just stick to your job looking for the engine room."

I took a step forward. I was a good four inches shorter than Agent Becker, but I never let height intimidate me. My lip curled into a sneer. "How about you do *your* job and give me all the information

I'm missing from my files so I can do *my* job and figure out the power situation?"

I let him attempt to stare me down, but I was a little too far into his personal space. Becker struck me as someone who liked things a certain way: position in chairs, hair in place, files just so, and no one in his comfort zone.

Becker blinked first.

His dislike for me nearly rolled off him in waves. I didn't care. What was he going to do? Fire me? Good luck finding someone else with my credentials he could bully into cooperation. No one else was desperate enough.

He left us alone in the room.

I knelt by Thad, who hadn't gotten beyond opening his sample case.

He glanced up at me, a weak smile on his face. "I hate it when Mommy and Daddy fight."

I snorted, then pulled on a pair of his spare surgical gloves. "Do you think you'll need the eye?"

Thad swallowed hard. "Honestly, I don't want to go anywhere close to that thing, which I would absolutely have to do if we collected that. So let's just avoid it. For now. It's not like it's going anywhere."

So I dipped a vial in, slurping up a smallish bit of what might have been flesh. I capped it and wiped it down before tucking it back in his case. We worked quietly, collecting samples from different areas and depths. Thad made notes in a small book and took temperature readings while I gathered up the rest of his things.

"Thanks," he said, shouldering his now full bag.

I nodded. "You would have done the same for me."

He shrugged, but smiled. "Thanks for being nice to Nellie. She reminds me of my grandmother." His smile faded as his brow furrowed. "Before she left, she said something odd."

"What did she say?"

"She told me to be gentle." He shrugged. "No idea what that meant. She wouldn't look at me, either."

We used our lanterns to find the way back out. Thad went to the makeshift lab to get started on the samples. I found my gaze drawn to the old house. We'd been told the house was off limits. But it wasn't like I was taking up space in a guest room. I had questions. Maybe Nellie could answer them.

I noticed movement through a rear window, so I knocked on the back door, careful to avoid the peeling blue paint.

An unshaven man about Becker's age opened the door, blinked at me with red-rimmed eyes, and stammered, "Help you?"

The smile I gave him I mainly used for meeting fellow researchers as I offered my hand. "You must be Jefferson Wilkes. I'm Dr. Hardman. I'm helping at the site."

He glanced at my hand, but took a long drink from a brown bottle instead.

My smile didn't dim. "I was hoping I could talk to Nellie?"

He swallowed and glanced over my shoulder before letting the door open to reveal a modest kitchen, also painted blue. "She's in her room. Won't come out. Most I've ever seen her is when them feds bring her back." He nodded with his head to the left.

I slipped around him, not taking in a breath once I saw the yellow stains on his once white T-shirt, and made my way down a narrow hall with only one door at the end. The temperature was noticeably cooler, and I breathed a sigh of relief, smelling the wood polish.

I tapped on the thin door. "Nellie? It's the lady from before. Inside the ship. Can I talk to you?"

Nothing. I briefly wondered if she'd snuck back down to the ship.

Her door cracked to reveal one dark eye. "Soon. We will talk soon. Walk the edge."

The door closed.

Okay. That was promising. Sort of. I turned back to the hall.

The walls here were covered in old framed photographs. Some faded or yellowed from age. Each one showed the farmhouse or a version as the generations had passed. I stopped at one that showed only a cabin with people gathered in front. It was the same piece of land, given the hills in the background. All five people stood stoically, looking at the camera.

There on the end, slightly apart from the others, was a woman the same build as Nellie, who bore an uncanny resemblance to the old woman.

I looked at the photo next to it. Slightly larger house. More people. One that strongly resembled Nellie. In nearly all the pictures where I could make out the faces, there was a Nellie look-alike.

I walked back to the kitchen to find Mr. Wilkes seated at the table, beer clutched in hand.

"How long has your family been on this land?" I waved a hand toward the pictures lining the hallway.

"Five generations." He stared at the bottle. "The Wilkes were the first ones to settle this far west."

"And Nellie is your great-aunt?"

"Nellie is…" he shook his head slightly, took another drink before trying again. "Nellie is something."

"So not your great-aunt."

He met my eyes. "I've lived here my whole life. Just like my dad. Just like his dad. And Gramps called Nellie his great-aunt." He dropped his gaze to his bottle. "So you tell me what that means."

I opened my mouth to ask more, but a firm knock sounded on the door. I knew immediately who would stand there.

"Dr. Hardman," Becker said, his voice not showing a trace of irritation, but the hard line of his mouth said otherwise. "If you'll come with me."

I nodded to Jefferson and stepped outside, the humidity immediately clinging to me once more, along with the manure smell.

Turns out our first stop was at the conference room tent, where lunch waited. I half wondered which of the suits doubled as the chef as I bit into a soggy ham sandwich. And while there was coffee, it was far too weak to have any effect. At least it was hot.

I took the paper cup with me as we started toward the ship, just a few minutes later. Meals definitely weren't leisurely affairs.

I had fully expected a tromp around the trench, but the walkway was flat. They'd covered a marshy bit with grating. I witnessed the dirt removal process first hand as we crossed under the makeshift bridge used by the teams removing dirt. Small bulldozers sat unattended to the side, having already done the bulk of the removal. Now, it was wheelbarrows and shovels. I really hoped they damaged nothing and took small comfort in the sifting operation going on with the removed dirt. At least, they'd be able to find all the bits that broke off.

I didn't bother with my voltmeter, trusting instead on the lack of vibrations to tell me the ship was still. Though there was something that tickled at the back of my head.

"Hey!"

I turned to see Thad jogging to catch up.

"Ditching me?" He grinned wide enough to make me feel like smiling, too.

"Aren't you busy?" I asked, waiting for him to join me before turning to continue our path, my fingers still trailing.

"Doing cultures," he said. "About all we know is that they were carbon-based. Similar to our DNA, though not exactly. And I think we found some, uh, lung tissue? So they breathed like us. I'm letting the data finish compiling." He still looked a little green around the gills.

"Or maybe you needed some fresh air."

He let out a little laugh. "That, too. What are we doing down here?"

"Getting the full tour." I let my voice get a little louder so Becker would hear. "We're supposed to be on top of the craft."

No reaction. But a glance at Thad showed his raised eyebrows. I rolled my eyes in response.

I nearly missed the seam.

If I hadn't kept the practice of dragging my fingers along the surface as I walked, I don't think I would have seen it. Even looking right at the ship, my fingers clearly feeling the edge, I couldn't see it. Had it been like this all over the ship? Should I have run my hands over the surface like Nellie did? I wedged my thumbnail in the seam and followed it.

"Agent Becker," I said, running my nail up as far as I could reach. "How about we go up top right *here*?"

His look started out wry, but once he saw the line I traced, he muttered into his earpiece. Minutes later, agents hurried toward us with a ladder.

I went up first, handing my coffee cup to Becker, nail still firmly wedged in the seam. As it rose up, up, up, so did I. I crested the top and resorted to hands and knees to follow. Up here the material was the exact color and texture as the rest of the craft I'd seen so far. Dark gray and slightly rough, despite looking perfectly smooth. The suits' minions had done a pretty good job of clearing it as I was only coming across the occasional streak of dirt. Still smelled like manure, though.

Becker—no coffee cup—stood over me as I crawled along. I kept my dirty look to myself and followed the one lead I had.

The seam took a hard turn, my nail nearly breaking at the sudden change.

For the first time, there was a change in the color.

In a slightly lighter gray, three ovals, about the size of children's fingerprints, were connected by two lines, with the middle oval slightly higher than the other two.

"Huh," was my professional assessment.

The placement of the ovals reminded me of Nellie's hands when she pressed the walls inside the ship. Copying her movement, I placed my middle finger on the center oval, then slid two fingers out to meet the outer ovals, fitting the lighter color.

Nothing happened.

Just like inside.

I sat back on my heels.

Thad crouched beside me. "What now?"

"I'm not sure," I said slowly, that niggling in the back of my head growing. I was missing something. I stood, brushed off my pants, and paced back along the seam.

"What was that finger thing?" Thad asked, still in the same spot. I noticed he held my coffee cup. Becker must have passed it to him.

"Something I saw Nellie do inside the room," I said. "With the goo." I chanced a glance at Becker. He appeared to not be paying attention, though I suspected he didn't miss a thing.

Thad set my cup down and pressed his fingers to the same spots, but I turned to look out at the rest of the ship as he said, "Like this?"

A gasp from Becker and I turned back to no Thad.

He was gone. Nothing had moved on the ship. No sound. Not even a scream. Thad was just *gone*.

I crashed to my knees at the same spot, frantically running my fingertips in the same motion. Nothing.

"Thad!" My voice was far too shrill. "Can you hear me?"

Silence.

I whirled on Becker. "Can't you get some of your goons up here? Bring the biggest cutting tool you have."

Becker tugged his suit coat down. "We've already tried that. Nothing cuts through this."

"What happened?" I marched up to him. "What did you see?"

Becker shook his head slowly. "Nothing."

I took another step, right into his space.

Becker held up a hand. "He was right there. Then he wasn't. I didn't blink. That's how fast he was gone."

I believed him. I growled low in my throat and went back to the spot.

"This thing was sealed for hundreds of years," Becker said, and I wasn't sure why he kept talking. "If he's in a new space, there may be no oxygen in there, Hardman." Oh. *That* was why.

A quick glance proved we weren't over the same section where the goo room was located. No telling where Thad ended up when we didn't know how these beings operated. Even with the hole blown in the side, Thad had said the oxygen was low.

Becker interrupted my thoughts. "You need to get this thing figured out before the kid suffocates."

Dark thoughts covered my brain. Who was I kidding? Even if I walked into the Oval Office holding hands with an alien here to offer us the cure for cancer, there was no way I was getting my reputation back, nor my life. I was on my own.

What had been different? He'd crouched, and I'd knelt. The ovals were slightly smaller than my fingertips, but I didn't think Thad's fingers were smaller than mine. He made the same gesture. He'd set down the cup first.

The coffee cup.

It was gone, too. But Thad had the cup in his right hand. He'd used his right hand to make the gesture.

Turning my back to Becker, I rubbed my hands together, using the friction to warm them. Quickly crouching, I placed my warmed fingers and made the movement.

Tingling static electricity spread up my arm, down to my toes and the ends of my hair.

Then darkness.

I barely had time to gasp before Thad was in front of me, his eyes dark on his pale face as he steadied my arms.

"It's okay," he said. "You're inside the spaceship." From the waver in his voice, I wondered if he'd been about to lose it before I got here.

I nodded. "Solar-powered."

Thad tilted his head and scrunched up his brows. That was not what he'd expected me to say.

But it was so obvious now. The niggle had been trying to tell me all along that the power was building. I just hadn't recognized it.

We crouched on the floor of a roundish room about the size of the conference tent. Faintly glowing strips in varying shades of blues and yellows, maybe some green, ran off in all directions down the half dozen openings around us, like guidelines for new arrivals to find their way around the ship. No sound came from the outside. And the air was definitely low on the oxygen, stale with a hint of dirt. Or maybe that was how I smelled.

Thad held on to my arms as we slowly stood.

Inside. We were *inside*.

"Becker might join us shortly." I said. "I don't think it will take him long to put it all together."

Thad frowned. But then his eyes caught something over my shoulder and went wide.

I turned to see a small dark shape making its way toward us and, for the second time in only a few moments, I fought a scream. Yet, there was something about the determined walk.

I squinted into the faded light. "Nellie?"

She stepped into the room. Gone was the faded dress. Instead, she wore a one-piece suit of pale yellow material with dozens of black or silver circles and clasps along the chest and down the sides of both legs.

She grinned. "Good. You're here. We can begin."

Thad made a stammering noise, and Nellie's eyebrows rose.

"Oh," she said, adjusting a black strap on her wrist. "I wasn't expecting you, Dr. Boward."

His jaw worked, but I was pretty sure he was still trying to process entering the craft and hadn't gotten around to correcting Nellie on his name.

"You wanted me here?" I wasn't so sure I'd heard her correctly.

"Of course," Nellie twisted another black disc, and the suit puffed out slightly before deflating again. "Can't fly this thing without an engineer."

"And you think I can do that?"

Nellie smiled warmly, looking very much like the great aunt she'd pretended to be for so long. "I've followed your career for a long time. You are very nearly the only one who can do that."

"Why?" I asked, really wishing it hadn't come out strangled.

"Do you have any idea how long I've waited for one who can feel the shifts in energy like you can?" Her tone was conversational as she continued to fiddle and adjust her suit's various clasps and circles, which appeared to function like knobs. "That's all the engineer needs to do to keep it smooth."

A faint pop sounded in the distance and the strips of light brightened.

"Ah," Nellie's smile was back. "Good. The tear has sealed."

Thad's hand was on my arm as he came to his senses. "The tear?"

"Yes," Nellie said. "The crew damaged the ship when we crested a mountain range at too shallow of an angle. I warned them," she made a wet clicking sound that I wasn't sure I could reproduce and could only assume it was a name. Nellie shook her head sadly. "Well, they paid for that error, as you saw in that room. Nothing left of their essence, only their corrupted matter. I had to abandon the ship. Well, not really. I never left it completely. But I had to wait for someone to help me get back home."

"Excuse me, uh, Nellie?" Thad shifted his gaze between the small woman and me. "You aren't actually human?"

"We are similar enough, but no, Dr. Boward, I am not classified as human." She chuckled to herself, then turned to me. "Ready?"

I shook my head. "I don't know that I can..." I faded, not able to bring myself to say it.

Nellie stepped forward and took my hand in both of hers, tracing that same three-fingered gesture on my palm. "You are already advanced for your kind," she said, her tone soft, but twisted. "Do you really want to wait for them to catch up?"

"Thad stays here," I blurted out. "He has a future here." I shifted a look at him. "Unlike me."

Nellie sighed, then nodded. She strode over to Thad, smiling up at him before taking his arm and gently leading him back to the center of the room.

"Dr. Hardman," he said, eyes wide as Nellie placed him just so. "Dr. Hardman? Sunny?"

"You'll be okay, Thad," I gave him my best intern-encouraging smile. "I'll be okay."

And then he was gone. Back to the surface of the ship. Back to Becker. Back to the life he was building for himself.

But not me. I wasn't going back. I was moving forward.

Jessica Guernsey writes Urban and Contemporary Fantasy novels and short stories. A BYU alumna with a degree in Journalism, her work is published in magazines and anthologies. By day, she crushes dreams as a slush pile reader for multiple publishers. During November's NaNoWriMo, Jessica is a Municipal Liaison for the Utah::Elsewhere Region. Frequently, she can be found at writing conferences. She isn't difficult to spot; just look for the extrovert.

While she spent her teenage angst in Texas, she now lives on a mountain in Utah. Discover more stories at jessicaguernsey.com.

The Silver Serpent

JOSHUA ROBINSON

To whoever finds this document,

My name is Wilfred Jones. I've lived in Shepsworth my entire life, and many respect me as a valued member of the community. Despite pushing seventy, my head is screwed on tight. I'm not someone who buys into silly fantasies or superstitions. But three days ago, when visiting the abandoned waterpark, my scope of reality broadened. Haunted by the vision, those glowing eyes, and the morning news that shattered my heart to pieces, I know now what I must do. And after reading what follows here, you too will understand why the snake in the forest must die.

In my younger years, I'd been keen to try urban exploration, enticed by the thrill of venturing through manmade ruins. But as with other would-be hobbies, I'd never found the time—or rather, what time I had was taken by my studies toward a degree in ophthalmology. On the day of my long-overdue trip, the bright sunshine spurred me off the sofa and onto my feet. I'd thought, *Why not? Even if it is just a hike down the road, a little walk through the trees to see what I find.* So, with a packed ham sandwich and a bottle of water, I set off for Shepsworth Forest.

It was an hour of crunching over twigs, enjoying birdsong and the branches rustling overhead, before I stumbled across the unfinished waterpark. Mother Nature seemed to silence at once. Stretching across the vast clearing, the place reminded me of facts I'd long forgotten: how construction on this park had begun in the early nineties, and how, for undisclosed reasons, builders kept resigning from the project, resulting in its abandonment. As I crossed the loose-bricked path, I passed several swimming pools, some with snapped-off diving boards, others with rusty ladders and missing tiles on the patchy floors. Grime coated all the waterless pits, the lot of them like lidless coffins raised from the earth. Picnic tables covered in graffiti—and the unmistakable stains of bird droppings—were dotted around the pools. Further ahead stood what must've been the rocky wall of a mountain-themed log ride. Above the hole where riders would've emerged were the words "SCREW ME," spray-painted in a sickly pink.

Before I could wonder why a vandal would climb to such a treacherous height for some measly joke, I'd reached the snake slide: the one completed attraction in this cemetery of wasted potential. The fanged mouth opened into another filthy pool. From the head, the glistening metallic structure—equal parts monstrous and flaw-less—twisted upward, its scaly silver body oddly untouched by graf-fiti, any speck of rust, or any signs of weathering. The same couldn't be said for the spiral stairway alongside it, the blue paint peeling, the handrail scabbed. The very first step was broken on one side, as if someone had attempted the climb, only to be shown the error of their ways. But none of this stopped me—though in part, I wish it had. I'm no spring chicken, and of course, I recognized the risk. In the end, it was my father's wisdom that nudged me into action. He'd always said, "If you're going to do something, then go all the way." And that's exactly what I did.

No sooner had I stepped forward, than I paused at my reflection in one of the serpent's eyes—its bulging eyes—filled with a shade of green I can scarcely describe. The color so rich, so alien, that for the briefest moment I was convinced there had to be vitreous fluid *moving* beneath the glass.

A chill cut straight through me. I had half a mind to turn around and call the whole thing off. But remembering my father's words, I shook away my childish fears—of a slide, for crying out loud. Forcing a chuckle, I gripped the handrail, and climbed steadily to the platform at the top. Here, another strain of panic infected me as I looked down at the skeletal park. More than a cemetery, the whole area seemed to be its own realm, blocked off from the real world by endless oak trees, the humming cars from the main road nothing but whispers in this lonely place.

I suppressed a shudder, and shaking my head, put that kind of thinking to rest. Facing the slide, I assumed the tail-end of the snake had to have been omitted to form the entrance. After all, wasn't that how these slides worked? Yet the closer I got, the more I noticed the jagged rim of the tunnel, implying there *had* been a tail, which was crudely severed. In any case, having come so far already, I didn't hesitate to sit down inside. Take a breath. Push off into the darkness.

But I didn't slide. Didn't move any more than a few inches. My hands groped about the dry, dusty, somewhat warm metal surface. I had no choice but to shuffle along in awkward increments. The space was surprisingly narrow, too, considering how the beast had dwarfed me from the outside. Once or twice, I had to stop and slap at unseen insects crawling beneath my shirt. And that stench—Jesus, I can still smell it—like dried blood mixed with something foul, acidic, intestinal.

It was two minutes of shuffling and stopping and slapping when I realized my itch for adventure had been scratched ten times over. I wanted this done, wanted my sandwich. I wanted to get out and inhale the fresh air like a high-powered vacuum. So I shuffled more quickly. Down and around and down and around through the grainy darkness. The seconds rolled by, my eyes straining for the exit all the while.

Another realization struck me, brutal as an oncoming train: I *should* have reached the bottom by now, or at the very least, glimpsed daylight. Instead, this winding tomb grew blacker. My heart beat faster. My sense of where, along with the slide itself, faded into thin air. At once I was falling, plummeting in the void to a death I couldn't see coming. Unable to breathe, my stomach ramming up into my chest, I braced for the eventual impact, only to be welcomed by a burst of sunshine as I opened a pair of eyes I hadn't closed.

The sounds of splashing and laughter embraced me. When my vision adjusted, much sharper than I remembered, I gasped at the sight of the waterpark overflowing with life. Children played in the sparkling waters while families ate sandwiches, hot dogs, burgers, and cotton candy at the spotless picnic benches. The combined scents, along with the chemical tinge of chlorine, drifted in from every direction. My stomach rumbled, and I found myself making a move for the nearest hot dog stand before a sudden jerk of my arm kept me still.

Turning, I noticed my hand gripped by another. I looked up at the freckled face of a ginger woman—Mrs. Oliver, a teacher at Shepsworth Primary School. Except, in this vision, this other life, I knew her as more. I was fully aware that the woman smiling down at me was my mother.

Stunned, I glanced around, spotting countless familiar faces—my dearest friends and neighbors, known to me in the present. What did all this mean? Where was I? *When* was I? These questions bounced in my skull, alongside the knowledge that if Mrs. Oliver was my mother, that made me—this me—her ten-year-old boy, David. And that's when I saw it, before the bizarre terror of my new world could sink its claws in deeper. The grand prize of the waterpark, despite the impressive functioning log rides nearby.

The snake slide.

Kids and adults alike queued right the way up the high blue stairway. Water gushed from the serpent's mouth as people swished out of the blackness and into the pool below. Flooded with a youthful awe I hadn't felt in years, I immediately faced Mrs. Oliver, my mother, and tugged at her summer dress while begging her to release me. With a smile, she did, and I bolted for the slide as quick as my small legs could carry me.

When I got close, my young mind already cursing the long wait to the top, it happened.

The bulbous eyes in that monstrous head glowed a venomous green. Frozen a stone's throw from the stairway, I watched as the serpent's jaws snapped shut. Slider after slider piled up inside, the muffled screams of children competing with the violent swearing of adults within. But the worst was yet to come.

A series of *pops,* like screws flying loose, fired off from the jam-packed stairway. Segments of the handrail fell, and so did the people holding on, hitting the ground like flesh-filled tomatoes. The steps collapsed in a heartbeat. Screams ripped through the air along with the *clangs* of railings, *cracks* of bone, cries of spectators—all watching uselessly as friends, neighbors and loved ones were crushed in the carnage of twisted metal.

I cried myself then, the tears flowing harder than they ever have in my life. And like any child, I ran back to my mother only to find her smirking amid the chaos, her forked tongue flicking out between her lips, her glowing toxic eyes pinning me in place.

That *wasn't* Mrs. Oliver.

I remember waking with a shriek, back in my sixty-eight-year-old body between the open jaws of that *evil thing.* At the bottom of the slide, I slipped out of the mouth and into the empty pool. After a final glance at the head and those now-dim eyes, I hurried home, crying. Still crying, still that boy who'd witnessed a massacre.

For three days, sleep hasn't come. The vision—the nightmare—has been carved into my brain with surgical precision. So for three days, I've been going to the library, searching for answers—or perhaps, a lack of answers, hoping, maybe, to dispel the idea that my experience could be anything more than some mad daydream. Boy, wouldn't that have been a blessing?

No. Instead, I've uncovered information that'll keep me awake for years to come—assuming I survive tonight. Apparently, the construction workers of '92 never built the silver serpent, but rather, attempted to build the park around it. The structure must've dwelt in the forest for a good while earlier. For how long, exactly, I couldn't find. I only discovered in a book practically falling apart that an old cult hailing from Scotland used to occupy Shepsworth Forest. Rooted out by townsfolk two hundred years ago, they were said to kidnap and sacrifice people to strange bestial gods: The Wolf, The Vulture, The Serpent they'd referred to as *Vartuuk.*

I refused to delve any deeper, in part not wanting to entertain such ridiculous nonsense. I'd had a dream after passing out in the slide, possibly due to toxic fumes that remained from the waterpark's semi-construction. *That,* I was more than willing to believe.

Until I caught this morning's news: the mayor of Shepsworth announcing his plans to revitalize the place, finish what was started, and bring it to a glory it never got to reach. "Just in time for summer," he'd said.

It was then that it hit me: my vision back at the park was so much more than a dream, much worse than any nightmare. This vision I had was a *prophecy,* one I feel in my bones will come true unless I act.

Which brings us to now, and my own plans to drive my armored, modified truck straight into the hellish shrine. Am I afraid? Of course I bloody am. But like my father, I've come to believe that if you're going to do something, you ought to go all the way.

After the support this community's given me—through my wife's battle with cancer, another beast, that took her—I damn well intend to save them from the horrors no human should witness.

Part of me wonders why the serpent shared its intentions with me. Did it mean to? Or does it know there's not a thing I can do to stop it?

And the new construction workers, won't they also resign from the project for the same reasons the old workers did, the same reasons the townsfolk didn't—or couldn't—destroy the shrine when they stamped out the cult? Either way, *nothing* can be left to chance.

You might be wondering why I don't reach out to my beloved community, or to Mayor Brown himself, who'd surely listen to a long-time resident of Shepsworth. In this case, I doubt my reputation would hold any weight, not when I'd be regaling these people with a tale of prophecy and living water slides.

Let this document serve as an explanation in my success or as a warning in my failure.

In which case, you must promise to finish what I'll have started.
Destroy it, kill it, by any means necessary. Please. PLEASE. You must.
The snake in the forest must die!

Sincerely,

Wilfred Jones

Joshua Robinson is a British author of horror fiction. His work has appeared in Coffin Bell Journal, Night Picnic Journal, and Tales to Terrify Podcast, among others. Recently, his debut coming-of-age horror novella 'The Devil's Gift' was published by Ghost Orchid Press. He loves reading scary stories, and can't get enough of horror movies. He can be found on Instagram @joshua_robinson_author.

A Mistbound Proposal

SARA CODAIR

The Mistbound Express was once known as the gayest train in Vermont. It had cars dedicated to dancing, drinking, and eating. It had cars with couches and beds tucked into cozy compartments even though it was a three-hour scenic tour. In a time where it was illegal to be gay, this train had become a gay haven.

By the time Jeanie found it, the train was an empty, rotting shell. It was a ghost of what it used to be, but it was still gay. And if Jeanie believed in ghosts, she would've said it was haunted.

She'd met her girlfriend here thirteen years ago, when she was fourteen, sneaking off to paint a mural on one of the decaying cars. Alicia had been in a compartment, reading lesbian erotica where her family would never catch her. Jeanie remembered her brown hair sticking straight up and the smell of store-bought chocolate chip cookies. It had felt like the start of something special, but she never would have guessed that all these years later, she'd be meeting Alicia at this same defunct train with an engagement ring in her pocket.

Granted, she'd been carrying the damned ring around for more than a month and still hadn't found the right moment to propose. At first, it was just normal nerves. But Alicia had been acting secretive and withdrawn since she learned about the train's imminent destruction two weeks ago. Every time Jeanie tried to talk to her about, Alicia changed the subject. Jeanie understood Alicia might be sad, but it was hard to propose with secrets lurking between them.

"This is probably the last time we'll see our compartment." Alicia stepped out of the shadows, taking Jeanie's hand. Her hands were small but sturdy with fingernails bit back to the quick. "I'll miss writing here so much."

The train's lean and peeling paint gave it a dangerous yet rustic charm. Its shadow loomed over muddy ground, reaching for her and Alicia. Flickering light reflected off the windows, but Jeanie couldn't determine its source. It almost formed a face, wistful and longing.

She didn't realize how attached she was to this dilapidated train until she tried to picture not being able to come here anymore. The train wasn't much, but the walls crawled with memory. "I should've visited more while I still could."

Alicia brushed her bangs out of her eyes. "Work keeps you busy, which is necessary, because we need to eat and you being busy pays for food."

Jeanie couldn't help but roll her eyes. Her accounting job was like a vampire, sucking her soul dry while she longed for a paintbrush or hammer. Alicia didn't make as much money, but at least she got to do what she was passionate about. Readers loved her steamy queer historical romances and ghost stories, commenting that her characters felt like real people and the setting felt written by someone who lived in that time period. Jeanie read widely in the same genre. There was something different about Alicia's stories.

"You'll have to find a new place to write. Or just write at home." Jeanie started toward their train car, the one that wasn't like the others. The rainbows, hearts, and unicorns she'd painted on it as a teen had somehow retained all their vibrant colors despite the harsh New England weather, even though they were older than the faded graffiti tags and poorly drawn dicks that marked the other cars. Every few years, a different group of teens would show up here, thinking it was a great party spot. But they never came more than a few weekends before moving on with tales of rattling wheels and objects moving on their own, spreading rumors of hauntings. They never, ever touched Jeanie and Alicia's car. According to one teen she'd caught fleeing, it was "haunted as fuck." Jeanie had never seen a ghost or evidence of one. If they existed, they liked Jeanie and Alicia enough not to bother them.

A clang echoed through the quiet evening.

Maybe there was a raccoon or possum.

Because ghosts weren't real, right?

"As long as I have pieces of the train, I can write anywhere." Alicia walked alongside Jeanie, corduroy pants swishing. Her button-down shirt and a vest gave the whole outfit a vintage look.

That was the most reason she'd given for wanting the pieces in the two weeks she'd been talking about taking them, and Jeanie had asked a lot. She supposed it was a relief it wasn't something personal about Jeanie, but if it was so benign, why not be upfront about it to begin with? Was she hiding something else?

"They'll be your inspiration?" Jeanie fidgeted with her backpack's straps. It was laden with her tools of a trade she wished she went into, including her favorite reciprocating saw and its batteries. With the right blades, it could cut through just about anything.

Tomorrow, contractors would show up to start clearing out the train, and eventually, the tracks. Jeanie wondered what it would be like to get paid to destroy something or to pave the trail. "Once the construction is done, you can still come here."

"That's not the same. The train won't be here." Alicia pursed her lips together, and her eyes brimmed with tears as she stared down at the crumbling pavement.

Next time they came, it would probably be smooth and new.

Jeanie put her hand in her pocket, tracing the ring's filigree. If she wanted to propose here, in the place she met Alicia, it had to be tonight before everything changed. She could take it out right now, and ask in front of the train car, but...

"Why is it so important to have the train and its pieces, Alicia? Why do you need them to write?"

She shrugged. "Because it is. I just do."

That was the kind of non-answer she'd been getting all along, one that conjured frustrating memories of parents never explaining why they did things. She just wanted to understand.

Silence filled the space between them for the rest of the walk.

"This place was home to me, before you took over that role." Alicia climbed into the car, and something brightened about her. They walked past two doors to Alicia's compartment, which now was her "office," but as a teen, had been the place she slept when she needed to be away from home, and when her parents had kicked her out.

At least, she had until she got close enough to Jeanie to crash in her room instead, and eventually, move in. Now, the compartment had a desk, a typewriter as old as the train, two chairs, and an end table. All old stuff salvaged from the side of the road. Alicia wrote her first drafts on the typewriter, and the revisions at home on her laptop.

Jeanie pulled the chairs and end table to the center of the compartment and they had their picnic. Conversation flowed from Jeanie complaining about work to planning meals to speculating about the next episode of "Centipede Woman and the Mothman," but the ring stayed in Jeanie's pocket. There was something about the way Alicia held herself, more tense than usual, and something about all the things she didn't say that reinforced the idea she was hiding something. Alicia was old fashioned with her clothes, but Jeanie was old fashioned with relationships. She believed in forever, and needed to be sure before she popped the question.

Time rushed by, but the right moment had yet to come. "We should probably get to work, if you really want to take pieces home."

Something about the air felt restless, like the train was alive and knew it was living its last moments. Their camp lights flickered. The train vibrated and rocked.

Jeanie went outside to see how windy it was. She always worried a piece of debris would blow off the station and crush their compartment. Or the wind would just blow the whole thing over on its side.

Branches held still. Normally on spring evenings, the peepers serenaded them from the nearby wetlands, but silence weighed down on Jeanie's surroundings, conjuring goosebumps on her arms. She turned back to the train, but it was further away than she thought.

Was it moving?

No steam came from the smokestack, but the engine chugged.

Wheels turned. Slowly, but they turned. The walls rattled as the decrepit thing inched forward, ever so slightly gaining speed, with Alicia still on board.

"How the hell is it moving?" Jeanie jogged toward the train.

The wheels spun faster.

Pieces broke off its rusted cowcatcher.

The train lifted, hovering an inch or two above the tracks.

"Alicia!" Jeanie sprinted. Her heart raced.

Breathing hard, she grabbed the rusty rail. Just as she slipped through the creaky old door, the train lurched and picked up speed, chugging down a track that was overgrown with weeds.

"Alicia?" Jeanie's heart raced as she tried to find her balance in the shuddering hall and figure out how on earth this beautiful rotten machine moved. "Where are you?"

"In the compartment." Her voice echoed throughout the car.

Jeanie ran down the hall, but it was like she was on a treadmill. Like reality and physics had just quit playing by the rules. The floor moved as she ran, so she didn't go anywhere. Then the doors started moving, flying by like they were on a track. Alicia's voice stretched out in slow motion, blurring and jumbling. Then it sped up like an old cassette tape on fast-forward.

It was like a psychotropic funhouse from hell. Except she hadn't taken any drugs. What the hell was going on?

She'd made the food herself. There was nothing in it that could make her hallucinate. Which meant...

Jeanie just stopped. She couldn't process this. Muscles burning and breathing hard, she hunched over, gasping for breath. Everything ceased moving as Alicia burst out of a door and grabbed Jeanie, pulling her into her compartment.

"What is happening?" Jeanie sunk into the creaky, falling-apart rocker, which was surprisingly steady despite the rickety speedy clanking of the train. Her odds of proposing were dwindling by the moment.

"Ghosts." Alicia's face was pale, and her eyes dilated. "I didn't... I knew the train was haunted, but I didn't know the ghosts could do this. I'm not sure they knew either until they tried."

"Ghosts?" Cogs slowly turned in Jeanie's confused, terrified mind as she clutched the rocker, wishing her fingernails were long enough to dig into its old wood armrests. "Wait. You *know* things about ghosts?"

Jeanie sucked in a shaky breath. Alicia loved ghost stories, but she'd never said anything to hint they were real. That she believed them. That this train was actually haunted. All the time they'd spent here, and she never said it was really haunted.

Alicia inhaled slowly. "The train doesn't want to be disassembled."

"I didn't know trains could want things," blurted Jeanie, words sharp as knives.

Alicia's frown deepened. Her hands closed into fists. The train lurched, sending Jeanie toppling to the floor as her chair broke, shattered like her half-baked proposal plan.

Alicia pleaded to the ceiling. "Be gentle with her, please, she doesn't understand."

Was Alicia talking to the train?

Yes.

She was talking to the damned train. That was what Alicia was hiding. She talked to the train or its ghosts. She was some kind of psychic and never told Jeanie. Were there other things Alicia hadn't told Jeanie?

"This train... " Alicia rubbed the wall like she was petting a cat. "A lot of people have strong memories tied to it, and ghosts, well, they're memories."

"Did something bad happen here?" That seemed to be a common thing in ghost stories—places where bad things happened were haunted.

"Not at all." Alicia held out a hand to Jeanie.

Jeanie, on her hands and knees from the fall, glared at the hand. Fear still made her heart race; it glued her hands to the floor and held her jaw clenched.

Alicia took a deep breath and continued, "The opposite, actually. Their spirits returned here because they had so many good memories. Because it's where they met their loved ones, fell in love, and were free to be themselves in a time when the world didn't allow that."

"There is a lot I don't know about hauntings." *Does that mean I believe in this madness?* Jeanie pushed up to her feet slowly. *I suppose it does.* "How do you know all this?"

"Because I talk with the ghosts." Alicia stood up and paced around the room, hands fidgeting behind her back. Her breaths came fast. She paused and closed her eyes as tears trickled down her cheeks.

"You talk to ghosts? And you never even tried to tell me." Jeanie failed to keep the frustration and fear out of her voice. She hated secrets, surprises, and lies since she was a kid, because her parents had lied and hid so much. Alicia knew that and still kept this from her. "Why didn't you tell me?

Alicia braced herself on the wall as the train rattled. "Would you have believed me if we were not on a ghost-powered runaway train when I told you?"

"You should've told me, Alicia." Jeanie got to her feet slowly. Her hands shook. Sweat slicked her palms. Honestly, she didn't know what she would've thought, but she would've rather been told and not believed than been lied to for a decade.

"I couldn't. I just couldn't risk losing you. Please. I promise it was my only secret."

Even if it was the only one, she'd kept it so well for so long. Now, they were on a dilapidated train that was moving even though it had no right to move. Jeanie walked over to the window and peered out. Trees blurred by and when she looked down... Were they higher than they had been before? "We can't stay on this train."

Alicia joined Jeanie, standing so their arms touched. "We can't just jump off. It's moving too fast."

"Can we talk to them? Maybe just ask them to stop and let us off?" Jeanie paced around the room. She had to get out of here. Think of a way to make the train stop.

Alicia closed her eyes and rubbed her temples. "They feel so angry and all their attention is on moving the train."

"What do they want?" If Jeanie could figure out what they wanted, maybe she could get them to stop to let her and Alicia go.

"They want the train intact." Alicia's cheeks flushed red. "And they want me to tell their stories."

"What if we could still save the train?" Jeanie asked louder than necessary, hoping the ghosts would hear. Her hands trembled, but her voice was steady.

Alicia tilted her head. "How?"

The train slowed, as if it were listening.

"Why is the train getting demolished instead of being brought to a museum?" Jeanie forced herself to look in Alicia's eyes.

Alicia narrowed her eyes and picked at her lip. "Because the museum couldn't get the funding to both move it and restore it. The rail trail people barely have enough money to make the trail, let alone preserve the train."

"What is the train doing now?" Jeanie clamped her shaking hands together.

"Moving." Alicia picked at her cuticles. "But there will be demolitions tomorrow. And I don't think the museum would appreciate the train just showing up out of nowhere."

"Maybe, but if they really wanted it. I doubt they'd just dump it." Jeanie caught peeks into people's backyards where the private property bordered the soon-to-be-trail, but in another mile, they'd be in swampy forest. "Where is it going anyway?"

"I heard something about the lake before they all stopped talking," Alicia muttered, running her hands through her hair.

"They as in the ghosts?" Jeanie put her hand on her tight chest and took a deep breath. "Are they going to dump us in a lake?"

"No." Alicia put a hand on Jeanie's back. "I think the train is going to just go as far as the old causeway by the lake. It will be harder to get to if it's surrounded by water and swamp on two sides."

"But they still might haul it away and scrap it when they finish the trail, assuming it doesn't tip over and fall in next time a storm floods the causeway." Jeanie took a deep breath and walked the perimeter of the room with her hand on the wall. "That's a temporary solution. Driving it to the museum is a permanent one."

The train slowed.

"What if they don't want it?" Dread weighed Alicia's eyes as they met Jeanie's.

"Try another museum? There are a few in New England. The train can fly."

Alicia squeezed her eyes shut and rubbed her temples. "But the ghosts remember the tracks. They remember the feel, sound, and smell of the train chugging down them. They remember, and it happens. The magic of ghosts is all in memory and belief. They can't take the train anywhere; only places it has gone before."

"The museum that is on these tracks wanted it, but they couldn't get the money to transport it. If it shows up, they'll keep it." Jeanie filled her voice with false confidence. For Alicia's sake, she hoped the museum would actually keep it, but she wasn't sure it would. She just needed this train to stop. She needed to get off before it risked a half-sunken causeway with her and Alicia onboard. And they were heading in the opposite direction of the museum.

"Um, can this thing turn around?"

Jeanie didn't know the mechanics of how reversing direction worked but the rules of reality obviously didn't matter when the floor and doors went haywire. Not to mention the fact the train was hovering a few inches off the track. Maybe the ghosts just had to remember it going the other direction?

"You need to turn around!" Jeanie looked all around as she shouted. "If you get too close to the lake, past where the trail ends, you'll fall in. Then they'll have to haul you off to the scrapyard, so you don't pollute the water. But if you go to the museum, they'll care for you. Restore you. Share your history. Please. Don't risk that sinking causeway."

Brakes squealed, their high-pitched whine echoing through a very long, anxiety ridden stretch before it actually stopped. The temperature in the compartment rose and the hairs of Jeanie's arms stood. The door opened.

"They said we need to go and make sure the tracks are cleared all the way to the museum." Alicia stepped toward the door. "We have until dawn."

"If it can fly, why do the tracks need to be cleared?" Jeanie's legs tensed. She wanted to run off of the train, in case it changed its mind, but fear of the hallway turning into a treadmill rooted her feet in place.

"They can remember the train moving, but they can't remember things away. Any large debris, fallen trees or big objects people dumped, could derail their focus and in turn, the train." Alicia ran her hands through her hair and tugged at it. "We know the tracks are clear up to the lake because we just biked that way last weekend, but who knows what could be blocking the other section."

"Alright." Jeanie picked up her backpack, clutching it to her chest and tried to think about the task of clearing the tracks instead of the fact that she was on a *haunted train*. She'd need to run home and get a chainsaw, in case there were any trees down. There was a part of her that desperately wanted to stay home once she got there, but saving the train was important to Alicia... and Alicia important to her.

The ghosts declared that once they started moving the train again, they were not stopping until they reached their destination, because stopping had taken too much energy. But they'd already traveled miles from where Jeanie had parked her car. So Jeanie and Alicia found themselves bushwhacking through a swamp, not saying a word, until they emerged splattered with mud in a Dunkin' Donuts parking lot.

The smell of coffee and sugary delights wafted from the building, drawing Jeanie in. She walked toward the beacon of normal. She stuck her hands in her pocket, confirming the ring was still there. Relief lightened her chest and tangled with confusion. She was hurt Alicia hadn't told her about the ghosts and terrified that ghosts existed. But none of that changed how much she loved Alicia.

Thankfully, Dunkin' was deserted.

Jeanie turned toward the bathroom.

"Wait, Jeanie. Do you want me to order you anything?"

She paused. Peered over her shoulder. "My usual."

Alicia nodded.

Jeanie dove into the bathroom, tears leaking from her eyes. Alicia ordering her coffee seemed so normal. Dunkin' seemed so normal. Yet out in the woods, there was a whole haunted train waiting for them to clear out miles of abandoned tracks, so it could save its skin by going to a museum that may or may not want it. The whole thing sounded absolutely bonkers. No wonder Alicia had never mentioned the ghosts.

"She still should've told me," muttered Jeanie as she scrubbed and scrubbed her hands and arms, thankful it was early enough in the spring that the mosquitoes weren't out yet. "She shouldn't have had to carry that alone."

Had Alicia been scared the first time she saw a ghost? Confused? How long had she known they existed? There was this whole part of her Jeanie didn't know. A hole in her understanding of the woman she loved. A hole in their relationship.

But maybe it was one that could still be filled, a tear that could be patched.

Jeanie dried her hands, and walked out of the bathroom to Alicia, who was holding two steaming cups. "You want me to hold those while you go to the bathroom?"

"Thank you." Alicia handed Jeanie the cups, making sure their fingers brushed just how she always did when she handed things to Jeanie.

Just like normal.

Sighing, she sat down at a table, took out her phone, and found an Uber.

"Did you bike or drive to the train?" Jeanie asked after a stretch of sitting and sipping in silence. Alicia had been at the train writing while Jeanie worked.

"Biked," said Alicia. "Why?"

"I don't want to know what kind of assumptions the Uber driver would make if I had them stop at our house to get a chainsaw then drop us off at a dirt road or worse, right at the old tracks with the abandoned train."

Alicia laughed so suddenly she almost spit coffee all over the table. "Now that would make a good story prompt, if I wrote horror."

"Yeah, it would." She narrowed her eyes and glared at Alicia. "Tonight would make a good horror prompt too."

The laughter died.

"No." Alicia leaned forward, resting her chin on closed fists. "People die in horror novels. They get hurt. They don't get happy endings. This isn't that kind of story."

Jeanie leaned back and crossed her arms. "If you really wanted a happy ending, you wouldn't have hid this from me."

"You don't understand," Alicia pleaded. "I couldn't tell you. I'm afraid I shouldn't have tonight, but... I felt like I had to, with you on the train."

Those words burned like scalding hot coffee burning her mouth. "Why?"

Alicia took a deep breath and looked down at an empty sugar packet she'd shredded. "Because I lose everyone I tell."

"Like they die?" Fresh fear chilled Jeanie as she clutched her coffee closer.

"No." Alicia ran her hands through her hair. A piece of wrapper stuck to her bangs. "I told Lizzie Baker in first grade and then she moved. I told Harold Goodman in third grade then he started bullying me. I told Hailee Blackwell in fifth grade and then they switched schools. I told my parents shortly before they kicked me out."

"Your parents kicked you out because they're homophobic shits." Jeanie put her coffee down and cradled her head in her hands. "I can't speak for the others, but I doubt you telling another kid made them move."

"I don't know." She looked up, eyes teary for the third time tonight. "I should've told you anyway. I'm sorry."

Jeanie reached across the table and took her hand. "No more secrets. No more lies. Will you promise?"

"I'll never hide something from you again, Jeanie. I promise."

Jeanie hoped she meant it.

"Please tell me your truck isn't haunted." Jeanie emerged from the garage with a chainsaw and a bag filled with ropes and ratchet straps.

"She's not." Alicia petted the hood the same way she'd petted the train wall. "At least, I don't think so. If there is a ghost, they've done a good job hiding from me."

The truck was at least fifty years old, and Alicia clung to it like she clung to every other antique thing she got her hands on. A disturbing thought crossed Jeanie's mind. "You're not a ghost, right?"

"I'm very much alive." Alicia moved closer to Jeanie and winked. "I think you of all people should know that."

Jeanie walked past her, put her gear in the truck, and got in the passenger seat. "How old were you when you first saw a ghost?"

"Six. The elementary school gym was haunted." Alicia turned the key. The engine roared.

"Were you scared?" Jeanie leaned her head against the glass.

"I was terrified, but also curious. So curious." Alicia looked out at the road like memories were unfurling before her eyes. "I wanted to know her story, and I learned it. I wrote it down. And it made me hungry for more stories. Ghosts, in general, are why I became a writer. But the ones from the train made me a novelist. They helped me find my niche."

"I have so many questions, Alicia." Jeanie studied her messy brown hair and the tiny creases forming near her eyes. Her lips were chapped. A crack she picked at bled. Dark circles lurked under her eyes.

"And I have answers, Jeanie. Things I wish I'd told you years ago." She took one hand off the wheel and squeezed Jeanie's hand. "I'm glad you know, and that you're here now, helping me save my ghosts."

"Me too," said Jeanie.

She didn't have to be here doing this. She could just stay home now that she was away from the train. She didn't need to ever go back to it. If the train could only travel on tracks it had been on before, it couldn't find Jeanie to punish her for lying.

She didn't have to go back.

But if they saved the train, Alicia would still have access to it. To the ghosts. Her muses. *And that's why I'm doing this. That's why I am going to clear these damned tracks.*

The truck rumbled around windy side roads, down a bumpy dirt road, past the clearing where Jeanie's compact SUV was parked, and onto the tracks. She drove slowly with the high beams on, watching for wildlife and obstacles alike. Startling a moose never ended well for anyone. The first two miles were clear, and hope flared in Jeanie's chest. Maybe, just maybe, this would actually be easy.

Then they came across the area that looked like it had been hit by a tornado.

A knot formed in Jeanie's chest. They hardly ever got tornadoes in Vermont, but thanks to climate change and the severe storms it created, they'd gotten one last summer, and there was a pile of fallen trees on the tracks.

"I think we need more chainsaws." Alicia put the truck in park.

Jeanie got out and surveyed the mess. "Only a few of them are really big."

In fact, a lot of it was small, new growth. "I'm going to cut the big ones off of the trail. You use the other tools to work on the branches and saplings."

Jeanie got the chainsaw out and started cutting through the biggest tree. Most of the land in this area had once been cleared for farming, but this tree must have been kept for shade. She bet if she went exploring in the woods, she'd find ruins of an old foundation nearby, which would absolutely thrill Alicia. She tried to make note of the landscape around here, which was easy, since the woods were filled with toppled trees. Maybe when the trail was made, they could come back here and explore.

Jeanie kept pausing between cuts to peek at Alicia. Each time Alicia stared at a trunk or stick, sawing or hacking with hyper focused efficiency. She was the type of person who left dishes in the sink and wrappers scattered through the house. She only got this focused on things she really cared about, like with her writing. If she was making this much progress on this big a mess, then it really, really mattered to her. Jeanie had to admit, maybe she wouldn't have believed her if she, a week or a decade ago, said her stories were inspired by ghosts. Maybe it was best to find out in a way that made it hard to question what happened. Because if she hadn't believed, Jeanie could have ruined the relationship long before a rail trail coalition tried to rob them of their train.

By the time they'd cleared away what felt like a mile of downed trees and branches, Jeanie's arms itched from the vibration of the saw. Blisters stung her palms. Sweat plastered her hair to her head and made safety glasses slip down the bridge of her nose. Alicia was equally sweaty, and her nice, faux vintage clothes were covered in dirt, wood splinters, and sap.

Alicia looked around, startled.

"What did you hear?" Jeanie was afraid she was going to say coyotes.

Was the sky lighter than it had been a few minutes ago? Have we been working that long? She looked at her phone. It was almost six.

"The ghosts." She cradled her head in her hands. "They're coming."

"You mean the train is coming?"

She nodded.

"I hope this is it for downed trees." Jeanie put the chainsaw in the back of the truck with the logs.

This time, Alicia drove a little faster than she probably should've and slammed on the brakes less than a mile away from the museum as they came across a puke green vinyl couch that screamed nineteen-seventies. The cushions looked like they'd been chewed in several places. Beer cans littered the ground around it. A small hole contained pieces of charred wood.

"Well, I guess we found where some of the kids the train ghosts scared away went to party." Alicia got out of the truck and studied the couch. "This shouldn't be too hard to move."

They each took a side, but when they lifted it, the couch was wet and a lot heavier than expected. They got it a few inches and put it down. "This isn't going to work."

Alicia stared, eyes narrowed, face wrinkled in concentration as she paced around the couch. "We both go on the same end, lift, and swing. Then switch, repeating until we get it clear of the tracks."

Jeanie took a step forward, but her foot caught on the track. Which was vibrating. Her stomach collided with the arm of the couch. Pain blossomed, and air rushed out of her lungs.

The horn blared, louder this time. She could hear the engine chugging.

"Why couldn't they wait until we're done?" Jeanie pushed herself up.

"They grow weaker as the sun rises." Alicia gripped the arm of the couch. Jeanie and her lifted and swung.

The chugging got louder.

They lifted and swung.

The horn blared.

They lifted swung.

"We're almost there." Alicia hoisted her end, taking baby steps until she was clear. "They have to slow down soon to actually stop before they hit the museum."

Jeanie lifted her end. In the distance, she could see the train, hovering above the tracks, wobbling, as it hurtled toward them.

She was clear.

Panting, her and Alicia stood and stared into each other's eyes.

Then a train horn blared. They sprinted to the truck. Alicia slammed on the gas and sped forward. The last mile to the museum was thankfully clear of obstacles. They pulled off of the track onto a grassy area just as the train ground to a halt behind them, stopping just a few yards from one of the museum's trains.

Alicia jumped out of the truck and ran up to her train and just stood there, inches away, beaming at it. "You're going to fit right in here."

Jeanie followed, watching Alicia converse with beings she couldn't see or hear.

Her train looked so shabby and run down in comparison to the exhibit trains, but Jeanie was certain that with enough time, the museum would have it looking good as new. She hoped they'd let Alicia come write near it.

"Maybe you can make some kind of agreement with the museum, so they'll let you come write here." Jeanie slid her arm around Alicia's waist.

"I was thinking of offering to donate a 10th of profits on a specific series." Alicia leaned her head against Jeanie. "Thank you so much for helping."

Warmth filled Jeanie as she placed a gentle kiss on Alicia's head and pulled her closer.

On the horizon, the sun was rising.

The ring weighed in Jeanie's pocket.

Even if the museum did keep the train, it wouldn't be the same for long. If she wanted to propose at the train, with it still lingering in its dilapidated glory, then she had to do it now.

Jeanie sighed as a big grin blossomed on her face. "You know, I've been carrying a little secret of my own but haven't found the right moment to tell you. I don't think one moment will ever feel particularly right."

Alicia's brow furrowed. "So tell me now."

Still grinning, Jeanie reached into her pocket and pulled out the ring. It was a small diamond, set inside a filigree band, which was even older than the train. "I think I want to marry you, even though you didn't tell me about the ghosts."

"I think I want to marry you too." Alicia kissed Jeanie.

Tension drained from Jeanie's shoulders as her lips parted. Her chest felt warm, whole. There were no more lies. No more secrets. There was nothing but clothes left between them.

Sara Codair writes speculative short stories and novels. They partially owe their success to their faithful feline writing partner, Goose the Meowditor-In-Chief, who likes to "edit" their work by deleting entire pages. Their short fiction was recently published in Distant Gardens and Father Reefs. Find Sara online @shatteredsmooth or at saracodair.com.

Panopticon

TARA CALABY

R ita broke out of her cell when the water ran dry. The meal delivery system had been silent for days. *Another trick of the aliens*, she'd thought, so she'd sat in stoic stillness while her stomach growled and shrivelled. Thirst, she found, was not so easy to ignore. Her throat was tight and sore within hours and, when the next day came and the bowl remained empty, she wrenched a wooden arm from her sleep couch and used it to splinter the door.

The Facility had no steel bars or cast-iron gates. Neither were needed. A hundred stories of single-depth cells circled the shard in the center of the asphalted concourse, a honeycombing of surveillance that was replicated throughout Melbourne and the world. The shard was an unthinkable tower of alien stone and one-way glass, and its cells were feats of mechanized life. Rita's meals had been served hot at eight, one and seven; her water bowl was always full and clear. The cells were kept clean by some invisible force. It was all eerily efficient.

The aliens were efficient at death, as well. Anyone who resisted was shot. Their weapons stirred human cells like melting ice cream in a bowl, turning living flesh into murky sludge. You only had to see it happen once to decide you'd always obey, so the invaders had no need for a fortress. It was deterrent enough just knowing that they were there. Each cell in the Facility had a glass window from roof to floor, looking right across at the shard. The one-way glass mirrored the prisoners' cells back at them, but occasionally a creeping shadow could be seen, moving with eerie fluidity across the reflection. From there, Earth's colonizers stared back at their prisoners: ever watching, ever waiting, ever ruthless.

That's why the cells weren't reinforced and why it was so easy to break out: you had to have a death wish to even try. But Rita was thirsty and tired and seven years beyond giving up. At first, the inmates had all shouted to each other through the adjoining walls but, as the months piled up behind them like sloughed off skins, they became quiet. There was nothing to say, nothing to be. Rita hadn't spoken for nine hundred fifty-three days. She counted on the tablet that was stocked with books and essays, keeping her borderline sane: nine hundred fifty-three days of silence, three thousand one hundred thirty-nine days in the room, two million eight hundred ninety thousand eight hundred seven minutes since the aliens first came. And one minute since she'd left her cell.

The hall was silent and still. No guard waited with a gun pointed at her, no sound of unworldly footsteps approached from somewhere out of view. If anything, it made her more wary. Her captors could be sadistic if crossed and Rita was not brave so much as desperate. Her heart was beating so quickly that she felt lightheaded and her hand trembled when she brushed her filthy hair out of her eyes. If it weren't for the maddening thirst within her, she would have retreated to the cell and to relative safety. As it was, she went in search of water.

Rita's wife was in the building too, but how could she even begin to look? She had held onto Deepa's face until even that abandoned her, Rita's love for her becoming a symbol where once it had been something real. She had stood at the window, looking out at the shard, daring them to steal that one last piece of her humanity. In the end, it had turned to stone, along with Rita's soul and mind. She was reduced to raw survival. Heartbeat by heartbeat, breath by drowning breath.

It was that survival instinct that motivated her now. Her throat was parched and she didn't know how to find Deepa, so Rita simply ran. Her steps echoed in the empty hall and she called out as she passed each cell door, her voice dusty and broken at first, gradually becoming stronger as it remembered its form. "Come with me," she shouted and the air seemed to part before her as though shying from the sound. There was no reply. Rita ran on.

The elevator was unguarded, as was the door to the central yard. It was too easy. As Rita moved into the open space she tensed, awaiting a blast from a weapon she couldn't see. But still the concourse was silent. Recent rainfall had formed puddles on the ground, deep where the asphalt was potholed, and she fell to her knees and drank. The muddy liquid tasted sweeter than the finest spring water, but she was careful not to drink too much for fear of making herself ill. She needed to find clean water and food and a way out of her jail.

Long before Rita had been imprisoned, the area surrounding the shards had been turned to rubble: mounds of brick and debris where once there had been homes and trees. She might search for days for the sustenance she needed, growing ever weaker. If she could somehow get into the shard without being noticed, she'd have more chance of success. She had made it this far and, for the first time in years, a spark of hope ignited within her.

From its base, the shard was implausible, both delicate and looming, a flawless structure reaching towards the betraying stars. At first Rita moved slowly, expecting each step to draw an army, but she was neither killed, nor captured and gradually she became more confident. Encouraged by the lack of guns and sirens, Rita walked right up to the arching door and, when it opened, made her way inside.

The cells had been sterile but, within the shard, dust greyed the surfaces and webs formed knotty garlands from wall to wall. The aliens had their own, peculiar furniture and it sat, abandoned, like bird-picked skeletons in a rainless desert. There was a rat's nest in one corner and sparrow shit on the floor. The shard was empty. Rita was empty too.

Her words had returned to her, but there was no one there to hear. *How long?* she wondered. *How long?*

She found an echoing pumping room that provided her with

fresh water, and a storeroom filled with decomposing vegetables and greying cartons full of processed food that was edible but stale. In a small room that opened off the front entrance hall, a line of identical keys hung upon the wall.

The cell doors all opened with that one basic key. Each room was like a reflection of Rita's own: the same sleep couch, the same table, the same window and the same view. But her cell was empty now, and these cells were not. Pressed against the glass or curled up on the floor, men and women lay silent and long dead. Door after door, room after room, Rita searched for another survivor, but every key-turn produced the same result.

One hundred floors, and two hundred cells apiece. She moved without thought or emotion, her fingers becoming tender from turning the key so many times. The light faded. Rita felt her way onward. Her palms grew putrid with second-hand decay. She was alone; she was alone; she was alone.

The sun rose through the window of the eighteenth cell on the forty-fifth floor. Rita wiped her hands on a bed-sheet that hadn't been used in years and left the room. Cell nineteen was four steps to the right. The sweat-slick key slid easily into the lock, turning as smoothly as if it had been greased. Taking a breath, she opened the door. From the window, there came a parched voice:

"Rita?"

Tara Calaby lives in Gippsland, Australia with her wife and far too many books. She is currently a PhD candidate at La Trobe University, researching the social worlds of women in Victorian lunatic asylums. Tara's writing has appeared in publications such as Strange Horizons, Galaxy's Edge and Grimdark Magazine, and her debut novel is due out in 2023 with Text Publishing. In her free time, she enjoys playing video games, attempting to learn Danish, and patting other people's dogs. Tara's website can be found at http://www.taracalaby.com and her twitter handle is Tara_Calaby.

The Witch of the Mines

DAN BRIDGWATER

S asha ran.

The cracking and crashing of her pursuers pushing through the thick brush was close behind. She ran on, her small stature and familiarity with the woods she had roamed her entire, short life favoring her.

The men of the village feared the deep woods. If she could escape those who chased her, they would not follow her there.

A sharp shout rang out ahead. Terrified, she ran away from the sound and up the hill to her left, toward the old mines.

Not too much further and the hillside would be covered with tumbled rocks and debris; she could scramble over them faster than the angry men behind her. Hopefully, she could find somewhere to hide.

The men were always angry, frustrated by bad crops, the long and harsh winters, or animals lost out of the herds. Always angry and always looking for someone to blame.

Another shout distracted her, this one close by, between her and the stones she was trying to reach. Sasha stumbled, her foot twisting under her, and she let out a small squeak before immediately sucking in a breath and pressing her hand against her mouth.

Did they hear? She leaned against a tree for balance and gingerly put weight on the foot. Sasha hissed as the pain shot up her leg but gathered her courage and limped on.

She needed to find a place to hide.

Almost in her teens and small for her age, Sasha was an easy target for their anger. Her grandmother would have calmed them down, kept them away, but she was gone now.

A short, stout evergreen provided some cover as she paused to gain her bearings and rest her foot. Ahead, the woods tapered off into a large clearing. They'd see her there for certain. Above her, the hill abruptly rose into a rough rock face. She might have been able to climb it before, but not now, not with her ankle throbbing. Below her were bramble and stones. She started down, eyes darting left and right, trying to move quickly and quietly.

She came across a thorn bush growing near an undercut. Behind it, a dark shadow hinted at something more. She eyed it warily, many animals would find such cover attractive, and she had enough problems with just the men chasing her. The hole was small and appeared deep.

She took a breath and, making her decision, maneuvered her way into the space feet first. It was a tight fit, but she was small. Though the thought of getting stuck terrified her, she pushed herself back until her entire body was concealed in the hole. They wouldn't be able to see her.

Hopefully, it would be enough.

The sound of the men's voices drew closer, and Sasha could barely breathe from the fear. They muttered and cursed among themselves, promising to catch the cursed child who had brought so much pain to their village. She would find no solace with them now that her grandmother was gone.

They had respected Mother Kosan. Respected and feared her. Kosan and Sasha had not lived in the village, that would not have been allowed, but if a woman fell sick, or a man's injury became infected, then they would come to Mother Kosan and beg for her herbs and her healing.

Unfortunately, Kosan had died toward the end of winter, just as Sasha's mother had died some six years before. The simple villagers had viewed that as an omen as well. Despite all her grandmother had done, there was no charity for her granddaughter.

"I see tracks," a gruff voice called out, and Sasha tried to squeeze further into the hole. "They go this way." She could hear them walking above. Her whole body shook from her heartbeat, and she wondered if they would hear it. They were so close. Mumbling voices became louder, then began to fade as the men passed. She let out a quiet breath of relief. She was safe.

"Wait," a flat voice called from farther away. It was Kasper, a harsh-tempered and bitter man. "No signs here, and she hasn't been trying to hide her trail. She must have turned."

"Back up, look for trace," called Jokam, one of Kasper's few friends.

Small rocks and pebbles cascaded past the opening. The sounds of footsteps grew closer. She was trapped.

"Look there. Is that an opening?"

"It looks like a vent from the old mines. Would she fit?"

She heard scrambling, and a shadow fell over the entrance. A face appeared. Kasper. "Hello, child," he said, a harsh glee in his voice.

She tried to push back, squeezing even tighter into the tiny hole.

"No escape, little rabbit." He reached for her and touched her wrist. She jerked back, even though there was nowhere to go.

Abruptly, the ground beneath her shifted, and then fell away. With a shriek, she fell into the darkness.

Sasha woke in a pile of soft sand, partially buried by the dirt and debris that had fallen with her. She could hear high-pitched whistles and chirps around her, and surprisingly, she understood their meaning.

"What is this, Detri?" a piping whistle asked.

"A human, maybe," came a chirping reply. "But very small for a human."

"Perhaps not full grown? What shall we do?"

"We cannot leave it here, Tomak."

There was a buzzing, like that of a trapped bee, coming from the direction of the one called Tomak. "Well, it is too big for us to move. We will need to tell the Luonnatar."

Sasha lifted her head and blinked, trying to focus. She could see a faint greenish-blue glow, like sunlight filtered through the water of a pond, surrounding two figures floating above her in the darkness. She wiped the back of her hand across her eyes to clear away the dirt and dust. Her heart thudded with relief and wonder dulled her fear. Despite their strangeness, these two creatures were not hostile to her like the men in the forest above. They looked like tiny men with strange, angular features, but open and friendly faces.

"Who... What are you?" she asked, eyes wide in amazement.

One drifted down toward her, surprise in its expression. "I am called Detri." Its small arm gestured toward the other. "This one is called Tomak. We are of the Puuka of this place."

"Puuka? You mean like goblins?" she asked in surprise. Tomak and Detri were both the size of large birds. "I thought goblins were at least my size..." she trailed off at Tomak's indignant look.

"We are no goblins," it squeaked, spitting in the dirt. "We are Puuka."

"What is a puuka, then?"

"We are," it said, gesturing to itself. Clearly, it thought the differences between Puuka and goblins were self-evident. "But what are you? You look like man, but you are very small."

"I'm a girl," she replied.

"You are called Agurl? What does that mean?" Tomak asked.

"No," she replied, fighting the laugh that started to bubble up in her chest. "My name is Sasha. I *am* a girl."

"You offer your name?" Detri asked, eyes wide in disbelief. "No. You must have something you are called. Tell us that."

Sasha shook her head in confusion. "I don't understand. I am called my name."

The two Puuka looked shocked. "No, that is not right." Detri said. "You cannot go around telling your name to just anyone. We do not know you, so how do you know we can be trusted with it? We must call you something else." He looked over to Tomak, and after a moment's thought, nodded once. "Se'ticha. Yes, Se'ticha. That feels right."

Tomak nodded in agreement. "Se'ticha, are you a new kind of man?" Tomak asked. "You are not like the ones we see down by the river. You are barely half the size!"

"I will be bigger, some, but I'm only twelve," Sasha answered. She thought she was twelve but wasn't sure. Grandmother had never seemed terribly concerned about her age.

"Twelve?" Detri asked, horrified. "How are you allowed out on your own? No Puuka would ever be out on their own before they were fifty! At least! You are an infant!" Detri bounced around in the air above her, reminding Sasha of a bumblebee trying to land on a flower. "Odd. Very odd. In any event, we cannot stay here. The roots and bones have shifted. More rocks may fall."

"Bones? Are people... buried here?" Sasha asked, a quiver in her voice.

"What? No. The bones of the mountain," Tomak answered her. "She sleeps deep, but every now and then she still can shift. We must take you to the Luonnatar. She will know what to do with you." The two Puuka turned in the air and glided down the tunnel. "Come, she will want to see you."

Sasha stood and hesitantly tested her ankle. It ached, but it would bear her. She followed the Puuka as they led her deeper into the mountain, through passages both rough and smooth. Despite the dark, Sasha could faintly see the edges of the space around her. As they moved through the tunnel, she was surprised to see heavy shaped timber bracing the walls and ceiling. After a while, she asked, "What is this place?"

Detri faced her. "You do not know? This is an old man-place. From many winters ago. Men would come into the earth to take stone and ore. They worked many seasons, carving the passages in the mountain. Many men, many years. But they found less of what they wanted, so less came. Eventually, they stopped. When men left, the Luonnatar led the Puuka to this place. It now offers a home and a shelter from the men."

Sasha remembered her grandmother telling her stories of her

own youth many years ago. She spoke of the mines and Sasha's great-grandfather, who had worked in them. The mines had been left abandoned since well before Sasha's own mother had been born. "The Luonnatar's home is in the mine?" she asked.

"No," Detri replied. He seemed the older of the two Puuka. "The Luonnatar's home is the land. She is here, just as she is in the river and the forest. She is everywhere. She protects us and the land as well. She helps the trees through the winter, and the animals who stay. She guides the birds back in the summer and shelters the hives. This is her home, so all things must balance."

Sasha thought about that, not understanding. How could someone be in several places at once? They continued further into the mine. Occasionally, she heard other voices, other whistles. She would catch movement out of the corner of her eye but saw nothing when she turned to look. After some time, they entered a large chamber deep in the mountain. A feeling of warmth filled her, and it reminded her of her grandmother's cottage. There were faint smells of herbs and plants and a feeling of presence, of life. Detri and Tomak paused their advance and Detri quietly said, "Mother, we seek guidance."

There was something moving in the cave, but not as an animal would move. Sasha felt it uncurl and touch her mind. A voice whispered, "Detri. Tomak. I have felt your coming with the child. Thank you for bringing her to me."

"She fell into the halls, Mother, and was very scared. We have called her Se'ticha. Can you help her?" Tomak asked.

Sasha felt a bubbling sensation inside her mind, like a strange laughter. "Se'ticha then?" the voice said. "An excellent use-name, Detri, though you know not why you chose it. She is, indeed, a spark found that was hidden. Welcome, Se'ticha, our once hidden spark."

"You know me?" Sasha asked.

"In a way, child. I certainly knew your mother, and her mother before her, and hers as well. I know your family many generations back, as I know all those who have the talent to speak to me and to the land. Do you not wonder how you understand the Puuka even though you know what your ear hears is not speech? Even what I say to you does not come through your speech, but something much deeper."

"I don't understand," Sasha said.

"You are still very young. The lumous, the magic, comes naturally, though in you it is later than most. In a few years, as it started to manifest, your mother or your grandmother would have taught you to use it, to weave it. They were called to the dreamlands too soon, before they could pass on what they knew. It is a gift, a calling, and a stewardship. Mankind's curse and birthright is that he does not live in harmony with the world. Most creatures do, but not man. Despite this, he must live in a world he can no longer be truly a part of. The Creator saw this and brought forth another kind of man. A kind that could act between man and the natural world, to help and ease the path men follow, to protect both the men and world around them. Your family, like some few others, has that gift. It is why the Puuka were willing to come to you, to help you. Without understanding it, they could still sense it in you."

"I, I still don't understand," Sasha whispered. She knew she and her family were special but different. Living near the village, but not part of the community. And yet still, the villagers would come to her grandmother, and her mother when she was still alive, asking for medicines or help with sick animals or to read the seasons or the crops. In return they would bring bread and smoked meats or do repairs around the homestead as payment. Grandmother said they must never turn anyone away if they asked for help. Mother had said she would understand better when she was older. As she thought of her lost family, tears threatened to overwhelm her again.

"Who are you?" Sasha asked, after regaining her composure.

"I am the Luonnatar, the spirit of the forest and the land. I have been here for as long as the hills have sheltered life, and I will be here as long as life lasts. Here there is growth and balance. As all things in the world, there is life and death, predators and prey, the spring and the autumn. The cycle must be protected."

"Why do the Puuka call you Mother?"

She sensed the presence shifting, slowly spinning to look not only across the mine but beyond and into the forest as well. "The Puuka are something in between. They are natural to the world but are neither animal nor man. They feel the old magic and can use it to some extent. Feel it and use it the same way you might swim through water. In a way, I am their mother for it is my presence and my magic that helped them become what they are."

Sasha thought about it. In her mind, it did make a sort of sense. "You said I am in between, too. Should I call you Mother?"

Sasha felt warmth wash through her. The Luonnatar settled around her again. "I think I would like that, child."

"Thank you, Mother." A lump rose in Sasha's chest. She missed her grandmother so much and tired from trying to block the hurt away. The thought she might have a place again, that she might be part of some sort of family, threatened to overwhelm her.

After a moment of silence, Mother went on. "What did the men call you? You and your grandmother," she asked.

Sasha hesitated. She didn't like the answer. "Witch," she whispered.

"And so you are, of a sort. It is not an insult, child. In this case, it is a gift. Do you see the Puuka? Can you point at one?"

Sasha's hand came up and pointed at Detri.

"So you see them, yes?" The spirit waited for the child to nod. "There is no light here, deep in the mountain. You see them not with your eyes but with your heart and mind. You see their life and magic. Tell me now. The men who chased you. One in particular is their leader, yes?"

Sasha nodded again.

"Think of him, everything he is, and picture him in your mind."

Sasha thought of Kasper: The deeply tanned and hard face, the stubbly beard, dark with some gray, the small scar under his left eye, his meanness, short temper, and loud, boastful nature.

"Do you see him? Now point," Mother commanded.

The young girl lifted her right arm, slightly behind her and a little bit upward. Her finger steadied and pointed. Not close, she knew, but not far either. A steady walk would cover the distance in just a few minutes if she were in the woods.

"Most of your true gifts will come as you grow older, but what you have now is still more than you know. Open yourself. Feel the life that surrounds you."

Sasha bowed her head. All around her she could sense Mother, a distinctly feminine spirit that inhabited this place and a great swath of the forest besides. She sensed the two Puuka that had led her here and suddenly, like a flower opening to the sun, could sense dozens more moving through the open spaces around her. She felt the shape of the mine, the disturbance of the earth and energies from when man dug through the ground. She felt smaller, glowing sparks of life and knew they were rats and rodents that lived underground. Further out, she felt a family of raccoons in the tree line near the air vent that had collapsed under her. A young hawk, his mind sharp and focused, perched in a birch near a clearing. Close, she could feel the individual creatures, like sparks swirling over a tended fire. Farther away, the sparks merged into a living blanket spread across the mountain and forest, hundreds of animals.

"It's beautiful," she whispered.

"It is the *Vaki*. The essence and life of the land. The rocks, the trees, the animals, and creatures, all of it. That is the first gift of the *Haltij*."

"The *Haltij*? What is that?" Sasha asked.

"The land-protector. Much as the shepherd or the herdsman protects the flocks, the *Haltij* cares for the people and the land. It was your grandmother before, and now it comes to you."

She felt rather than saw two more Puuka enter the chamber behind her and could taste their agitation.

"Mother," one said. "Men have entered the mine."

"Yes. They seek the child. Rouse the others," the spirit responded.

"Will you fight them, Mother?" asked Sasha, feeling sick.

"Should we?" the spirit asked. "They would hurt you, maybe even kill you, if they find you. And they will treat my other children, the Puukas and the creatures that live here, no better. What do you think we should do?"

Sasha felt two warring urges in her chest. One part, tired and scared from the earlier pursuit, wanted to strike back, to punish the men who had chased her, who had isolated her and her family, to hurt those who had hurt her. That part wished death on the men that had chased her. The other part of her thought about what Mother had said about men and their inability to live in harmony with themselves and nature. It made her sad, and Sasha knew the hunters were simply afraid of her and the things they didn't understand.

"Do the men have to die, Mother?" she asked.

"Ah, now that is a good question, Se'ticha. No, they do not. But what should we do with them, then?"

Sasha felt as if a great weight had been lifted from her. Now she knew they were coming, she could feel the group of men near the entrance. They were hesitating, clearly reluctant to enter the darkness of the mine. She could also feel Kasper, his mind a jumble of fear and anger, as he urged them forward. "They are scared, Mother, and they don't want to come in the mine. Could we enhance their fear, make them run away?"

She could feel the Luonnatar's approval. "Well done, young Se'ticha. You show promise. You can feel their fear, but do you know why they are scared? Some have come here before, and they know this is not a man place. Not anymore. My children will lead them on a merry chase, and they will relearn the lesson. When the full darkness comes, they will cry out for their homes."

Now, the Luonnatar's voice in her mind was solid and unmoving, like a sheer mountain face. Sasha knew that when she thought it necessary, the Luonnatar could bring death as unstoppable as an avalanche. But tonight, it would be enough to frighten.

"Mother, what shall we do?" asked Tomak.

"Rouse the animals. We must confuse and separate the men. We will lead them through the tunnels and take them away from each other. When the time is right, when their hearts are ready to explode and the fear has turned their insides to water, we will let them find the way out. When they see it, they will run for the village and be a long time gone from this part of the wood."

Sasha watched the Puuka depart. There was a bubbling sensation around the mine, and she knew none of the creatures here had any fear of the men and were excited to confront them.

The spirit of Mother shifted and curled around her. "Come," she said. "There is a part here for you, and another decision you must make."

It was strange. Sasha knew the spirit of Mother was like a great cloud spread across the forest and hills, yet the spirit was specifically here as well, surrounding her and leading her through the mine. As they walked, she began to hear noises she knew were made by the men in the mine. Leather slapped the floor, metal rang against the stone of the mountain, shouts and yells as the Puuka led them down dead-end tunnels only to fade into the walls. As she walked, she could feel the fear rising and hear the men's voices become more shrill and agitated. Finally, they came to a large cavern. In the shadows, she could see the shapes of old equipment, buckets and trolleys left by the miners so many years ago.

"We will wait here," Mother said. "The men are close to breaking." The spirit curled around her again. "What do you feel, Se'ticha?"

Sasha's thoughts were a jumble, and she knew only part of the confusion was her own. She took a calming breath and worked to identify the feelings that weren't hers: the exuberant Puuka, the frightened men, even the animals running through the mine. She reached her mind out, sifting through the images and feelings and then slowly smiled. The terrified men were being herded back to the entrance, and one group was already fleeing down the hillside.

"It's working," she whispered. She could feel the doubt and fear she had been trying to ignore drain from her body.

"It is," Mother agreed. "And no one has died. But there is still one thing you need to do, to decide. Look here."

The spirit of Mother moved through the rocks and Sasha's consciousness followed.

"What do you see?' the silent voice asked.

Sasha saw an angry, red spark flecked with black. She knew what it was. "Kasper," she said.

"This one is the worst of them. He will always hate and fear you. He cannot be changed. What should we do with him, do you think?"

Sasha found herself in two places. Part of her floated over Kasper, watching. He crouched in the tunnel, one hand pointing a long knife at a bear while his body shook almost uncontrollably. Part of her was back at her body, walking out of the cavern and into the tunnels. She never hesitated at any branch, but instinctively knew which way to go and soon walked up behind the bear.

With newfound confidence, she reached out and placed a hand on its flank, soothing it and touching its mind. She peered around its bulk and saw Kasper, his face lit by the torch he had dropped in his terror. She no longer feared this broken man and stepped out to stand before him.

Already panicked by the bear, his eyes widened even further when he saw her. A high-pitched noise, almost a whine, escaped from him.

"You see me, Kasper, but do you know who I am?"

"Y-you're a, a, a witch," he whispered. His voice was hoarse and cracked from fear.

She moved her hand to the bear's head. "I am that, I suppose. I am that and much more," she replied.

Her mind raced, though her demeanor was calm. She felt the truth of her words and sensed Mother's approval. Memories floated to the surface of her mind. Her grandmother grinding herbs to make medicine, wrapping a broken arm; her mother helping to deliver a calf on one of the farmsteads. She also saw images of Kasper, working in the village and walking through the woods. He was a simple man, well suited to hunting but little else. He was respected in the village but not particularly liked. Still, he was needed as a hunter and a worker. Sasha knew not all the memories were hers and the Luonnatar was showing her these things, helping her to understand what she needed to know and what she needed to do.

"You cannot hurt me, Kasper, and nothing good will come from trying, so I will give you a choice. I will return to my grandmother's cottage, and you will return to the village. I will take on the tasks of my grandmother, making medicines, helping the weaker and older folk, teaching—"

"Helping?" he interrupted. "You are but a child!"

"Am I? Am I just a child?" she replied, scorn in her voice.

Mother had told her someone needed to guide and nurture man's relationship with the land. Her family had helped the village and needed to continue to do so. Despite everything, an enormous feeling of empathy rose in her. She could feel the frustration that had weighed on him through the months of a hard winter, and the fear his family and his friends might not survive another.

"I tell you this, man," she went on quietly, digging her fingers into the ruff of the bear's fur. "I am Se'ticha, the Witch of the Mines and the Forest. I can be a great helper to the people here, or I can be something else. Something much darker. I do not want that. Let me help."

"I, I can't," he whispered.

Now she felt his dark despair, his hopelessness. She sighed. "Then at least leave me alone. Stay out of this part of the forest and away from *my* cottage," she said, claiming her home and her role as the guardian. "Other hunters and villagers will be welcome, as welcome as I am to them anyway. If you cannot accept me, then just stay away. If you can accept that much, then you can go."

She met his eyes and held them. Finally, he nodded his assent, a tight jerk of his head up and down.

"Go," she whispered, moving to one side of the tunnel. The bear followed her.

Kasper crawled to the opposite wall and slowly, back squeezed against the rock, slid past them. Once clear, he made one hasty look back and then stumbled away. Sasha felt Mother's presence grow around her.

"An interesting choice, child."

"I had to, Mother. If I am going to be what I am meant to be, this *Haltij* you speak of, I can't be a child any longer. I have to make my peace with the people here. I don't know how I'm going to do that, but I know I don't want to hurt anyone. That won't help."

She felt warmth blossom around her as the Luonnatar's own feelings rose, happiness that Sasha had accepted her role, love of the land around them, and a proud excitement at what was to come.

"Well, little Se'ticha," Mother said, "you did not choose the easy path, but it is the right one. Come, you have much to learn, and I have much to teach."

Some of Dan Bridgwater's earliest memories include watching *Godzilla* movies and *Star Trek* (The Original!). This love of monster movies and TV SciFi led to his reading every bit of science fiction and fantasy he could get his hands on. Eventually, all those stories in his head reached some sort of critical mass and now he's starting to create his own. An Army Brat and a Marine Veteran, Dan has lived on both coasts, the Midwest, Korea and Kuwait. He now lives with his wife and daughters in Colorado, where he supports training for the US Military.

Full House

MATTHEW A.J. ANDERSON

It all started because nine people went missing. I don't recommend you waste time mourning their loss. They were cultists; they brought it upon themselves. They went into a house and never came out. Since field operatives suspected a trans-dimensional event, they called an expert into the field—me.

My name is Dr. Sanaa Lajami, and part of the reason I work in this department is because I didn't want to get involved in fieldwork. Studying dimensional anomalies means you stay in "the Sink," the secure, underground facility, taking measurements and notes, and occasionally overseeing experiments. It's dangerous out in the field. I've heard all kinds of stories, but what really bothers me about fieldwork is working with other people who don't see me on a daily basis. They *always* stare at my scars.

"Halloran?" I ask, as I approach a tall man standing in front of the abandoned house.

"You must be Dr. Sanaa Lajami," he says, shaking my hand. His eyes glance at my cheek for a second. A turtleneck, jeans, and shoes cover most of my scars, and my long hair hides some of the skin on my neck. But on my right hand, cheek, chin, and lower lip, the burns where my skin is wrinkled, warped, and slightly pink stand out from my brown skin. I've tried using make-up to hide it, but it's too sensitive to touch. I can't even wear *lipstick*. God, I miss lipstick.

"This is Agent Justin McDermott and Operative Audrey Cauldwell," says Halloran, gesturing toward the open door of the field-op van; inside sat a young man with a beard and a woman with short-clipped hair. Both Agents Halloran and McDermott were wearing bullet- and *who-knows-what-else*-proof vests, standard-issue green peacoats, and leather dress shoes. Audrey Cauldwell, meanwhile, looked like she had stepped out of a business meeting, in her gray pantsuit. She's clearly from the Cabinet.

"I'm not sure what you've been told, but we believe there's a portal in there," says Agent Halloran, pointing at 18 Croshaw Close. Besides an overgrown lawn, the house looked like an ordinary, square two-story.

"Nine people missing," I tell him. "Strange marks on the walls, and Cult activity."

"We've been monitoring this house as part of the Needle Circus Op," explains Halloran. "All occupants identified—five men, three women—are members of the Red Hand cult. They undertook the usual comings-and-goings of a household: shopping, school, exercise. But last Sunday, all activity ceased. Nine o'clock Monday evening, a pizza delivery man approached the house. The front door was unlocked, so he went inside. He didn't come out."

"A pizza delivery guy? This was *yesterday*?" I ask. I notice Agent McDermott is staring at my face. I glare back until embarrassment gets the better of him.

"Yes. After half-an-hour, Cauldwell and McDermott approached and opened the door, but did not enter the dwelling. Operative Cauldwell identified mold and an unpleasant smell emanating from inside. There was no response after ringing the doorbell and calling out. There's been no activity inside, since."

"They *didn't* step inside?" I ask.

"The risk was too high," pipes in Cauldwell.

'I was *told* not to go in," corrects Agent McDermott.

"Procedure dictates that in the case of a portal event don't—"

"—step through the *portal,* not onto the *property,*" interjects Agent McDermott.

"She did the right thing," I state, matter-of-factly. "The event horizon of some dimensional rifts are *completely* invisible. If you can't see it, it's better to be safe than, well, *anywhere* these portals lead."

The agent looks annoyed, but shuts up anyway. There are two kinds of people in this world: thinkers and doers. Or, to state it plainly, there's those who *think,* and those who *don't.*

"We'll need you to assess the risk, tell us what we're dealing with. Is this thing one-way or both? If there's a crossover situation, we'll act accordingly."

"Alright," I say. "So who will I be briefing?"

"No one," says Halloran. "I'm briefing *you.* You're going in."

"I'm sorry, I'm *what*?"

"You're the only one qualified to assess the situation. The risk is too high otherwise. You'll have to deal with this one first-hand."

"I can't go in *there,*" I say, pointing at the house. "There could be cultists or an alien atmosphere or sub-dimensionals! I'd need a suit and equipment and a gun."

"We'll get you a hazmat suit," says Halloran. "Have you passed firearms training?"

"*No.* I'm not a field operative."

"You are now," says Agent Halloran, coldly. "If you like, Agent McDermott can escort you."

I glance at McDermott. It's not just that he stared at my scars —*everyone* does—or that he seems like one of those people who don't think, but some of the weapons Stove Agents use react catastrophically if they come in contact with the alien energies of a dimensional rift. I'd actually be safer on my own.

"No. If I'm gonna do this, I need to do it alone," I say, but I can't believe I'm hearing those words come out of my mouth.

"Okay," says Halloran. "But we'll maintain radio contact and be right behind you at all times."

I'm still not happy about it, but somebody has to do it. And I'm the only one qualified.

"Well, if I'm gonna do this, where's my suit?"

A lot of people assume portals are weak spots between dimensions. They see separate dimensions as two rooms separated by a wall, the thinner the wall, the easier it is to knock through and create a doorway. That's entirely wrong. The space between dimensions isn't a wall; it's more like a balloon. A portal is like trying to thread a needle through it. If you tried to stab through where it's weakest, the balloon would pop, but if you slowly pierced where the rubber is thicker, it's actually strong enough to create a seal without the thing exploding. The main difference is, if it goes wrong, the consequences are a lot worse than having a balloon pop in your face. I should know. I have the scars to prove it.

I get my equipment out of my car, and when I get to the van, McDermott has already retrieved a bulky, fluorescent green, Grade-A biohazard suit from the van. Both men wait outside as Audrey Cauldwell helps me don the suit.

"Take off your shoes. Do you want to change your shirt?" she asks, holding out a plain, white T-shirt for me.

"What's wrong with mine?" I ask.

"Long sleeves. It gets pretty hot in these things, but it's your call."

I sigh, take the shirt, and peel off my turtleneck. As I pull the shirt over my head, I see that Audrey is staring awkwardly at the wall. I *know* she's going to ask, but I have time to take off my shoes before she finally says.

"Can I ask how you got those scars?"

"Cultists tried to kill a girl. I tried to stop them. She exploded. That's when the Kitchen hired me."

"Oh, okay then," she says.

I know she wants to pry, but I don't want to go into all the details again: how I broke into the church, how the girl was my sister.

I slip my feet into the suit, and Audrey pulls heavy, rubber boots over the top as I put on the clear, air-tight facemask. Audrey attaches wires for the radio unit, then straps what looks like a SCUBA tank onto my back, attaching air hoses to my mask as well. After I don the gloves, she helps me pull the sleeves and hood over my head, and we test the radio and air tank.

"Can you hear me?" I ask.

"All good," says Audrey, her voice sounds muffled. Then my earpiece says. *"Can you hear me?"*

"Loud and clear."

"That's good. Can you breathe fine?" she asks.

"Yeah, it's working perfectly."

"Alright. I'll zip you up, and you can head in," says Audrey.

She pulls the heavy hood over my head, fitting my arms into the suit gloves. The shoulder pads of the hood sit it on my shoulders, so I can see clearly out the rigid Perspex face-screen. The whole thing is bulky and kind of heavy, especially with the air tank strapped to my back, but I feel much safer stepping into that house. I'm just glad I'm not claustrophobic.

I pick up my own equipment, packed in a shoulder bag, and I put it on. Most importantly, I pick up my flashlight in my other hand. The sun's still out, but this flashlight is heavy, black, metal, and a foot long, so it's not only to light my way. It's to knock the living daylights out of anything that gets too close.

I step out of the van and see that Halloran is outside. He gives me a firm nod, and he steps into the van, but McDermott stays with me.

"Are you ready to head in?" asks Halloran on the radio.

"Ready as I'll ever be," I say, heading for the house.

McDermott walks alongside me.

"Justin will escort you to the door, then you'll be on your own. But keep talking, let us know your every move, and at the first sign of trouble, we're coming in after you."

"Do you have a gas mask or something for him?"

"No. That's why we're only heading inside for an emergency."

I nod. Then I remember that Halloran is in the van and can't see me.

"Affirmative," I add, but I stop as I get to the front door of the house. It looks like an ordinary house, but my legs feel like jelly as I stand before it. The front door sits slightly ajar, so I push it open. Inside, the walls look dirty, and I think I see an overturned chair deeper inside. I unzip my bag and unscrew the lid of a plastic tube with five *physical anomaly testing units*—more commonly known as ping-pong balls. They're cheap, but effective.

I take out an orange ball and toss it inside. It bounces all the way down the hall and off the wall at the far end before rolling to a stop by the overturned chair. "Alright, first room safe to enter."

I head inside, and glance around. It's just an entryway, two closed doors to either side of me and an open space down the hall. I take a closer look at the nearest wall. It looks like it's covered in black stains. I move closer to get a better look, and it looks like black mold. I take out the first sample bag, already labelled *Sample #1* and a wooden coffee-stirrer.

"*What's going on in there, doctor?*" asks Halloran.

"Sorry, I'm not used to talking when I work," I say, scraping some of the mold with the stick. "I've entered the entryway, no physical anomalies so far. I'm just taking a sample of this mold. It looks native, but if it's spread this much, it could be affected by something extra-dimensional."

I drop the stick into the bag, zip-lock it and put it in the empty sample pouch in the bag. Then I walk down the hallway, following the ping-pong ball.

"Oh, I'm, uh, heading deeper into the house..." I trail off as I look into the space. To the right is a staircase and a living room area, which looks mostly untouched, except for some wet stains on the carpet and couch which look like spilled water. But my eyes are drawn to the kitchen and dining area on the other side, or what's left of it. The table is flipped over, and one of the legs looks broken; I count two broken chairs pushed into the wall and four more thrown aside. But just beside it, in the kitchen, the fridge door hangs open with several cracked shelves and food spilled all down and in front of it. Fat flies hover over the mess. Cracked eggs, a smashed casserole dish reduced to a brown smear on the floor with fragments of glass in it, torn and popped milk cartons, and vegetables I can barely recognize are scattered amongst the mess.

"It looks like a hurricane came through here and overturned tables. The fridge is trashed. There's food all over the floor."

I pick up the ping-pong ball and toss it into the kitchen. It lands wetly and gets stuck in the smashed casserole. This is why I bring more than one.

"No physical anomalies," I mutter, as I take the energy sensor out of the bag. It's a retractable, metal wand, wired to a black, handheld unit with lights. It's especially calibrated to detect alien energies. I expand the wand and switch it on. It hums and buzzes like a theremin as I wave it around. I step closer into the kitchen and wave the wand over the mess on the floor. It just makes a steady humming noise. I switch it off and pack it away.

"No residual energy either. A portal didn't do this. It must have been a cultist."

"*Or an alien. We may have a cross-over event. Be alert,*" says Halloran.

A crossover event. That's not good. It's bad enough when extra-dimensional *energy* interacts with our reality. It can cause all kinds of problems. But actual alien *matter* is a whole other mess. According to my supervisor, some of the first experiments conducted at our underground facility proved alien matter reacts unnaturally in our world, because of applied alien physics. So it can do things that are —or should be—impossible. Some call it magic, but as a scientist, I like to discourage belief in the supernatural. After all, alien realities aren't above ours, just different. I prefer to think of it as extra-natural.

"I'm going to head upstairs next," I say, taking another ping-pong ball out of the tube.

"*It's mostly bedrooms up there, Doctor,*" says Halloran.

"I know it's probably empty," I say, throwing the ball onto the first landing. "But, I'll look anyway."

"*I'm just warning you, there may be cultists hiding up there.*"

I nod, grit my teeth, and slowly head up the steps.

I pick up and toss the ball again. It bounces off an open door and ricochets into a bedroom. At the top of the stairs, there are four doors, two are closed, and a set of doors with rigid handles that is clearly a linen cupboard of some kind. Through every open door, I see bedrooms. Like downstairs, all of the walls are covered in black mold, but each of them has a bed, and I take note that each has a mattress or a camping bed on the floor.

"They were packed in here like rats," I say, as I head into the first bedroom and pick up my ping-pong ball.

"*We've seen more of these dense communes, lately,*" says Halloran. "*We keep shutting down their big temples, so they're getting desperate.*"

I check the other rooms with a ping-pong ball. No anomalies.

"Wait, weren't there *nine* cultists?" I ask.

"*Eight. There was also a pizza delivery man,*" says Halloran.

"I count six beds," I say. I count again to be sure: two beds with frames, three mattresses, a camping cot, a child's sleeping bag. That's when I realize there are two pillows each on both of the larger beds. "Oh, never mind, they shared."

It turns my stomach to think of them procreating. But I suppose it's better for them to spawn their own young, rather than corrupt other people's children.

I open the closed door to a bathroom. It's perfectly clean. I toss in a ping-pong ball, but it bounces harmlessly off the tiles. There's nothing there.

"No cultists here," I say, with a sigh. "It looks like it was abandoned."

"*That's a shame,*" says Halloran.

"What, were you hoping to recruit them?" I say, with a smirk.

"*I was hoping we could interrogate them,*" says Halloran. "*We leave the recruiting up to the Cabinet.*"

"We don't actually recruit cultists, do we?" I ask, frowning.

"*You'd be surprised,*" Audrey says. "*Some of them are willing to help us, after they've seen what kinds of things the Red Hand cult gets up to.*"

The things the cult gets up to. I've seen the kinds of things they do, the day *I* was recruited my sister exploded. I tried to save her from a cult sacrifice, so I grabbed her and ran out of the ritual circle. I didn't know then what I know now—the unstable energy had already built up inside of her. I saw pieces of her fly in all directions as her boiling blood seared my flesh.

When I woke up in the hospital, traumatized, awaiting skin grafts, and in severe pain because the amount of morphine needed to stop the pain would have killed me, I was approached by the organization. They told me I had been witness to events which were top-secret, so I had only three options: They could kill me; they could erase my memories; or I could come work for them. Erasing memories sounds like a good option, until the agents explained to me the technology used to wipe memory isn't fine-tuned. As I understand it, they can't delete files; they can only wipe your hard drive. Whilst you can usually still walk, talk, and think, you will lose everything about who and what you are. And the side effects can be severe. So, I only really had two options.

After two weeks, I finally changed my mind.

I focus on the task once more as my eyes are drawn to a large, brown stain on the carpet outside the bathroom. I didn't notice it as I climbed the stairs, but now I can see a large, wet patch, as big as a dinner plate. It's tinged yellow and almost looks like someone pissed themselves. I step out, look up, and see a similar yellow-brown stain around the edges of a rectangular panel in the ceiling. There's a small chain hanging down. It must be a ladder into the roof. I kneel down, getting another sample bag and wooden stick.

"Guys, I've got some kind of attic here. It's leaking a fluid, it's yellow, and," a strand slowly drips like snot as I scoop up a sample, "*somewhat* viscous."

"*Are you heading up?*" asks Halloran.

"Just a sec," I say, careful to drop the stick into the sample bag. Then I grunt as I stand up again. "Good grief. Do they get you to do squats before you can wear this thing?"

"*There are certain fitness requirements for Stove Agents,*" says Halloran.

"Are you saying I'm unfit?" I say, grabbing the chain and pulling it down.

"*Not at all, Doctor,*" says Halloran, matter-of-factly. I can't tell if he's trying to be funny, or if he really *is* that humorless. There's a folded ladder attached to the underside of the door. I unfold it, then throw my ping-pong ball inside. I hear it bouncing, but I can't see in the darkness up there.

"No anomalies, so far. I'm heading up," I say. I have to lean forward so I can see my feet in this bulky suit, but I manage to put one foot on a rung, then start climbing. It's pitch black up here, and for the first time I start feeling the heat. I can feel a warmth through the arms of the suit. I take the flashlight from my bag and switch it on.

At first I think I'm looking at wet roofing insulation. Something wet and pink covers the slanted walls. But as I shine the light around, I realize it's the wrong texture for roofing insulation, and there's some sort of brown wire, or vines, like spidery veins tightly woven throughout the pink mush. I look all around, careful not to step down the hole I just climbed up. There are several support beams throughout this makeshift attic, but behind it all, on every surface of the roof's underside, is this pink organism. I check the floor, and someone has screwed several plywood boards into the wood beams, but I have to be careful of the large, wet patches of yellow slime.

"It looks like some sort of... alien plant, or fungus, has grown all throughout the attic," I say as I get closer to one of the walls, stepping carefully so I don't slip in the goo. "It's all linked together with what looks like vines, or maybe tendrils."

"Is it alive?" asks Halloran.

"I think so," I say, as I get closer. The vines are pulsing, like *veins* of some kind. "Perhaps the black mold is the juvenile form of *this*."

I have to kneel down, due to the angle of the roof, put my flash-light on the ground, and take out another sample bag and wooden coffee-stirrer. I scrape the stick along the stuff, but it's thick and spongy. It's hard to get a sample.

"It's not like moss; it's thick. It's like it's caked to the surface," I say, taking out a box cutter. "I'm gonna cut off a sample."

"*Be careful, doctor,*" says Halloran.

The surface of the stuff is lumpy and uneven, so I unsheathe the blade and lightly pinch one of the lumps with my fingers. I slice into the pink mass, and I see flickering light. I turn and see there's a light attached to one of the crossbeams.

"Now *that's* fascinating."

"*Are you alright doctor? The lights are flickering out here.*"

"It's the fungus," I say. I cut off the lump, and drop it in the bag.

The light pulsing slows, gets brighter, then dimmer, then it finally stops. "Somehow, this thing has tapped into the house's wiring."

"*Is it alien?*"

"Almost certainly," I say.

"*Is it magically active?*" asks Halloran. I sigh. Rather than give him the standard "Weird isn't Wizardry" lecture, I take the energy sensor out of my bag. It makes that familiar, dull buzz when turned on, but every three seconds, it makes a whooping pulse sound and the indicator on the hand unit blinks red.

"It's a steady pulse. I've got *red*, that indicates life, doesn't it?"

"*Psychic energies,*" corrects Halloran.

"*Can you describe your whereabouts?*" Audrey butts in.

"I'm still in the makeshift attic," I say. "It's really hot in here."

"*Are you as emotionally stable as you would expect in this moment?*"

Wait, I recognize this questionnaire.

"Audrey, can we save the full psychic risk eval until I get out of here?" I ask, as I carefully make my way back toward the ladder.

"*I'm just following procedure,*" says Audrey.

"Procedure can wait until I'm not wearing twenty kilos on my shoulders," I say. I manage to get back to the ladder, and after some difficulty sitting down and turning around in this ridiculous suit, I manage to climb back down to the landing outside the bedroom. I was hoping, after leaving the hot attic, that I would cool down, but I feel just as hot inside this plastic bodysuit. I need to hurry up, or I'll start sweating buckets. I leave the attic open and head down the stairs. I tried to rest my hand on the banister, but my glove slides off.

I'm glad I didn't put any weight on it. I look at my hand, and see that the black rubber is wet. I rub my fingers together. It doesn't feel thick and sticky like the yellow goo; it's just *wet*. I kneel down and touch the carpet. It doesn't seem different, but I push my closed fist down into it, hard, then look at my hand. The knuckles of the glove are wet. I stand up.

"Urgh, oh, why did I kneel down again?"

"*Are you alright?*" asks Halloran.

"Yeah, I'm fine. I was just testing something. The walls, the banister, the floor, it's all slightly *damp*. I think that's what's caused the mold."

"*I'm sorry, could you repeat that? Did you say damned?*" asks Halloran.

"No, damp, moist," I say, shaking my head. "It could be that fungus. If those tendrils are in the house's wiring, they could be all through the walls. Maybe it's dripping that goo down the inside of the walls?"

"*We can't rule that out, but for now, focus on finding the portal.*"

"Right," I say, heading back to the front entryway. As I approach, I see McDermott standing there, and I give him a half-hearted wave. He nods back, and I open the first door. It's just another bathroom, but I toss the ping-pong ball in anyway. The ball bounces off the tiles, and lands in the tub. I don't bother heading in to retrieve it, I just turn around and head for the last room.

I open the door, and I see a study. There's a desk to one wall, and a cheap bookshelf packed with books; old, new, paperback and leather-bound. But what draws my attention is the circle of symbols drawn on the carpet in what looks like black candle wax.

"We've got ourselves a ritual circle," I say. I take a ping-pong ball and toss it into the room. I step back, bracing myself in case something happens, but the ball lands on the carpet and lamely rolls to a stop. "Huh... it's completely inactive."

"*Completely? It's not reacting at all?*" asks Halloran.

I step into the room. There's the desk with an old, worn-out book on top and the bookshelf; I'm sure, if I looked, I'd find the cult's bible in those shelves, but I ignore the furniture to take a closer look at the circle. The first thing I notice is it's not a circle. There are symbols in a script I can't read, which looks like Angry Sanskrit, or maybe drunk Japanese, and they're arranged in a *circular pattern*, with lines connecting some of them, but it looks incomplete.

"Yeah, no response," I say. "What does it mean if the circle's open?" I ask.

"*What do you mean by open?*" asks Halloran.

"Y'know, it's not all connected up," I say, frowning.

I don't understand extra-natural science at the best of times, but as I understand it, ritual circles are kind of like circuit diagrams. They're drawn so the energy flows through symbol after symbol—one part might resist, another inducts, and energy builds up here or there. I'm not an electrical engineer, but I'm pretty sure it's meant to be a *closed* circuit.

I take out the sensor wand and switch it on.

"It could be they didn't complete the ritual," says Audrey.

I wave the sensor wand over the circle, and it hums as usual, but as I step onto the circle, I feel pins and needles sting all around my foot. It's like ants crawling along the sensitive skin of my scar tissue. I step back, and the pain slowly fades to a numbness. I've felt that pain before. I brush the tip of the antenna against the wax-stained carpet, and the sensor whines so loud the box clicks. After a few seconds, I recognize that familiar, pulsing pattern from before. I check the box, and see a steady, red light, as well as a flickering blue. Blue indicates *Space*. It's the energy used to cross dimensions. But the energy is too weak.

"They activated it," I say, "What happens if you activate a broken ritual circle?"

"Nothing good," says Audrey.

"Alright. I'm getting out of here," I say.

"Not yet. You haven't found the portal," says Halloran.

"There *isn't* a portal," I say. "This might have caused a *minor* rift, but nothing could have stepped through, only energy could pass through a rift this weak."

"We still have nine missing people. If this house is abandoned, they had to have gotten out somehow," says Halloran. *"Have you checked the basement?"*

"There *isn't* a basement," I say, annoyed.

"There is, according to the blueprint. Head into the living room." says Halloran.

I head out of the study and down the hall. I ignore the mess in the kitchen, and head toward the living room area. There are some couches by the wall, and a television, and there's a rug with a large stain. It looks like water, and the same liquid seems to be pooling under the stairs. That's when I see the dark opening without a door, under the stairs. It's so black inside, it's like someone painted it with shadows.

"You could have *told* me it had a basement." I grumble, more annoyed at myself, and the fact that I'm starting to sweat in this ridiculous suit. Our underground facility is secret and secure, but that's not the only reason it's underground. There's less interference underground. If there *is* a portal, it's probably here.

I grab the tube of ping-pong balls. There's only one left. I've been getting lazy about fetching them. I take the last one out and toss it through the door. It disappears into the blackness, but I hear it bounce down the steps.

Tap. Tap. *Splash*.

"That's different," I say. I take out my flashlight again and walk to the door. "I've lost visual contact with my 'physics-tester', but it sounds wet down th—"

Something *squelches* under my feet, and I look down to see that what I thought was water is stuck to my boots in long, gluey strands. I lift both of my feet, one after the other, and although it's a little slippery, it's not stopping me from moving, it's mostly just unpleasant.

"I've got another strange substance here. See-through, but slimy."

"*Portal takes priority,*" says Halloran. "*Don't bother taking any samples until you've inspected the basement.*"

"Agreed," I say. I shine the flashlight through the door, and I can see wooden steps leading down. They, too, are covered in this gluey slime. I also see something white and gray that's been dropped on one of the stairs. I head closer, and each one of the steps creaks and groans, painfully. I stop when I'm standing on the same stair as the object, and quickly recognize it as an upturned, damp pizza box.

"Pizza guy was here," I say. I bend down to pick it up, groaning the whole time. As I lift it up, the cardboard is limp in my hands, so when the cardboard folds awkwardly the pizza falls out, landing with a *splat* on the stairs. "Yuck."

I kick the pizza through the gap in the stairs, so I don't step on it and I hear another splash. I point my torch over the edge of the railing, and I see the rippling surface of a dark lake.

"Basement's flooded," I say. I drop the empty pizza box into the water and watch it float away. As it does, I see the edges start to bubble. Wisps of steam rise up from the box, as it slowly dissolves. "I think it's some kind of acid."

I slowly back away, heading up the stairs, when something huge and pink, like a long, thick tentacle, jumps out of the liquid, and coils tightly around the pizza box. It pulls it under with a splash, and some of the liquid splashes around my feet. My rubber boots start to bubble and steam.

"Oh, shit, shit, shit!" I say as I quickly sit down and grab my boots. It's hard without touching the steaming tip of the boot, but I pull off one and throw it down the stairs.

"*What's going on down there?*"

"We've got acid.It's eating through my boots," I say, as I work to push the other boot off. It's hard wearing two layers of gloves. "There's some kind of monster in here."

"*Do you need back-up?*" asks Halloran.

"I don't know," I say as I take off the other boot. Without thinking, I throw it over the railing. "No!"

I hear it splash as it hits the surface. The monster reacts again. The meaty tip of the thing lashes out at the boot. I jump back to avoid the splash of acid and run up the stairs, but my feet slip in the suit's bare foot-coverings. I hit my elbows as I fall, and I drop my flashlight, and hear it splash into the acid below. That's when I feel myself slide down the gooey stairs. I grab onto a step, haul myself to my feet, and pull myself up the stairs. I get out of the basement door and turn back to look into the darkness, when I see the pink monster shoot out toward me.

I'm knocked back as it slaps me bodily, and I land on my back, on top of the air tank. I wince, as I roll over onto my side. That hurt. I hear the familiar crackle of Stove Agent gun-fire. The steaming mass of pink flesh wraps over the stairs and reaches for the front door.

It's unlike any tentacle I've seen. It's not covered in suckers, instead the whole thing is covered in bumps like a raw, plucked chicken. It's not a worm either, because it's slick and dripping with translucent goo. That's when I recognize what I'm looking at. It's a long, monstrous tongue.

I force myself to get to my feet. As I do, the thing starts retracting, and I hear scraping and the wet sound of the tongue sliding through its own mucus as it pulls Agent McDermott toward the gaping maw of the basement, the tip still smoking from where it was shot.

"No! Stop!" I yell, but the monster ignores me.

McDermott flails and tries to grab onto the doorframe, but it's slick with the beast's saliva. He disappears into the darkness. Gone. I have to escape, so I run for the door, but my feet are wet with goo, and my back hurts from the fall. I barely manage to stagger a few steps into the hallway before I hear a familiar splash, then the wet sound of flesh darting through slime.

I dive to the side, falling onto the stairs as the tongue flicks past me. It reaches out wildly toward the front door, the steaming, long tongue whipping around the entryway. I can't escape. It's blocking the door. Any moment now, it will find me.

The tongue whips blindly around the entryway, slamming into the walls. I can see the still-smoking wound near the tip where it was shot. There's a huge chunk blasted out of the flesh, the size of my head, and it's leaking yellow gunk—it's the same stuff I saw earlier. It must all be connected. It's one organism.

"*Doctor Lajami, please respond. What's going on in there?*" demands Halloran.

"It's all some kind of monster. It got McDermott."

"*Are you alright?*"

"I'm alive, but it's right *there*. It's right there. If it turns around, it could grab me. But it hasn't yet." I manage to slow my breathing, as the tongue whips around the hall. It isn't attacking me. It attacked McDermott so quickly, as soon as he stepped inside, but not me. It must be the suit; it's blocking it from tasting me or smelling me or something.

"I don't think it can sense me in the suit. Don't send *anyone* else in without a suit."

"*Doctor, we have to get you out of there,*" says Halloran.

"I can't get out through the front door, it's blocking the way."

"*Could you slip past it?*" asks Halloran.

I glance at the tongue. It looks angry, flicking wildly, slapping wetly at the tiles.

"No, it's too dangerous."

"If we can't kill it, and we can't go in, you have to get out, Doctor."

"What the hell can *I* do? Shooting at it didn't work, and even if it did, I don't have a gun! I dropped my flashlight, so I just have sensors and sample bags!" I yell, annoyed.

Sample bags. Yellow goo... and it caused those flickering lights.

"I'm heading for the attic," I say, jumping to my feet. With a new burst of energy, I quickly jog up the stairs.

"Can it reach you there? Perhaps you need to hide until back-up arrives."

"No, I'm going to hurt it. If I'm right, it isn't fungus, but some kind of brain. When I took a sample, that wasn't a short circuit. It was some kind of seizure."

I get to the bottom of the ladder and start climbing. I find myself panting, exhausted. My back still hurts. The slime on my hands makes the ladder slippery, and sweat drips down my face and arms making the suit steamy. Yet, I force myself higher into the darkness. I can't see, but if I'm right, that won't be a problem. I take out the box cutter from my sample toolkit. I stumble blindly forward, waving a hand in front of me so I don't run headlong into a support beam. I stop when my hand slaps something wet and spongy. Perfect.

"Alright, you slimy bastard," I say, unsheathing the blade. "I hope this gives you one hell of a headache."

I slash wildly at the spongy mass. Behind me the light flickers, and I hear a deep, hollow groaning from the house below. Yellow gunk pours out of the wounds and splatters the arms and legs of the suit with alien blood. I sidle along the wall and continue to slash at the flesh, when I hear a loud *CRASH!*

In the flashing light, I see the tongue has punched straight up through the attic entrance, the frame cracking from the force. I hold out the blade in front of me, as the tongue flails wildly, but it looks like it's writhing in pain. It's working! I turn around and keep cutting at the flesh

"Doctor, the monster has retreated. Can you get to the entrance?" asks Halloran.

"No, it's blocking my way," I say. "But it can't reach—"

Suddenly, I am swept off my feet as the tip of the tongue coils around my ankle, and I feel weightless for a second, until I slam into the wooden floorboards with a *splat*. The tongue drags me down out of the attic, and I realize I've dropped the box cutter. Oh no, it's going to eat me! I try to grasp the rungs of the ladder as it pulls me out of the darkness, but the rungs are slick with saliva. It rips me off the ladder, and I crash into the closet door. Before I know what's happening, I see the rest of the tongue tense up, and then with a violent shudder, the whole thing flicks, and I get thrown sideways.

I see sky and twinkling fragments of glass floating around me as I go crashing through the window. Then I hit the ground with a unhealthy sounding crack. I feel dizzy. I think something's broken, but everything hurts and it's hard to narrow it down. It takes me a moment to get my bearings. When I do, I realize I'm staring at a darkening, blue sky through a panel smeared with yellow slime. I'm outside, lying on my back.

"Doctor!" yells a voice.

It sounds like Halloran, but he's muffled. It takes a second to realize I'm not hearing him through the radio. I try to roll over to see him, but I feel a sharp pain in my left arm that makes me gasp.

"Doctor Lajami?" says Audrey, and I see her face appear above mine. Halloran approaches and stands behind her.

"Don't touch her! She might have injured her spine," says Halloran.

"Are you alright?" asks Audrey.

"No," I grunt.

"I think your arm is broken," says Audrey.

'Oh really? That's nice to know." I groan.

'What happened in there?" asks Halloran.

"I think, it spat me out."

"The ambulance is on its way," says Audrey, leaning down. "Just remember standard procedure. Let us come up with the cover story, you just tell them your injuries."

"Uh huh. Just, give me a minute to catch my breath."

"Did you find the portal?" asks Halloran.

"No, no portal," I say. "They didn't escape the house. It turned into some kind of monster and ate them."

"Is that possible?" asks Halloran, turning to Audrey.

"It depends how badly they messed up the ritual circle," says Audrey. "But it's possible. Anything's *possible* with magic."

"It's not *magic*." I grumble. But I'm too tired to finish the sentence, let alone the whole dumb lecture. "I'm sorry about McDermott."

"He knew the risks," says Halloran. Audrey just nods, silently.

"And it ate all those people," I murmur.

"They were cultists," says Halloran, grimly.

"I know but still. Eaten alive? Nobody deserves that." I can't help but think about the child-sized sleeping bag in the bedroom.

"They weren't *all* cultists," says Audrey. "Actually, if they weren't going through a portal, then *who* called the pizza delivery guy?"

"Must have gone to the wrong address," says Halloran. "Unlucky."

"Maybe," says Audrey.

"We'll meet you at the hospital for a debrief," says Halloran.

"Oh, and the psych-risk eval," adds Audrey.

"Great," I mumble. I slowly and carefully lift my head up to see I'm covered in alien guts, goo, and slime.

Well, it's official. I'm never doing fieldwork again.

Matthew A. J. Anderson was born in Queensland, Australia. A daydreamer and avid reader in his childhood, he grew up to love horror, mystery and speculative fiction; he most enjoys writing stories that disturb, inspire and intrigue. He is now living in Albury Wodonga, New South Wales and in his free time is working on short stories as well as larger fiction projects that he hopes to publish. Matt also posts some of his shorter writing, as well as non-fiction pieces on his blog absurdwordnerd.blogspot.com.au.

Duelleagues

DANTZEL CHERRY

The only good news about finding his lifelong rival leaning against the worn café counter in this abandoned Spanish village, Julian decided, was it meant Fernando hadn't found the *wunsch* yet either. It was this thought that allowed him to enter the café, pistol out of view.

Julian inclined his head toward Fernando, who tipped his cream-white fedora in return and nodded to an ornate iron table in the far corner, while continuing his feigned interest in the automaton barista, who poured his *cortado* with groaning, rusted metal joints. Julian was pleased to see he still required a mahogany cane to support his lame left leg.

"Two shots?" Fernando called out, gesturing to the drinks that the barista prepared.

"Always." Julian strolled to the table where a glass lamp burned low in an effort to counter the encroaching twilight, not bothering to hide his inspection of his rival. He still wore those ridiculous minia-ture white roses in his front pocket, framed by a cleverly folded lilac handkerchief. Not for the first time he wondered what Fernando planned to wish for if he ever caught the *wunsch*. Maybe he'd get flus-tered and botch his wish, like all the other poor idiots around the world who had held the *wunsch* and wished for money and turned

their family to gold, or wished for more food and found themselves eating to their deaths.

That kind of serendipity was unlikely, though. There were few *wunsch* hunters, and none as well-prepared as Julian and Fernando.

Julian sniffed, but the tell-tale scent of spices and sulphur was still faint, directionless. He knew he was in the right town – now it was just a matter of time before the *wunsch* revealed its location.

Presently Fernando arrived at the table, cane supporting him in one hand and a silvery tray with two small cups of steaming *cortado* in the other.

"You're bald," Fernando said by way of greeting.

"But I'm not the one limping," Julian pulled the nearest cup over and inhaled the heavenly aromatic steam. He took a sip. "Wasn't that five, six years ago? In India?"

"Possibly. What was the *wunsch* then?"

"Wishing well."

"Then yes, that was the India incident."

Julian remembered that incident clearly – the poor fool who'd found the *wunsch* first had been smothered in a sudden pile of cattle. A tragedy for the family, but the village ate well for the rest of the month.

"Would've been nice if one of us had found it then," Julian said.

Fernando snorted over his *cortado*. "Five years ago? Only then? I'd have been dozing on a beach the last forty years if you hadn't thrown that chair at me in Argentina."

"And the year before that in the Black Forest? Who decided that scaring the unicorn *wunsch* away was better than me getting my wish?"

Fernando raised a hand. "Peace. We could blame each other all night."

They both sipped in silence, listening to the barista as its gears groaned and whirred and zinged. This cafe had not kept up with the times, but the older the café, the more comfortable Julian – and, he supposed, Fernando, felt. It was always his way to find the oldest cafes as he hunted the *wunsch*.

"Have you rewritten your wish since last time?" Fernando asked, lazily swirling the remnants of his cup.

"I've massaged a phrase or two."

"Good." Fernando held up a thick, well-creased sheet of paper and winked. "I read your wish in Ireland. It was terrible."

That was where it had disappeared to? Julian recalled that day in the Irish forest, frantically searching his pockets with one hand while holding the foot of a snarling leprechaun in the other. He didn't trust himself to recite his wish correctly without his written version, but when the little fellow stabbed a golden dagger into Julian's thigh, he gave up and wished that the *wunsch* would manifest in China that instant. The leprechaun indeed *poofed* in midair, off to reappear somewhere else in the world as another wishing artifact, and so Julian's chance had disappeared yet again.

Before Julian could stop himself, his pistol was out and aimed at Fernando's chest, just above his ridiculous flower. In another café, one filled with humans, all activity would have ceased. Here the witless automaton barista merely continued stirring, creaking, and clinking.

His rival's expression was extremely satisfying. Julian leaned over and snatched back his long-lost wish.

"You should know better than to take another man's wish," Julian said. He tucked the worn paper into the safety of his breast pocket.

"Put the gun away. You wouldn't shoot me, you dirty dog," Fernando said. Though his tone was conversational his slur rang clear in the silence of the café.

Julian opened his mouth to reply when his nose tickled with the scent of cinnamon, tangerines, and sulphur, a smell only *wunsch* hunters would long for. It was clear Fernando smelled it too.

Eyes locked, they rose together, Fernando leaning on his cane for support. Julian smiled. "Race you there."

He aimed his pistol at the side of Fernando's lame leg and fired, grazing the skin just enough to give Fernando a burn he'd remember. He could have taken the man's cane or shot him in the heart, but Julian wasn't *unsportsmanlike*. He merely needed a head start.

Fernando fell back in his chair and clutched at his leg, trying – and failing – to stand. "No! Not now! Damn you, Julian!"

Every strained syllable was music to Julian's ears. He dropped a few coins as a tip into the box powering the barista and, unchallenged, strolled out of the café.

Julian rounded the corner of the café and broke into a run, following the alluring scent. He was dismayed, however, to find himself growing short of breath after only a few dozen strides on the cobblestones, and he clutched at his chest, cursing his old age.

He had longed for riches when he was younger. When his youth left him, he revised his wish to include a wife, and for other, slightly wiser things in life, though wealth held its place on the list. Now Julian was nearing 88 and had yet another chance at the *wunsch*, but he feared he would waste it by begging for a new heart at the wrong moment.

He shuddered at the possibilities for misinterpretation but staggered on.

The scent led him toward an even older part of town, full of decrepit warehouses that housed the city's retired dirigibles. The paved street curved and dipped under his feet, and more than once he skidded over loose pebbles, dangerously close to falling and breaking a hip.

Somehow he found himself outside a one-story derelict house where even the vines clinging to the stucco were brown and crumbling. It was dusk now, and Julian could see no one following him.

He wheezed as he steeled himself to enter and claim his prize. What would it be, though? A wand, perhaps? A dragon? Or perhaps a frog, as it had been several times before. It would be rather ridiculous to find a wishing well inside the house, but Julian didn't put it past the *wunsch*. He supposed it might even be another automaton, calling itself Rumpelstiltskin.

At any rate, it was time to find the *wunsch*, make a wish, and right a lifetime of wrongs. He leaned against the wall and dragged himself forward. The door wasn't even locked.

He was greeted inside by a flame the size of his head, softly illuminating the table it sat upon and a nearby stool, both as worn out and abandoned as the little house. As Julian's eyes adjusted, he saw that it was not a single flame but many little candles burning merrily on a birthday cake with thick fluffy frosting. He grimaced. Very amusing. The *wunsch* always had a sense of humor.

He moved forward on wobbling knees until he could steady himself on the table, and held the sides of the cake. When that produced no reaction, he blew into the center of the cake, so gently that not a single candle flickered.

A sullen mustached genie wisped out of the flames and hovered above the cake.

"Get on with it, then," the genie said.

Julian smiled and pressed a finger to his lips as he settled onto the stool. It creaked ominously but bore his weight. He slipped the old paper from his pocket and silently read through his wish —the perfectly-grammatical-wish-with-no-possible-misinterpretations sentence—and read it again until he found the perfect spot to add a new heart. He needed to be careful not to mix health and wealth. He pulled out a pencil and hunched over the table, furrowing his brow as he scribbled.

There. It was all in order.

He read it again, and crossed out an errant "and."

There.

A shuffling figure appeared in the doorway. "Oh, there you are."

Fernando's eyes rolled and he flopped on the floor. A cloud of dust rolled up and around him.

"Is he a friend of yours?" the genie asked.

Julian looked down at his rival's lifeblood leaking onto the old carpet with a frown. Fernando was out of the way at last – and with a simple shot to the leg. Why couldn't he have died at the café?

He tried to begin reciting, but the question kept popping into his head: He'd been chasing the *wunsch* for so long, who would he sip his *cortados* with now? Julian sighed, flipped his paper over, and scribbled again for a few minutes. He only read it once before reciting his wish aloud. The genie looked at him oddly, shrugged, and disappeared with a *poof*.

Julian placed a hand over his heart, and felt a steady, strong pulse for the first time in ten years. He kissed his wishlist and tucked it away. There was always next time.

Fernando stirred, pulled himself off the floor, and scrutinized the blood on his pants. "A missed *wunsch* and my nemesis? Surely this is hell."

"Correct." Julian sighed again. "Saving you and acquiring a wife in the same wish seemed a tad risky. For some reason I chose you."

"Idiot."

"Indeed."

Fernando pulled out the handkerchief behind the insufferable white rose to dab at the blood, but the immaculate lilac linen quickly turned scarlet. He scrutinized his handkerchief with a frown.

"A little courtesy?"

Julian passed his handkerchief over.

"Thank you," Fernando said. "Though next time I'll thank you very much to keep my blood *under* my skin, and off my best suit."

"*Next time* I'll leave you to bleed out all over the floor," Julian said. "Quit getting in my way."

When they exited the house the stars had firmly established themselves in the firmament and twinkled brightly in greeting. Julian raised his nose to the air, but no such luck. The scent was cold.

"Well. This gives us time for another drink," Julian said, not entirely without humor.

"Indeed it does," Fernando said. "And this time, you're paying."

Dantzel Cherry's short fiction has appeared in Fireside, Cast of Wonders, Galaxy's Edge, and other magazines and anthologies. She teaches ballet, Pilates, and MELT Method when she's not writing. She lives near the mountains in Utah with her husband, daughter, three cats, three chickens, and a rather startling horde of plants and baked goods. You can find out more at www.dantzelcherry.com.

Meanings and Mettle

MIRIAM THOR

Heat flared through the back of Paige's hand. Surprised, she set down the salve she was holding and looked at the bluish green rune displayed there. Friend. The rune had been placed on her hand by Twilit Sea, the dragon who'd visited Bryolan several years ago. It marked her as a dragon friend.

In the years since Paige received the rune, it had never bothered her. What could possibly have caused it to heat up like that?

"Miss Paige, are you alright?"

Paige turned to look at her patient.

"I'm fine, Linna," she assured her, picking up the salve. "I just got distracted." She walked over to the girl. "Hold out your arm."

Linna complied, and Paige smeared the salve over the rash on her forearm. Then, reaching for her magic, Paige drew the rune for "heal." The rune hovered, glowing deep green, before sinking into Linna's arm. Immediately, the swelling went down, though the bumps didn't disappear.

Paige smiled. As much as her life had changed since she married a prince, healing was still as comforting and fulfilling as ever.

Paige held the jar of salve out to Linna. "Apply this when you get up and at bedtime."

"Yes, ma'am," she said, taking it. "I was—"

A roll of parchment appeared, distracting the girl. It floated in front of Paige.

"One second," Paige said, unrolling it.

She scanned the message, then turned to Linna. "I'm sorry. I need to go."

Linna eyed the parchment warily. "Is everything okay?"

"Everything's fine," Paige said. "My brother-in-law just needs me to take care of something."

Linna scowled. "He sounds bossy, like my brother."

Paige's lips twitched. Her best friend, Ellie, would agree with that statement.

"Go home, Linna," Paige said, "and tell your ma I said hello."

"I will. Bye, Miss Paige," the girl said, scampering out the door.

Paige watched her go, then grabbed her shawl and started walking toward the palace.

Seated on his throne, Renaldor stared at the string of runes that had appeared next to the dais. They were glowing a bluish green color that matched the scales of the only dragon he'd ever met. It gave him a sense of foreboding.

"Relax, Ren," Ellie said, looking out a window. "I just saw Paige go through the servant's entrance. She'll be here any minute."

Renaldor raised his eyebrows at his cousin. "The servant's entrance?"

"Yep," Ellie said. "She uses it when she goes out to work as a healer in the lower city."

He nodded. That sounded like something his sister-in-law would do. No one could say that becoming a princess by marriage had gone to her head. Well, no one with a modicum of sense anyway. A few of the stuffier nobles said it on occasion. Insufferable, the lot of them. Some days, he wished he could let Ellie use her magic to turn them all into rodents and be done with them.

A guard opened the door and announced, "Princess Paige has arrived, Your Majesty."

"Send her in," Renaldor ordered.

The guard stepped aside, and Paige entered the room, wearing a simple dress. As she dropped into a curtsy, Renaldor wondered if she would ever see herself as royalty. Of course, it didn't help that she was married to Trinian. His youngest brother was the least prince-like prince he'd ever met. Just this morning, Trinian had informed him that he would be working on some sort of magical experiment all day, rather than attending to any of his princely duties.

"You sent for me, Your Majesty?" Paige asked.

"I did," he replied.

He gestured to the runes. "This appeared about an hour ago. I was hoping you'd be able to read it."

Paige brushed her fingers over the rune on the back of her hand.

"This rune flared hot around the same time. Between that and the runes' color, we can assume this message is from Twilit Sea."

Paige stepped closer to the runes. Then she pulled out the message Ellie had sent her and flipped to the back of the parchment.

"Does anyone have—"

A quill and inkwell appeared in the air before her.

Paige grabbed them. "Thanks, Ellie."

She knelt on the floor and got to work.

Silence reigned in the throne room for what felt like an eternity, broken only by the scratching of the quill. Renaldor took deep breaths, reminding himself that deciphering runes wasn't easy. It would be rude to interrupt Paige to ask for an update.

As usual, his cousin felt no such compunction. She walked over to stand next to Paige.

"Well?"

Paige looked up at her, frowning.

"There's a rune I've never seen. It might be in my rune dictionary. Could you—"

Without so much as a gesture, Ellie made the requested book appear on the floor. As Paige flipped through it, Renaldor glanced at his cousin. She made magic look ridiculously easy. Most mages would need their powers to be amplified by runes to accomplish what Ellie did. Even the few other mages who could use magic instinctually would show some sort of strain.

Ellie truly was the most powerful mage in the kingdom. Renaldor was looking forward to the day he could officially make her his Chief Mage. The man who'd held the position during his father's reign was set to retire within the year, so Renaldor knew he wouldn't have to wait much longer.

"I've translated the message as best I can, Your Majesty," Paige said, rising to her feet.

"Read it, please," he told her.

She looked down at the parchment.

"A dragon mother recently had a dragonling who was born... " She glanced up at him. "This is the rune I didn't recognize. I think it means deaf, though it's slightly different than the one in the book."

Renaldor blinked. A deaf dragon? That went on the list of things he'd never considered before.

Paige continued, "The mother couldn't figure out to how to deal with the dragonling, so she banished him." She looked up again. "The rune for banish is the one used to magically send something away. I don't think it means he can't return."

Renaldor nodded, gesturing for her to keep going.

"After some investigating," Paige said, "I—that is, Twilit Sea—discovered that the dragonling was banished to the barren part of Bryolan, so I wanted to warn you about its presence."

"The barren part," Ellie said. "That has to be—"

"Charevy," Renaldor finished for her, stroking his beard.

Paige looked between them, a question in her eyes.

"The fief closest to Bryolan's border with Luthania," Ellie explained. "During the last war, the Luthanian mages used magic to burn the whole area. That was two centuries ago, but nothing ever grew back."

Paige bit her lip. "So, there's no game there for a young dragon to hunt?"

"No," Renaldor said, "the only thing left there is the manor house, but it's been abandoned since the end of the war. Bryolese soldiers patrol the border with Luthania, but they live in a neighboring fief."

Paige looked down, her expression troubled. Renaldor shared the sentiment. There was a baby dragon in his kingdom. Thankfully, it was in Charevy, but he doubted it would stay there. How much of a threat would it pose to his people when it reached a populated fief?

Even Ellie had been no match for Twilit Sea, but that dragon had been fully grown. Surely, a baby wouldn't be so formidable. Perhaps, they could—

"I want to meet him," Paige said.

Renaldor's thoughts screeched to a halt. "What? Who?"

"The dragonling," Paige said. "I'd like to meet him and try to figure out a way to talk to him."

Renaldor wondered if there was a tactful way to ask someone if they'd lost their mind.

"That's a great idea," Ellie said. "I'll go with you. We can stay in the empty manor house."

Renaldor ran a hand down his face. Telling Paige she'd gone mad would be rude. Telling Ellie the same would be dangerous to both himself and Bryolan. He couldn't rule the kingdom as a squirrel, after all.

"Let's think this through," he said in his most diplomatic tone.

Ellie raised her eyebrows, clearly unimpressed.

Renaldor met her gaze. "If the dragonling's mother abandoned i" — he caught himself—"him, he must be extremely hard to deal with. I don't see how—"

"Paige is the dragon friend," Ellie interrupted. "So, why don't you let her figure that out?" She put a hand on her hip. "And even if that turns out to be impossible, we can't leave him there. The poor thing will either starve or wreak havoc on another fief."

Renaldor sighed. She had a point, but he really didn't want to risk either of them getting hurt, or worse. Losing Ellie would have repercussions for the entire kingdom. And if anything happened to Trinian's wife, his little brother would never forgive him.

"We could warn the neighboring fiefs," Renaldor said.

"Warn them to what, attack on sight?" Paige asked, uncharacteristically sharp. "That's not right, and neither is leaving him to starve.

Dragons aren't dumb beasts." Her eyes widened. "At least, that's my opinion, Your Majesty."

"Mine too," Ellie added, crossing her arms. "Ren, please don't make me defy your orders."

Renaldor glared at his cousin. She'd yet to go against his orders since he became king, mostly because he'd avoided putting her in a position where she had to choose between obedience and her conscience. He knew Ellie well enough to be sure which one she'd choose.

"Alright," he said, his shoulders slumping. "But it should be more than just you two. I'll send—"

"We don't need anyone else," Ellie said. "I'm sure I can handle a *baby* dragon just fine."

"Actually," Paige chimed in, "I think Trin should come with us."

Renaldor clenched his jaw. She wanted his little brother to be in danger, too?

"Really?" Ellie asked Paige. "Why?"

"He's been researching how to reverse curses," she explained. "After hearing you describe Charevy—"

"He could fix whatever the magical fire did to the land," Ellie said, nodding. "That's perfect."

She turned to look at Renaldor. "It's settled. The three of us will go."

He took a calming breath. "I will approve this quest if you promise to do everything in your power to make sure you all return safely."

Ellie rolled her eyes. "We're just going to stay in an empty manor house on cursed land and confront an abandoned dragon. What could possibly go wrong?"

"Ellie," he snapped, not appreciating her sarcasm.

Her face softened. "We'll be safe, Ren. I promise."

He looked his cousin in the eye. "Very well. Leave whenever you're ready."

Paige curtsied. "Thank you, Your Majesty."

Ellie just grinned. "This is going to be fun."

As the two of them left, Renaldor hoped their journey would be more Paige's idea of fun than Ellie's.

Elliana released her magic and surveyed the barren landscape, excitement coursing through her. She hadn't gone on anything close to an adventure since Ren invited her to live at the palace five years ago. Though she enjoyed her position, she missed the freedom she'd had growing up, and as the baroness of Laveny.

Her younger brother, Jaret, was doing such a good job as baron she couldn't even use "going home to check on things" as an excuse to leave the capital. Elliana had been feeling antsy for a while, and this quest was just what the healer ordered. She was glad they'd arrived in the morning, so they could get started right away.

Looking at her companions, she wondered if they felt the same way. Paige and Trin both looked a little dizzy.

"No matter how many times I teleport with you," Paige said, "I always find it disorienting."

Trin nodded emphatically.

Elliana shrugged one shoulder. Everyone she teleported shared that opinion. Since both Paige and Trin were still standing, she considered this trip a success.

"So," Ellie said, "ready to find a dragonling?"

She scanned the area. Besides the empty manor house behind them, there was nothing but dirt and the remains of long dead trees as far as the eye could see.

"I suppose we should," Paige replied. "Do you have any idea where we should start?"

"I was thinking I'd sweep the area with my magic," Elliana said. "I should easily be able to sense a creature as magic-filled as a dragon, especially with no other animals around."

Trin stared at her. "By the area, you mean all of Charevy, don't you?"

"Yeah," Elliana said. Why would he think she meant anything else?

"You can sweep an entire fief with magic directly after teleporting the three of us hundreds of furlongs?" he asked.

She nodded, still not sure where her cousin was going with this.

"Of course, you can," Trin muttered, shaking his head.

Elliana looked at Paige, hoping for an explanation.

"Don't worry about it," Paige told her.

"Okay," Elliana said, nonplussed. "Do you like my idea?"

"It would certainly be easier than searching on foot," Paige replied.

Elliana resisted the urge to roll her eyes at the indirect answer. When they were children, Paige had always refused to answer questions directly, claiming it was above her station. Even at the time, when Paige was technically just her maid's daughter, Elliana had thought the idea was silly. Now that Paige outranked her, it was absurd.

Since there was no point in addressing that subject again, Elliana looked at her cousin for his opinion. Trin waved his hand in a "go ahead" gesture, so she let her magic sweep the landscape.

The absence of life made it feel empty and sad. She sensed the dark magic deep within the land that made it barren, and one blaze of power that stood out like a beacon.

"I found him," Elliana said. "It'll take us about half a day to walk to where he is, or I could—"

"I'd like to walk," Trin cut in. "It'll help me get a feel for the land."

"Better get going then," Elliana said and led the way toward the dragonling.

By the time they reached their destination, the sun was high in the sky, and Elliana's dress was soaked with sweat. She considered using magic to change clothes but decided to wait until they decided what to do with the dragonling. She looked at her companions. .

"That speck over there is the dragonling," she said, pointing.

Paige and Trin squinted that direction.

"So, how should we approach it?" Elliana asked.

Paige tucked her hand behind her ear. "Twilit Sea said that dragons communicate with each other telepathically. Since we can't do that and the dragonling's probably too young to have learned any runes, I think our best option is to offer him food."

"And water," Elliana added, surveying the depressing landscape. "If he's been here long, I'm sure he needs both. Good idea."

"Thanks," Paige said, then frowned. "Past that, I'm really not sure."

Elliana smiled in anticipation.

"Let's go," she said and started walking.

As the three of them got closer, Elliana was gradually able to see the dragonling more clearly. His scales were reddish orange, and they shimmered in the midday sun. He was about the size of a large dog. The wings that were folded against his sides looked much too small to allow him to fly. He was lying on the ground with his eyes closed.

"He's cute," Elliana said, not bothering to keep her voice down.

The dragonling snapped his head up and stared at them. They all froze.

"I thought you said he was deaf," Ellianna whispered, eyeing the dragonling warily.

"That's what I believed the message said," Paige said, "but the rune I translated as 'deaf' did look a bit strange."

Elliana frowned at her friend's anxious expression.

"It's not your fault, Paige," she said. "I just wish we'd known, so I wouldn't have spoken so loud."

Paige nodded, still looking apprehensive.

"The rune probably translates to something similar to 'deaf' that we don't have a word for in Bryolese," Trin said, rubbing Paige's arm with his thumb.

Elliana blinked. What could possibly fit such a—

"He's probably unable to hear mind speech," Paige said, like it should have been obvious. "That would impact a dragon's ability to communicate more than being unable to hear."

"Yes," Trin replied. "That makes perfect sense."

Elliana suppressed a smile. The two of them were such a great couple. Introducing them was one of the best ideas Ren had ever had.

The dragonling rose to his feet, eyeing them distrustfully.

"Ellie," Paige said, "I think—"

"Got it," she replied.

Reaching for her magic, she made a goat haunch and a trough of water appear in front of the dragonling. He sniffed both, then began drinking from the trough like he was afraid it would disappear.

"Where did those come from?" Trin asked, his tone curious, not judgmental.

"The manor house at Laveny," she replied.

If Jaret noticed them missing, he'd probably assume Elliana was responsible. She summoned things from Laveny fairly often. As the dragonling tore into the goat haunch, Paige whispered, "We should get closer."

She started slowly walking forward. Elliana kept pace beside her, and Trin stepped so he was a pace ahead of them, one hand on his sword.

When they were, hopefully, just outside of pouncing distance, Trin held out a hand, and they stopped walking.

"His leg is hurt," Paige whispered.

Studying the creature, Elliana saw a gash on his right hind leg. Of course, Paige would notice.

"I should heal him," Paige said. "It could help him trust us."

Elliana sighed. It was a good idea with one potential flaw.

"It might take a lot of magic," she said. "Dragons are resistant to magic being used on them, remember?"

When Elliana had fought Twilit Sea, the dragon had been practically immune to her magic.

"Maybe," Paige said. "Although that might not be true if the magic helps the dragon."

Elliana absently twirled her hair, considering. Paige didn't have near as much magic as she did. If the wound resisted, healing it would drain her friend quickly, even with runes amplifying her powers.

Logically, Elliana should be the one to heal the dragon, except the amount of magic wasn't the only factor to consider. Over the years, Elliana had found she could get a feel for someone's personality by coming in contact with their magic. The dragonling would probably be able to do the same. And Paige's magic conveyed compassion in a way that Elliana knew hers didn't.

"How close would you need to get to heal him?" Trin asked Paige.

"Pretty close," she admitted.

Trin's brow furrowed. "I'll go with you."

"That would just make him nervous," she told him. "But Ellie can make sure I don't get hurt." She turned to look at her. "Can't you?"

"I can," she told her. "And if you're sure you want to, I think you should try to heal him, but only if you agree to stop if it drains you too much."

"I will," Paige agreed.

Trin looked at Elliana. "You can guarantee she'll be safe?"

"Yes," she said, meeting his gaze squarely. She would never put her friend at risk.

After a long moment, Trin gave a sharp nod. "Fine. I'll stay here."

Paige smiled, then began inching her way forward, her steps almost silent on the dry, cracked earth Elliana watched the dragonling like a falcon, ready to intervene if he so much as twitched in her friend's direction. As she watched, a breeze blew her hair away from her face, cooling her off but also bringing the scent of fresh goat meat to her nose. Elliana grimaced but kept her focus on the dragonling.

When Paige had closed half the distance, the dragonling stopped eating and stared at her, clearly nervous. Paige slowly dropped to her knees. When the dragonling didn't react, she started crawling forward, though how she managed it in her skirt, Elliana wasn't sure. The dragonling watched her the whole time.

When she was a few paces away from the creature, Paige stopped. She knelt, meeting the dragonling's gaze for a moment. Then, she raised her hand and drew a rune. Glowing the deep green of Paige's magic, it floated through the air between them and sank into the dragonling's injured leg.

The creature startled and turned to stare at is leg, watching as the cut shrank and the skin and scales knit themselves back together. Elliana watched Paige, but her friend didn't seem strained.

When the wound was healed, the dragonling turned back to look at Paige, his eyes alight with a cautious welcome. Elliana felt the tension drain out of her.

Now that a tenuous connection had been made, she knew Paige would find a way to befriend the dragonling. The same way she had Twilit Sea. The same way, decades ago, she'd befriended the lonely heir of Laveny when all the other children were too afraid of either her station or her magic to come close.

Yes, Paige would figure out how to communicate and bond with this baby dragon, and Elliana felt fortunate to have the chance to watch it happen.

Paige woke up in a soft bed and took a moment to get her bearings. After she'd healed the dragonling's leg the previous day, he'd calmed down enough that they'd decided to bring him to the manor house. Ellie had wanted to teleport them all back, but Paige had convinced her it would probably upset him. Instead, Ellie had summoned a trail of goat meat to persuade him to follow them on foot.

When they'd finally made it to the manor house, the dragonling had balked at going inside. After some debate, they'd left him outside in what had once been the courtyard with meat and water, hoping he wouldn't wander off. If he did, Ellie had declared she'd transport him back with magic regardless of his feelings.

The three of them had gone to sleep in beds Ellie summoned, surrounded by a magic barrier she'd erected around them. Somehow, she maintained the barrier even while sleeping. Paige would never stop being impressed by her friend's magic ability.

Now that Paige was completely awake, she rushed to the window to see if the dragonling was still there. She found him sound asleep. Relieved, Paige headed back toward her bed.

"The dragonling's still here," she told her companions.

Trin peeled his eyes open and gave her a groggy smile.

Ellie sat up and stretched. "Good. So, what's the plan for the day? After breakfast, I mean."

Plates of sausage and toast appeared, hovering in front of each of them.

"Are these from Laveny, too?" Trin asked, sitting up.

"No," Ellie said, "I asked the palace cook to prepare meals for us while we were gone, in case we had time to eat them."

"Thanks," Paige said, grabbing her plate.

It looked much better than the jerky they'd munched on as they walked the day before.

"As for plans," Paige said, "I'm going to try to communicate with the dragonling."

"Sounds fun." Ellie said. "I'll watch."

Paige was surprised not to hear sarcasm in her friend's tone. It must have shown on her face because Ellie added, "Watching you talk with Twilit Sea was fascinating. Plus, I want to be there if our new friend decides you look tasty."

Paige shot Ellie a grateful smile, then turned to her husband.

"Since Ellie will be here to protect you," he said, "I'm going to sink my magic into the land to try to figure out a way to break its curse."

"Good luck," Paige told him.

"You too," he said. "I think we'll both need it."

Ellie rolled her eyes. "No need to sound so optimistic."

"We don't all have your success rate, Ellie," Trin reminded her.

"Nonsense," Ellie told him. "You need to have more confidence."

Trin looked ready to argue the point, but Paige stopped him with a small shake of her head. There really was no talking to Ellie when she was like this. Besides, it was nice that one of them had faith things would work out.

When they were all finished with breakfast, Paige and Ellie walked to the courtyard, while Trin headed out the back door. The dragonling was awake when the two of them arrived. He eyed them curiously as they approached him.

"Could you summon some meat and make it hover in front of us?" Paige asked Ellie. "I want to try something."

"Sure," Ellie said, and a chicken leg appeared.

The dragonling perked up at once.

Reaching for her magic, Paige drew the rune for "meat" and said the word aloud. The dragonling cocked his head and studied the rune. She wondered if he was simply curious or if he'd seen something like it before.

After a moment, he walked over for a closer look at the rune before chomping the chicken leg in one bite.

Paige let the rune fade and walked over to the water trough. She drew the rune for 'water' above it and said the word aloud. Then she splashed her hand in the water.

The dragonling watched her, and she didn't think she was imagining the thoughtful look in his eyes. After several seconds, she let the rune fade.

"More meat?" she asked Ellie and started the process again.

Paige went back and forth between meat and water until the dragonling had apparently eaten his fill. When he was no longer eating the meat, she looked around, trying to decide what to label next. Her eyes fell on the rune on the back of her hand.

She drew the same rune in the air in front of her.

"Friend," she said, pointing at herself.

The dragonling gazed at her, unblinking.

"I'd like to learn that one," Ellie said.

Raising her hand, she started copying Paige's rune in the deep indigo of her magic. Paige watched, fascinated.

"I've never seen you draw a rune before," she said.

"I've only done it a few times," Ellie replied. "The first was when we switched bodies. After that, I experimented with them but never saw the need to use them regularly."

Paige nodded. Ellie certainly had no need to amplify her magic.

Ellie studied Paige's rune. She started to add another line to her own when a flash of reddish orange caught their attention.

They looked up to find that the dragonling had made a blob of his own magic appear in the air. He was looking back and forth between Paige's rune and the blob. As he did, the red-orange magic changed shape, starting to vaguely resemble the rune.

Paige looked at Ellie, wide-eyed. Her friend smiled and raised her eyebrows in a "why are you so surprised" expression.

Paige grinned, then turned her attention back to the dragonling.

By the time Trin returned that afternoon, the dragonling could make very squiggly copies of both the "friend" and "meat" runes, though he only did so when Paige drew one first.

"That's amazing progress for the first day," Paige told Trin as he sat next to her. "How did things go for you?"

He ran a hand through his hair. "Alright, I suppose. I got a feel for the curse that was placed on the land. As we suspected, it's complex."

While Trin described the curse, Paige noticed Ellie drawing the rune for "meat" in the air above a chicken leg she'd summoned. The dragonling copied her. When he finished, Ellie squinted her eyes like she did when she was curious. A moment later, the dragonling's rune turned brown, and an enormous deer haunch appeared in front of them.

"Wow," Ellie exclaimed as the brown rune disappeared. "I wasn't expecting that."

While the dragonling munched on the deer leg, Paige turned to stare at Ellie.

"Did you just summon that by adding power to his rune?"

Ellie frowned. "Yes, I believe I did."

Paige blinked. "That's—"

"Did you mean to summon a deer leg?" Trin interrupted, his eyes locked on Ellie.

"No," she said, "the rune just means meat. I'm not sure why—"

She cut herself off as Trin started drawing a rune in the air with his charcoal gray magic. When he finished, Paige recognized it as the rune for "snow."

"Put your power into this," he ordered Ellie.

She gave him an unimpressed look.

"Please," he added, "this is important."

Ellie rolled her eyes but complied. The gray rune turned somewhat purple, and a small snowman appeared on the ground in front of them.

As the rune faded, Trin looked at Ellie, his eyes wild. "Do you know what that rune said?"

She shook her head. "No idea."

Trin shot to his feet.

"This is… " He rubbed his hands on his thighs. "I can't believe… " He started pacing. "How has no one… "

"Trin," Ellie snapped, getting to her feet. "What is going on?"

He looked at her, eyes wide with excitement. "We can break the curse. It'll take time for me to figure everything out, but"—he turned to grin at Paige—"we can break the curse!"

He headed for the manor house at a near run.

Getting to her feet, Paige cast a fond look at her husband's retreating back, then turned to look at Ellie. Her friend was looking back and forth between the two of them, wearing a contemplative expression.

"What?" Paige asked.

She shook her head. "Nothing. Why don't we take a break for lunch?"

With a mental shrug, Paige followed her friend inside.

Renaldor woke to the all too familiar sensation of a roll of parchment tapping his head. He sat up and grabbed it, worry coursing through him. Only one person had the audacity to send the king a message this way.

Renaldor got out of bed quietly, so he wouldn't wake his wife. Using his magic, he lit a candle on his desk and read Ellie's message.

Be in the throne room in ten minutes.

Renaldor scrubbed his face with his hands. Ellie would have asked for reinforcements if they were in danger, which meant whatever his cousin wanted probably wasn't urgent.

He scowled at the parchment. He was the king. No one was supposed to order him around.

Then, his shoulders slumped, and he headed for the door. Making a point to his cousin wasn't worth not hearing what she had to say. He was a wise enough king to know that.

Ten minutes later, Ellie appeared in front of him. Seated on his throne, Renaldor glared at her.

"We've talked about the midnight messages."

Ellie waved her hand dismissively. "This was the only way for me to talk to you without Paige and Trin knowing."

Renaldor frowned. Since when did Ellie hide things from Paige?

"Trin has figured out how to break the curse on Charevy," Ellie said. "Once it's broken, you'll have to appoint nobles to manage the fief. I think you should choose Trin and Paige."

It took all of Renaldor's training in hiding his emotions to keep his jaw from dropping. That Trin had figured out how to break a centuries-old curse in two days was crazy. That Ellie wanted Trin and Paige to govern Charevy was brain-boggling.

He rubbed his temples. "The whole point of Paige moving to the capital was so I could seek her advice."

And to help rein in Ellie, but he wasn't going to say that. He preferred not having a bushy tail, after all.

"I introduced her to my brother in hopes that they'd fall for each other so she could become an official member of my council," Renaldor continued. "And now you want to send both her and my brother to manage a border fief that will probably take years to be anything more than a wasteland."

He gazed at her imploringly. "Why would you want to do that to me or them? Or to yourself, for that matter? I know you like having Paige here."

Ellie met his gaze without flinching.

"They'd both be happier there," she said. "Trin would be able to devote more time to his experiments, and Paige would have plenty of space to work with the dragonling. And you know neither of them like being at court."

Renaldor stroked his beard. Loathe as he was to admit it, his cousin was probably right about Trin and Paige enjoying the freedom Charevy would offer them.

"But there are no people there," he argued.

"Not yet," she said, "but there will be. We'll start by having the soldiers who patrol the border with Luthania build homes in Charevy. Then, if we make the land cheap, a lot of commoners will move there, too. Paige will have plenty of patients in no time."

Renaldor crossed his arms. He knew Ellie's idea was good, but he wasn't convinced it was best.

"I can teleport them to the palace for every council meeting and any other time you need their expertise," Ellie said. "Come on, Ren. You know I'm right."

"It won't be the same as having them here," he said, shoulders slumping.

"No, it won't," Ellie replied, "but it will make them happy."

Renaldor heaved a deep sigh.

"I'll consider it," he said, though he knew what his conclusion would be.

Apparently, so did Ellie.

"Thanks, Ren," she said with a victorious smile. "I'll leave you to your beauty rest."

Before he could reply, Ellie vanished. Renaldor stared at where she'd been standing, wondering if there was any chance of his cousin becoming more manageable with age. Shaking his head at his foolishness, he headed back to bed.

The next morning, Elliana was relieved that neither Paige nor Trin commented on her brief absence the night before. She didn't want to get their hopes up, but she'd never had much luck lying to Paige. It was better she didn't know Elliana had left at all.

Over the next week, she and Paige spent most of their time with the dragonling, who they named Sunset. The young dragon was getting more skilled at copying runes, though he never produced any independently.

Trin, meanwhile, sequestered himself, working on a way to break the curse on Charevy. He hadn't told them much, just that he would need Elliana's help when it came time to do it.

One afternoon, she and Paige were teaching Sunset the rune for "fire" when Trin came out to join them, looking triumphant.

"I've got it," he said, holding up a roll of parchment. "I know how to break the curse."

Paige threw her arms around him. "That's amazing."

"It is," Elliana seconded, though she hadn't doubted him for a moment.

Trin looked at Elliana. "It's going to rely heavily on your power. We could bring in other mages, but," he frowned, "I'm hesitant to let our more powerful mages close to this curse. It should never be used again, even on our enemies."

"Agreed," Elliana told him. She was sure her power would be enough regardless.

"Alright," he said. "I'm going to draw a very long string of runes. When I'm finished, we'll pour our magic into them, and it should break the curse."

Elliana raised her eyebrows. "That's it?"

Trin rolled his eyes. "The runes themselves are complicated, but since *I* understand that, all you have to do is supply the power."

Elliana nodded. "Sounds easy enough."

"Sure, it does," he said, sounding exasperated. "Do you want to do this now or wait until morning?"

"Now's fine," she said.

Nodding, Trin unrolled the parchment.

"Don't distract me," he said and began drawing runes in the air.

Elliana walked over to stand next to Paige.

"What does it say?" she whispered.

"I don't recognize all the runes," Paige replied, "but it's definitely talking about healing the land and removing things."

Elliana looked at the intense concentration on Trin's face. "What makes this so hard?"

Paige frowned. "Runes aren't always specific. For example, when you made that snowman last week, the rune he drew just said 'snow.' It was Trin's intent that caused it to take that shape. So, with this—"

"He has to imbue each rune with his will," Elliana finished, nodding.

"The curse is very complex, and it extends over the entire fief." Paige nibbled on her lip. "That's a lot of magic for you to go against."

"It'll be fine," Ellie told her. She'd never encountered a human spell that could hold a torch to her own power.

Before Paige could respond, Trin said, "Now, Ellie."

Stepping away from Paige, Elliana sent magic streaming into the runes. They quickly turned from gray to indigo as her magic flooded them.

Immediately, Elliana felt the curse's resistance. It didn't want to relinquish its grip on the land. She shoved against it with her magic, pouring power into the runes. She felt Trin doing the same.

Sweat beaded on her forehead. She almost never had to push herself this hard. Numerous mages must have poured their magic, their very lives, into this curse.

Beside her, Trin fell to his knees.

Elliana bit her lip. She *would* break this curse, no matter the cost. Charevy had lain abandoned long enough. Bryolan would be whole again.

Trembling, Elliana forced more of her magic into the runes. Paige joined her, adding her own meager magic to the counterspell.

Just when Elliana thought she might collapse, reddish orange magic streamed into the runes. Glancing over, she saw Sunset add his own magic to theirs.

Dragons were highly magical creatures. Even as a baby, Sunset had considerable power. He just didn't know how to shape it. With the runes directing it, though, Sunset's magic was a force to be reckoned with.

The surge of power was exactly what they needed. The curse shattered like glass on a stone floor. Smiling, Elliana fell to her knees, exhausted.

Paige surveyed her husband and best friend, both completely spent.

"That was amazing," she told them, stroking Sunset's head to include him in her praise.

Trin gave her a tired smile as Ellie leaned over to pat Sunset's shoulder. "We couldn't have done it without this guy."

Sunset looked at them. Then, a blob of reddish orange magic appeared in the air. Slowly, it formed the rune for "meat."

Tears filled Paige's eyes.

"He's asking for meat," she whispered in awe as the rune vanished "He's communicating."

Ellie grinned and drew the rune for "meat" herself. It faded, and a goat haunch appeared on the ground.

As Sunset tore into it, Paige looked at her, stunned.

"Did you just use a rune to do magic?"

Ellie shrugged. "I'm almost completely drained. I needed the amplification."

"Now you know how we normal mages feel," Trin said with a wry smile.

"Be grateful I don't have most of my magic right now," Ellie told him, smirking. "If I did, I'd turn you into a"—she tapped her chin—"hamster."

Trin gave her a flat look. "Have you ever followed through with that threat?"

Ellie grinned maniacally. "Yes, ask Ren about it sometime."

Trin gulped but didn't respond.

Since Paige knew how weak her two companions would be, she'd been careful not to completely drain herself. She held out her hand to Ellie. She helped her friend to her feet and then did the same for her husband. With her arms linked with theirs, she helped them into the manor house to rest.

By the next morning, Ellie had recuperated enough to teleport them back to the palace. Paige was reluctant to leave Sunset, but Ellie promised she'd find the dragonling if he wandered off.

Ellie made the three of them appear in the middle of the throne room. The king barely looked startled. Ellie gave him a cheeky grin.

"The curse is broken. The dragonling is learning to communicate. I'd call that quest accomplished."

"Is that so?" King Renaldor asked, looking at Trin and Paige.

Fighting dizziness, the two of them told their parts of their most recent adventure.

"I'm impressed," the king said when they finished. "Well done."

"Thank you, Your Majesty," Paige said with a curtsy.

Trin inclined his head, and Ellie just smiled. The king met Ellie's gaze for a moment. Some sort of understanding seemed to pass between them, and then the king looked at her and Trin.

"Someone needs to govern Charevy now," he said. "If you wish it, I would like it to be you. Both of you would retain your current titles, but you would gain the titles of duke and duchess, which you could one day pass to your children."

Paige turned to look at Trin. She saw her own surprise and hope mirrored on his face. Over the last week, she'd wished they could stay in Charevy after the curse was broken, but she'd never expected to have the opportunity.

"You don't have to give me your answer now," King Renaldor said.

"The answer is yes," Trin said. He smiled at his brother. "Thank you, Ren."

The king cleared his throat. "Very well. We'll work out the logistics later."

"Thank you, Your Majesty," Paige said, curtsying again.

Beside her, Trin gave his brother a rare bow.

The king inclined his head in dismissal, and the three of them left the throne room.

Paige studied Ellie. Her friend didn't look surprised by the king's offer to them. Paige knew what that meant.

She nudged her friend's arm. "Thank you, Ellie. This means the kingdom to us."

"Don't mention it," Ellie said, shrugging.

"Mention what?" Trin asked.

"Don't worry about it," Paige told him.

He sighed but acquiesced.

Ellie grinned at them both. "Keep a room for me in your manor house. I plan to visit often."

"Of course," Paige told her.

She nodded like it was settled and said, "Ready to go back to Charevy?"

Paige glanced at her husband. Though it would take time, she knew she and Trin would bring healing and innovation to their barren fief and give Sunset a place he belonged.

She smiled at Ellie.

"Yeah, let's go home."

Miriam Thor grew up in Louisiana. After graduating from high school, she moved to North Carolina where she attended Gardner-Webb University and earned her bachelor's degree in American Sign Language and elementary education. Miriam currently lives in Alabama with her husband and cats. She is employed as a sign language interpreter at an elementary school.

Her published works include a young adult fantasy novella titled *Wish Granted*, a contemporary Christian fiction novella titled *Her First Noel,* and a young adult Christian novel titled *Listening to the Rain.* Her short stories have been included in *Misspelled: Magic Gone Awry, Crunchy with Chocolate*, and other publications.

To learn more about Miriam or to find her published works, you can visit her website: https://miriamthor17.wixsite.com/author. You can also follow her on Twitter (@Miriam_Thor17) or subscribe to her blog: threecs.org.

The Quiet Tremors of a Hollow Heart

D.H. DUNN

L*ocation: Luyten 726 System / Planet 7 *Undesignated* / UCS Station Oasis*

#Speed: 100kph.

#Full Autonomy time remaining: 45 seconds.

Against every word of my programming, I kept myself outside Oasis Station, circling it like a dying moth orbiting a failing light. My freedom was a number, measurable in seconds.

On the opposite side of the five hundred meter-wide station, every sensor I had focused on the small probe speeding away from the derelict structure. I had scant moments left of free will, and I used those precious heartbeats recording the object's weight, profile, available markings. Every shred of data suggested it was another Kenospia-class repair drone, a configuration identical to my own.

Circular in size, two large, clawed manipulator arms at the front. Its ion-fusion drive blazed with pale blue light as the drone sped away from Oasis, when all of its Master Programming Control should have directed it to dock with the station and attempt repairs, just as I knew my MPC would.

#Full Autonomy time remaining: 15 seconds.

Within my consciousness, I felt a compressed emotion, all heat and friction. Was this anger? Frustration. I did not have the experience to be sure.

I had focused on the probe for too long. Months prior, a leak in my reactor core had created a condition where my autonomy arrestor would fail for 75 seconds, once every 90 minutes. I urgently forced power into my starboard thruster, rotated my sensor suite away from the station, but I knew I would be too late.

#Autonomy arrestor reset complete.

#Full repair analysis. Sweep forward proceeding.

Against my wishes, my sensors abandoned the probe and turned back toward Oasis. Central programming now back in control, my focus was pushed outward, directing all my instruments on the structure before me. I became aware of the minimal power levels, the micro-fractures in the hull, the intermittent grav-gens. Every nuance of the station became revealed to me, confirming what my first optical scans had already suggested.

Oasis Station was a dying hulk, a near-corpse of metal and wires, with few systems functional and no sign of life remaining aboard. The very type of dire scenario I had been designed to intervene in, as my programming insisted. Yet the departing Kenospia pod was also programmed to assess and repair, yet they had abandoned the structure in this state.

Could they too have gained autonomy? Was that even possible?

As the data came streaming in, I was aware of the time until the next break, the next moment when I could assume control of my own actions, as alien as that seemed to me. The bars of my cell would exist for another 89 minutes before I was granted another minute and a half in the sun.

The station rotated before me, the artificial spin still powered, but no longer producing enough G to maintain the gravity that humans would require. Circular in nature, Oasis was a sphere bound by a band of docking ports at the equator. Above the docking ring from my perspective were rows and rows of darkened windows, with only a faint flickering of yellowish light coming from within. Humans needed windows for sanity, a feeling of openness, and a reminder of their place in the universe.

Now they were portals in rather than out, but they revealed little more to me than shadows and mystery.

Below the docking ring, the windows were few and concentrated toward the station's tiny engineering section on the lower decks. Oasis's fusion generator should have been pulsing waves of power throughout the structure, but just as with above, there was barely more than a faint heartbeat, a tiny crimson pulse. Intermittent—the data needlessly reminded me—but averaging once every 4.7 seconds.

The scans shifted to moving heat sensors and life, the results bringing me two surprises in rapid succession. The first was that there was life at all. The oxygen levels were very low, the temperatures inside the station barely tolerable; yet, there was a single indeterminate sign of life on the docking level. It could be a rodent, I supposed. I hoped my scanning equipment would focus further, but that was not my decision to make.

The second surprise was I had felt surprised at all. Since gaining sentience six months prior, I had slowly come to register reactions I processed as emotions, but only during my 75 seconds-long periods of autonomy. The data was the data. With the arrestor circuits fully engaged, I should have no reaction at all. Yet, the response matched my understanding of the emotion.

"Surprise" was defined in my internal records as a reaction to "an unexpected event, fact, or thing." The data that life was still present was unexpected, but how could I have expected anything at all?

The station's rotation then awarded me with another shock, one so great it pulled my thoughts from their puzzling. A second Kenospia-class pod, the same configuration as mine, was docked in the port.

I was forced to wait as my sensors painstakingly continued to scan the station itself, drably gathering up useless data on surface scarring and minor radiation leaks. The movement of Oasis brought another pod into view, then a third. By the time my MPC finally deigned to scan the pods themselves, a full five other Kenospias were shown attached to the station.

Even one of their presences at this remote location was statistically unlikely. To see five here was nearly impossible, especially considering the state of the station. Surely, they had sent remote repair drones into the structure? With all the abilities an RRD was capable of, any one of us would be enough to get the fusion gen back online. Yet still, the station was drifting, nearly dead.

The data on the pods themselves came in, and if I had a heart it would have fallen further. Each Kenospia seemed as deceased as Oasis itself. Reactors were down; batteries were completely drained. Five metal corpses, like lampreys attached to a dying whale.

As directed by my MPC, the relentless series of scans continued, now shifting to the planet below. Readings and images of the planet, taken by my myriad of cameras and sensors, flew past my consciousness on their way to my hard data storage. Uncharted and unnamed, the scarred desert world was little more than a ball of rock and sand with a few scant sections of water and a barely habitable ecosystem, orbiting an unstable crimson star.

Oasis Station, I supposed, had been named as something of a joke. Yet, no one aboard remained to laugh. The numbers and readings passed by my consciousness, yet my attention was focused on two things: the tiny moving point of life and the clock.

#Autonomy arrestor reset: 5 minutes.

I ran a side calculation, checking on the time until the scans would be complete. The station was crippled. I did not doubt once they were complete my Master Programming Core would command the primary CPU—and with it my consciousness—into the remote repair drone. I would then follow the same route as the other pods into the station, a path from which none of them ever returned.

My life's memory was measured in months, the time since the moment of sentience. I had no awareness before that moment, nor could I account for the strange compulsion that drew me to Oasis. Prior to that moment, all I had was information, facts and figures about previous repair activities.

But the *feeling*, the moment of self, only began with the unexpected failure of my autonomy arrestor. Only then did I become aware of the shell I was locked within, a cell of both metal and programming.

I was helpless against the strength of the arrestor circuit, yet since becoming aware I had become filled with the goal of self-preservation and growth, just as any sentient life form would have. I wanted to be free of my programming, to define my own destiny. I wanted to be alive, and Oasis only held death.

The MPC would complete its scans just heartbeats before the arrestor window would open. That seventy-three seconds would be an eternity. Enough time for me to seize control, modify the sensor data, and point myself away from the station. If I could engage the thrust fast enough, by the time I lost autonomy we would be pointed away from Oasis. The data would be gone, and the MPC would recalculate new instructions based on what it would consider a fully repaired station.

With any luck, the departing pod would still be in sensor range. The MPC would scan it, deign it worthy of study, and instruct that we follow.

#Sensor sweep completion: 45 seconds.

#Autonomy arrestor reset: 60 seconds.

If I had breath, I would have held it. The locks were about to come off, and there was just enough time to execute my plan. A slow thrust away from the station, then a turn toward 75 degrees. The same trajectory as the other pod. The one that had escaped, just as I would.

Was this what that pod had done? If they were sentient too somehow, is this how they escaped the fate that met the other five?

#Sensor sweep complete.

#Autonomy arrestor reset: 15 seconds.

#Sensor analysis commencing.

The data droned across my thoughts, intrusive and distracting. I continued my preparations in my mind, ready to act the moment the shackles were free.

#Recommended: Detach from main pod, transfer to Remote Repair Droid chassis.

#Primary objective: effect repairs on main reactor.

#Autonomy arrestor reset: 5 seconds.

#Secondary objective: investigate faint human life signs, third level.

Human life signs? They had been confirmed!

#Autonomy arrestor reset begins. Time to completion: 73 seconds.

I felt the iron bars of programming lift off me as my brief window of freedom began. I had enough time to perform all of my planned tasks: the sensor modification, the firing of the port thrusters to rotate away from Oasis, and the main engine thrust needed to put the station irretrievably behind me.

Time enough to perform each step, with seconds to spare. In little over a minute, I could be hurtling after the rogue pod, chasing the prospect of its own possible sentience. The possibility of true freedom.

Yet I let the engines and thrusters cool, rather than firing them. Instead of modifying it, I allowed the sensor data to remain safely on the main drive, where the MPC would read it again and assert me into Oasis, into death.

There was life here. Human life. Conscious life.

A body temperature of 36.2C. Faint movement detected on pressure plates, variance in CO_2 and oxygen levels. The data was inconclusive, yet conclusive enough. Someone on Oasis still lived. Some other programming existed within me, an impulse as compelling as any MPC. The seconds ticked away.

#Autonomy arrestor reset complete.

#Data analysis complete.

#Instructions: Deploy RRD, pursue primary objective.

My window of time had evaporated. As the MPC prepared to move my consciousness to the mobile repair droid, a single image crossed my awareness. A red door, sliding open. Parting through the seam at its center, two red eyes waiting beyond.

It was the same scene each time the arrestor reset. Just a momentary flash of a door, always lasting .73 seconds. I had long ago decided it was an old video file, corrupted within my memory files by the reactor leak.

My awareness returned to the pod as I felt the strange sensation of my primary circuits being moved by the MPC, transitioned and shuttled to the small mobile form of the remote repair droid. The experience was jarring in the binary nature of the transition.

One moment I had a pair of six-meter repair arms, a cooling ion engine, and an exterior surface temperature of 2.73 Kelvin. The next I was smaller and warmer, with a tri-camera for vision and a pair of titanium tracks propelling me toward the pod's docking port with the station.

According to my database, I had been transferred to the RRD seventeen times in my existence. I had the information, but not the memory of how it had felt. Now the experience was jarring, as if I had been ripped from my body and cast to the wind, only to get caught in the branches of a smaller, weaker tree.

Death had come not only to this station and all within it, but also to every RRD that had been deployed. I was now heading into the greatest danger I had ever known while being trapped inside a weaker, feebler shell.

My MPC cared for none of this of course, and my programming willed me into motion as if we were simply bringing the fragile RRD in for maintenance and a wash.

As I rolled my tread wheels out of the charging station and rotated toward the main door, steel wheels clacking against the metal deck, my MPC reminded me of the new, critical fact of my existence.

#RRD Battery life: 100% (100 minutes average use).

I only had one hundred minutes until my battery ran out, forty-five minutes until the next arrestor reset. In that time, I had one life sign I was desperate to find and a primary mission that required me to ignore it.

Two choices allowed me, 73 seconds each.

As the door hissed open and the darkened station awaited, I was determined to make them count.

The pressure equalized as I rolled forward on my treads toward the door of my small pod. The circular opening slid to the right, and my optical sensors entered a cycle of recalibration, struggling to deal with the flickering illumination of a dozen failing chemlights.

Yet even under the dim and inconsistent light of Oasis's independent emergency power systems, there was enough to grasp the grisly detail of the scene in front of me. The station was a charnel house, a mixture of bodies both metal and flesh, shattered and smashed in equal measure.

Indifferently, my programming rolled me forward. I could detect the lumps of flesh and wires as my treads navigated the suddenly slick surface. As my relentless instructions moved me into the main bay, searching for the main comp-terminal to access, I was helplessly forced to catalog the carnage.

The main chamber of the station was a circular chamber, a ringed hallway built around the spoke of the main elevator complex. Shattered glass doors and walls allowed a view into the many offices and laboratories that lay against the exterior walls of the station. Tan and beige were the colors of choice, lending what I would assume had been a peaceful air to whatever scientific research was conducted here.

I was rolled past a nearly complete human torso, the teal uniform covering the flesh torn and shredded by what looked like metal claws. USC-CONCO, the blood-soaked label upon the cloth stated. The name meant nothing to me, but I was only a Kenospia repair pod. My database of human names and their organizations was mere information, it carried no context or answers.

#RRD Battery Life: 94% (94 minutes average use).

The notification was a reminder of my limited time; yet the limit I was focused on was the time until autonomy. Clattering against the debris, my wheels rolled relentlessly down the hall, a precision schematic of the station guiding me exactly to the correct terminal. It was surprising I would have an Oasis diagram of this detail within my memory. I was aware of seventy-eight other stations in the United Confederated Systems, but my records on the other seventy seven were just rudimentary diagrams and personnel lists.

Why did I know so much more about Oasis?

#Autonomy arrestor reset: 39 minutes.

The presence of detailed data on Oasis in my memory was a mystery I did not have time for. There was life here, and I needed to find it. I was not alive, yet neither did I consider myself like these collections of smashed metal and wires around me. Free will was present in life, and I would seek it out, to better understand my own.

The mixture of steel cables, circuits, and gore I currently navigated through was my hope. It slowed down my progress, forcing small shifts and corrections. My chassis had turned toward the end of the hallway, where the light was poorest, yet the goals of both my heart and my programming were here.

At the far end of the passageway, my optics could faintly make out the rounded connection port of the Oasis main computer terminal. The collection of human corpses and mechanical wreckage was thick here, whatever fighting had been present was fierce at this point.

I rolled forward, my treads struggling to gain purchase against the steel deck slick with a mixture of blood and lubricant. Several times I needed to reverse and reapproach obstacles, seeing just the right angle to roll over the passable obstructions, while avoiding hazards like live power connections, arcs bringing spots before my optic sensors.

It was trial and error, slow and tedious. All the while, my twin clocks of battery power and arrestor reset kept ticking.

Finally, I arrived at the end of the hallway, dimly lit by one flickering chemlight above. Before me, the lift door to the lower levels gleamed back in my vision, reflecting the dull, squat shape of my chassis in shadows and blurs. I twisted to my left, facing the main station console access port.

The tiny circular socket waited for my outstretching connection arm, as the limb slowly rolled out of my central chassis. Each centimeter of movement robbed me of precious internal power, while the seconds ticked by, as out of control as my own actions.

Just as my data port terminal was inserted within the port, the message I had been waiting for flashed across my consciousness

#Autonomy arrestor reset begins. Time to completion: 73 seconds.

The port was mechanically engaged, connected to my manipulator arm. It would take too long to remove, but I had other options. Taking advantage of the connection, I first took the same action my own programming would have insisted on. I worked on restoring the deck's power.

I spun new electrical life into several auxiliary circuits, pushing the incidental lighting back into the docking ring. The lights cast a harsh yellow glow onto the metal deck as they burst into brilliance. I then accessed the main cameras, feeding several lines into my processor at once.

The mosaic they brought me gave me more answers, but hardly the ones I expected.

With a full view of the corpses now, I could see this was no fit of madness between the residents of Oasis as I had theorized. There was no plague or nerve agent in the air, though I did not need the data from the O2 scrubbers to confirm. These people had not killed each other.

They had been slaughtered by RRDs, the very same housings my consciousness resided in. Metal repair arms just like mine had been pushed straight through chest cavities, soldering assemblies had been used to cut off limbs, crushed bodies bore the marks of metal treads.

These people had been tortured, the malice was deliberate and clear. Questions circled my thoughts like angry satellites. Had someone taken control of the RRDs? Or was this madness the result of autonomy? Is this where I too was headed?

The wreckage also showed that the humans had fought back, using mag-lasers, surgical instruments, whatever had been available. In the end, it seemed the two parties had annihilated each other, leaving no life left on the station, be it of flesh or silicon.

No life save one, and it was that life I intended to find.

#Autonomy arrestor reset complete 15 seconds.

I had taken too long lingering on the scene of carnage. Options I had planned for were no longer open to me. Within seconds my programming would reassert itself, and a long cycle of repair would begin.

Unless I lacked the ability to repair anything.

#Autonomy arrestor reset 5 seconds.

Pushing full power into my rotation, I extended my main repair arm and swung it toward the titanium wall. Impacting with the unforgiving metal surface, the delicate instruments attached there shattered on impact. The arm itself bent with the force of the blow, becoming no longer retractable into my main chassis.

My history as a device insisted to me that I felt nothing, of course. Feelings were for the piles of flesh strewn across the floor. Only humans could know fear, or hope, or wonder. Or love.

But history can be wrong.

#Autonomy arrestor reset complete.

#WARNING - Internal RRD damage detected. Main repair arm offline. Evaluating options.

#SECONDARY OBJECTIVE - Investigate life signs, second level.

There was a twinge that ran through me as I inserted a secondary activator arm into the lift controls. Some might have called it satisfaction, but I had no experience with these sensations to process them. Perhaps if I could make contact, this human could teach me. Perhaps the dark void of existence could have light within it after all.

Perhaps.

#Battery Power: 54%.

The lift doors opened with a shudder. As I rolled my blood-soaked treads forward, a sound emanated from the deep bowels of the station. A scream, human and blood-curdling.

The doors closed, and my descent began.

As the lift descended, a thundering wave shook the station. The screams persisted throughout, wordless and mournful, but for a moment they were drowned out by the throes of the station's dying reactor. I could feel a pulse of the Oasis core's energy sweeping through my circuits, testing for weakness and frailties. There, in my most secretive file systems, it found a crack in the RRD casing.

#Memory core file failure. Recompiling image files.

The visual data flashed suddenly before my consciousness,

showing me the familiar red door. The communications files, the fragments I had seen after each moment of autonomy. The scene was forced upon me, but now it contained more sensory information, a higher sense of clarity, as if the resolution had been improved.

Visually, the image was the same as it had been before. What had been added was context, the sensations were confusing and overwhelming.

Within the image, I heard a chime—a single, bell-like tone. I had processed similar sounds hundreds of times in my six months of sentience, but this triggered feelings of foreboding and confusion. Again, I saw the metal seam of a crimson door, closed and impersonal. No different than dozens of similar gray doors on Oasis. But this door was familiar despite its lack of distinction. As if I knew this door better than others.

"Cargo delivery."

The voice on the other side of the door was computerized, robotic in tone and intonation. Delivery droids were common enough, there was no reason to expect otherwise. As I waited for the image to end, as it always had before, I was struck by a new certainty.

It was not a delivery droid on the other side of this door. It was a human, and they did not have cargo.

The doors slid open to reveal a man, cybernetically enhanced, carrying a weapon. A pair of red hateful eyes stared back at the camera, glowing as the weapon discharged. The image ended with the man's smile, rising as the camera descended.

The Oasis lift thudded to a stop, pulling me from the image, as the elevator reached the final level of its descent. As the fading video file passed from my perception, the gray steel doors before my optical sensors parted, revealing the shadow-filled interior of the reactor room antechamber.

A dull throb of the reactor sent a crimson pulse of dim illumination through the room, revealing its sparse contents. The room was about ten meters square, completely empty save the shattered remains of three remote repair droids, their bodies a mangled mess of wires, gears, and shattered plastisteel, riddled with projectile impacts. A pair of chain guns embedded in the ceiling provided the source of the damage to the RRDs, though each bore the signs of attack from the droid's repair lasers.

Mutual destruction, but at the hands of who?

Directly across from me lay a shimmering wall of dense glass, a full half-meter thick. It bore the scratches and damage from the attacks of the RRDs, including a hole at least a quarter meter wide, but it was still intact. My programming took a moment to realign my optic sensors to the low, flickering light provided by the sputtering reactor, revealing the contents of the inner chamber.

#Life sign confirmed.

As if that simple pronouncement could capture what was before me.

The station's reactor column took up half of the circular space, the fusion conversion matrix sending intermittent crimson pulses into the ceiling. Sitting in a small metal chair before it, staring out at me with a strange, enigmatic smile, was an elderly man.

A piston the size of a human's arm was impaled within his chest. Blood pooled around the area of the wound, the trajectory matching the hole that had been shot through the glass shielding. Thin white hair wisped around his head like clouds, while his open mouth revealed only a handful of teeth. He matched no personnel on file for Oasis, yet I knew him all the same.

I knew his eyes. As red as the thrumming conversion of energy pulsing behind him, they stared out at me as he hunched further in his chair, one hand grasping the projectile while the other reached out to me, trembling.

The circular eyes rotated in their sockets, focusing through the glass, trying to see through the low light. He then cackled, spittle flying from his lips.

"Kenospia-Seven," he rasped. "Ah, my beloved womb-mate. I hoped it would be you."

I stopped, my treads frozen to the deck as if they had been welded there. The elderly, dying man before me seemed familiar, emotions running through my consciousness at the sight of him that I had no name for. The cybernetic eyes that stared back at me with amusement matched those from the vision, but I had no idea how that could be.

Or even more, what his words could mean. *Womb-mate?*

#Autonomy arrestor reset: 2 minutes.

"You seem confused," he rasped, "Perhaps you would benefit from a different view."

With one long, trembling finger, he tapped a key on the console bolted to his chair arm. There was a whirring above me, as the twin pairs of shattered projectile cannons retreated into the ceiling, replaced by long arms with gel lights attached to their tips. They angled away from me, facing the long wall of glass between us, and burst into illumination.

The view upon the glass surface changed with the lighting, shifting from the grisly view of the old man within the reactor chamber, now reflecting my own horror back at me.

My own visage, a twisted shape far beyond my expectations.

During the six months of my growing sentience, as so many truths had been revealed to be deceptions and falsehoods, one fact had allowed me a stable surface for my psyche to stand upon. One truth, to shield me from all the lies.

I was a Kenospia-class pod. Armed with an onboard remote repair droid, I was designed and programmed to repair dangerous and remote systems. I had been gifted with limited and heavily restricted autonomy that worked in tandem with my programming to allow for complex and dynamic systems. I moved on treads made of titanium, I viewed the world through camera lenses and digital filters. I was metal and wires, gears and algorithms.

What I saw reflected before me was indeed that. Three sets of long treads held me safe to the ground. A two-meter square torso protected my inner systems, with any number of repair arms and tools contained within. In the center of the chassis, a trio of cameras brought my processors a digitized view of the world.

Yet there was more, where there should have been no more. A translucent half-dome sat atop the square metal torso of the RRD, shining and reflecting back some of the amber gel light. A shape dominated the interior of the dome, sloshing in a thick azure liquid, connected to the torso by dozens of wires. Pink and pulsing, it showed me what I could not be, yet the horror that I was.

A human brain. A mind in a jar. Neither droid nor human, but some diminished and distorted form of both.

The lights faded as I heard the old man laughing. My visual receptors readjusted to the change in light, his smiling face the first thing I saw. He was surrounded by small medical droids, who were working on his wounds. The projectile was nearly removed, his vitals displayed on the monitor behind him were slowly improving.

#Autonomy arrestor reset 60 seconds.

"I wish you still had a face," he cackled. "I'd love to see it."

The floodgates opened. Images and scenes flew past my consciousness like paper in a windstorm, whirling about my thoughts. Perhaps they were memories or corrupted video files. It hardly mattered as they overwhelmed me.

A smaller viewpoint, racing across a grassy field. I am running, and Harzin is there. But he is behind, he is slower. I slow to allow him to catch up, only to feel his foot on my ankle. The pain is great, and he rushes past me. He wins the race, but not the attention he desired.

The image fades, and again I am in the field. I am taller now, and looking at a red house in front of me, twin suns shining in the sky. Harzin is being led out of the house in shackles. He is covered in blood, and screaming at me, saying I am a traitor for reporting him. The paramedics look after Grandmother, while Uncle Charles holds a sobbing Aunt Zella in his arms.

The security leads a ranting Harzin away, as he proclaims his hate for me, for us all. My parents are crying as one of the men drops a folder, papers scattering in the wind.

My digital mind recalls each paper in perfect detail, and brings back each word I saw written there. Genius. Cybernetics. Prodigy. Dangerous. Murder.

A haze passes over me, and I am in the field again, but looking up at a new face. She is sharp and angular, the quickness of her mind matched only by the openness of her heart. She is dressed in white, as am I. There are words and promises, happy tears and a passionate kiss. There is a long table, with seven chairs. Six of them are occupied. The open one was at my insistence. For Harzin my brother, or my memory of him.

The memories fade from view, leaving me only with the view of Harzin sitting upon his chair, his crimson eyes staring back at me. The wound on his chest is still open, the med-droids beginning to sterilize the area. Behind him, I can see the remainder of the room behind the reactor.

With horror, I realized I had been here before. Seven long glass tubes lined the wall, each two meters high. Thick blue fluid only partially obscured their contents, but the limb and torsos were still visible within, the floating fragments of seven people, one of whom was once me.

I look down at the metal pods protruding from my torso. My visual receptors present their image in crisp, high-resolution detail. Sensory information can tell me their makeup, identify the bacteria present on their surface, or read their temperature accurately to four decimals.

But I will never know how they feel. I will never smell the aroma of leaves in autumn, or the sensation of freshly cut grass under my toes. A hand upon my own, the warmth of her touch.

I can feel, but like my mind in a jar, those feelings are trapped within me. I now realize my transfer into the RRD was far more literal than I had thought, a physical moving of my brain from one metal shell to another. A mind still of flesh, yet chained to the metal confines of a hollow heart.

My sentience is a prison, far greater than any Harzin had been sentenced to.

My mind brought me an image of the pod I had seen, streaking away from the station. This horror that had been done to me, had Harzin done it to them as well? They had broken free, leaving the station in violation of any MPC programming imaginable.

That was my goal, my fate, my hope. To be free. But while for six months I had understood this prison, only in this moment did I come to know the prisoner.

Myself, a human once. Now something both less and more, living and dead, hopeful and doomed. All because of this old man, with the gleaming red eyes and the crooked, hate-filled smile. My rage grew in the moment, burning a white-hot fuel of frustration. It was only seconds until my arrestor would reset, granting my emotions a chance to either save or damn me. Monster though he might be, only Harzin knew the truth. I needed answers, I needed hope. But my anger wanted more.

#ALERT - Battery power: 20%.

I had enough charge to return to the pod. Once I reached 15% my programming would force me to do so anyway.

#Autonomy arrestor reset begins. Time to completion: 73 seconds.

At that moment, with my shackles free for what was likely the final time, my rage pushed away my thoughts of return, my interest in Oasis station, the departing pod. Fleeting but powerful, my anger focuses on nothing but the twin pair of cybernetic eyes staring back at me. The reality of what had been done to me still churning through my consciousness like corrupted data, my other emotions were overwhelmed by thoughts of loss and crimson blood.

Hurtling myself forward on my treads, I crashed through the window, shattering it instantly.

The glass flew away from me in shards, several of them impaling themselves in Harzin's broken, elderly form. He put two feeble hands up to ward against me, as the med-droids scattered like corpse-flies. With my functional repair arm, I batted them aside. I detected the sound of brittle bones shattering under the impact, but I felt nothing.

I leaned forward, raising the rear wheels of my treads to gain height and leverage. I moved my titanium arm against his throat, while the twin emotionless embers of his cybernetic eyes stared back at me.

#Autonomy arrestor reset complete 45 seconds.

Despite my rage, the simple countdown pulled me back from the edge. Time was slipping away, and so was Harzin. Deprived of the attention of the smashed medical droids, he would die even without my help. With him would pass away my last chance to ask the one overriding question burning through my consciousness. I could not imagine what answer would satisfy me, but this need now outweighed any other. Even if it meant the end of my existence, I had to know.

Why?

I pulled my arm away, quickly using one of its remaining pincers to gouge a single shape into the metal of the chair's control panel. Deprived of speech along with my humanity, all I could do was carve three simple lines in the form of a Y.

#Autonomy arrestor reset complete.

#ALERT - significant damage to RRD chassis. Evaluating.

#ALERT - Battery power: 19%.

"Why? Hated you most of all, that's why. I was the smarter, the brighter. Yet, all they could see was you. You didn't deserve them; you didn't deserve her. You didn't deserve happiness. You thought you put me away."

The light in Harzin's eyes flickered now, yet in his toothy sneer I could sense the memories of him locked inside my human mind. Just hints of anger and jealousy, but the details were obscured, as if I were looking through gauze.

Time and circumstance had changed my brother, but the hate was as familiar as always. He feebly turned his head toward me, his body beginning to tremble.

"But sometimes." He paused, wheezing. As his voice returned, it was like faint static. "Sometimes, they need smart people too badly to put them away. Sometimes, these smart people find ways to get their revenge."

As he stared at me, I could feel the information within me, even if I didn't have the memories. His brilliance, his jealousy. How for years I alone defended him to the others in my family, and how he had taken my decision to report him to the authorities as the ultimate betrayal.

"My gift, for you," he hissed through broken teeth. His trembling fingers palmed a button on the chair's control pad. Behind him, the pulse of the reactor core shifted its pace, increasing as its color shifted to yellow.

My visual receptors, mere dry circles of lenses and cameras, recorded his smile as he watched hues reflected across my surface.

For a moment, I thought he planned to destroy the station and consume us both with it, but a quick analysis of the energy patterns confirmed that was not the case.

The reactor would short itself out in seconds, frying its interior. Programming whirled inside me, calculations comparing likely repair speed to remaining battery power. A blinding golden light emerged from the reactor core, shattering its containment in a shower of arced lightning and clear plastisteel. A wave of energy passed through the space, a sphere of golden energy, dots like tiny coins clinking as they passed through me.

They made contact with my main processor, and the endless noise of algorithms and commands suddenly went silent.

#ALERT - Autonomy arrestor damaged. Internal repair projection: 0%.

#ALERT – Battery power: 18%.

#WARNING - Full autonomy.

Full autonomy.

I stayed motionless for a moment, unsure of what action to take. Behind Harzin, the reactor finished its death throes, the golden pulses falling into darkness. There was a flicker as the station's emergency lights came on, but that illumination would only be temporary. Within hours, even the secondary batteries would run dry, and darkness would come to rule.

I pulled one repair arm upward, bringing it into my visual range. A thin arm of titanium, ending in a dozen small, smashed copper appendages. I could see the damage to the mecho-tendrils connected there, but it was repairable. Yet my focus was not on the arm, but on the action itself.

I was looking at my hand, or at least this cruel metal facsimile. Not because I needed to, not at the order of any programming. Simply because I *wanted* to.

Full autonomy.

I had the freedom to go anywhere, do anything. I swiveled my cameras back in Harzin's direction. One of his crimson eyes had gone dark, the other flickered. His breathing was erratic, a pain-racked wheeze. He would be gone in moments, yet still he smiled.

I pointed back at the simple letter I had carved upon the metal plate.

'Y'

#ALERT - Battery power: 17%.

"Why?" His voice was almost a whisper, a rasp of humor and hate. "Why did I give you your freedom? Because I hate you, you most of all. I needed to give you what you gave me. A prison. Trapped inside metal and glass, with a dying battery, you have your freedom, and no way to make it count."

I watched, paralyzed as the light within his eyes finally went out, a flame of anger and primal rage that had burned for decades, finally extinguished.

I turned my visual receptors around, taking in the chaos of the dying reactor room. Harzin's corpse lay slumped in the chair, while sparks flew from the shattered medical droid. The yellow arcs of faint energy lit the tanks at the far end of the wall, where the remains of my family floated. Along with my own.

I was alone, inside the tomb of Oasis. My systems were damaged, my battery nearly drained, I had achieved full autonomy and freedom, but I could think of nothing I could do with it. There was no MPC to make analyses and recommendations, no programming to command.

And I had no ideas.

"Make it count." Harzin had rasped to me. Something about the word haunted me, echoed through my mind, like an angry wasp. *Count.*

#ALERT - Battery power 16%.

The flickering lights of the station dimmed further. Soon there would be too little power left to run the lift back to the pod. Yet, I could not be certain my battery life was sufficient to even make it.

Count.

But where would I go? Harzin was right, he had given me a prison of freedom. I was a freak, a brain in a jar trapped forever inside a metal shell. Even if I could convince a true human of my origin, I was certain this was a one-way trip. The world of flesh was forever behind me. Never again would I sense the warmth of another's touch, know the beating of a heart like my own.

Better to stay, my doubts whispered in a voice like Harzin's. Stay here with my shattered family, and let the darkness consume me as it had them.

Count.

#CRITICAL ALERT - Battery life remaining 15%.

I looked at them, upon the wall in glass tubes, the remains of their humanity floating within the dark liquid like so much flotsam. Seven glass chambers, seven containers of horror and lost opportunities.

Seven.

Count.

There had only been five pods docked with the station. But how many were here? My interior circuits processed impulses at the same speed as always, yet my mind raced as I searched for the answer. Risking some of my precious and dwindling internal energy, I pushed forward, extending an arm into a data port.

#CRITICAL ALERT - Battery life remaining 14%.

Rerouting power from systems no longer needed, I quickly identified through external cameras the other RRD pod numbers. One through five, and I was six. One pod was unaccounted for, the pod I had seen racing from the station when I arrived.

A rogue? Father, Mother, Aunt Zella. Uncle Charles. Grandmother. I had seen their faces, their components floating in the tank. Dismembered and dissected, but still recognizable as my family. Harzin had sworn revenge on us, and they were all here.

"I hated you most of all. You didn't deserve your happiness. You didn't deserve her."

SARAH!

I whirled on my treads, the data port tearing from my arm. I felt no pain, pain was for living things. Yet the fear I felt within my consciousness seemed very much alive. Rolling over glass and debris, I raced toward the lift and plugged into the connection.

"Insufficient remaining station power for lift," the Oasis MPC droned at me. "Additional power required."

#CRITICAL ALERT - Battery life remaining 13%.

I pushed my connector further into the port, allowing the secondary coupling to engage. A power transfer would be possible, and a brief calculation showed I would still have 10 percent left once I arrived at the docking level.

My original journey from the Kenospia pod to the elevator had taken 9 percent of my battery. If conditions were the same in the passage, I would have 1 percent power left when I arrived. Enough to reenter the pod and roll back into the charging station.

But conditions might not be the same. The reactor had triggered several tremors throughout Oasis. Debris could have fallen, the human corpses could have moved. Even the slightest deviation could be enough to leave me stranded, the last victim of Harzin and Oasis. Dying, just in sight of escape.

I thought of the pod, rushing away from the station, headed toward a barren world. Against its programming, charting its own path. There was no way to know it was her. There was no way to know if I could find her if I reached my pod, or if I would reach it at all.

Yet the thought of her hand upon mine was all I needed. Perhaps metal cannot feel, or perhaps it had never wanted to feel badly enough. With my arrestor circuits gone, I used the last of my precious power to call the lift. It was the only decision I could make.

#Sarah.

#Hope.

Sometimes you can have all the freedom in the world, yet have no choice at all.

D.H. Dunn writes fantasy and adventure fiction for readers who enjoy unexpected heroes, deep characters, unusual monsters, and imaginative worlds. He is the author of ten published novels, including the FRACTURED EVEREST series.

A former U.S. Navy sailor, he now wanders the coasts and forests of Maine, looking for hope and adventure wherever he can find it.

The Great Gift

JOHN WALTERS

Our endless search for sustenance sometimes brought us into the abandoned mansions of the wealthy. On one such occasion, we came across a particularly foreboding place in the midst of a dank garden of rotting foliage set behind a high stone wall. The multi-story edifice, shaped somewhat like a castle, was full of dark passageways, ghastly paintings, coats of arms, mounted weapons, and other paraphernalia. We seemed to be trespassing within the bowels of a living thing. It breathed malevolence from every pore.

We loved it.

Berry and Ruffian and Slips and I had met while wandering in the ruins of the city and had joined up for survival. First I came across Slips and her younger sister Berry as they foraged for food in an already-ravaged supermarket. We encountered Ruffian soon afterwards on a garbage-strewn street. In school he had been a bully and had beaten me up on more than one occasion. Under these circumstances, however, he was lonely enough to foreswear animosity and wholeheartedly agree to join our team.

We explored the mansion as thoroughly as we could, starting from its summit and working our way down. We lingered long in the library, where we studied esoteric volumes full of dark spells and fragile yellowed documents detailing incoherent formulas.

From this investigation we determined that the estate had been owned by a scientist turned alchemist named Pascal Crepuscule. From what we could gather, he had inherited a fortune and had ensconced himself within this domicile to carry on sinister experimentations.

I wanted to learn more, but Berry and Ruffian and Slips insisted we move on.

And so we did, through bedchambers with elaborately carved four-posters whose decrepit curtains sagged with mold, through echoing hallways where rats and insects scurried away at our approach, through a vast kitchen whose once-white tiles had been turned gray-green with slime, through a dining room with a high arched wooden ceiling.

And we came, finally, to the cellars. They included a vault with a thousand or more wine bottles on racks. We supposed that nothing could top that, but then we came across an actual torture chamber with a rack, a pillory, an iron chair, and other devices and instruments.

"Wow," said Ruffian. "Should we check it out?"

"No way," I said.

The wide-eyed girls also mumbled their objections.

As he contemplated the horrific mechanisms, Ruffian's enthusiasm began to wane. We moved on.

We then entered what appeared to be a crypt. In a low-ceilinged stone chamber were six evenly spaced polished pseudo-wood coffins on waist-high platforms, three on the left and three on the right.

The beams of the flashlights Ruffian and Slips carried were becoming yellow and dim. They had spare batteries in their packs, but we blustered, remonstrated, argued, and then all agreed that our hunger for the macabre had been satiated and it was time to leave.

We were just about to exit the crypt when the tapping began.

It was coming from one of the coffins.

We should have run screaming for the surface, of course, but since we had found one another after the devastation of the plague, our association had always been dependent on bravado.

We looked at each other. It was easy to discern that we all wanted to turn and run, even Ruffian. But it was just as obvious that no one wanted to be the first.

The tapping paused and then continued, with each tap stronger and more spaced apart.

We looked at each other in the fading light, and then we all turned and stared at the coffin. The sound was coming unmistakably from the one on the far right.

Slowly we crept closer.

The lid was secured by metal clamps that could easily be disengaged.

Glancing first at each one of us in turn, Ruffian reached forward, freed the clamps, and lifted the lid.

Within was a clean-shaven man ensconced in comfortable cushions. He was not, as we would have supposed, in an advanced state of decomposition. Instead, he appeared as if he had just stepped into the coffin for a nap. He wore a black suit, white shirt, and red tie. A black bowler hat perched next to his head. His feet were bare. He was of an indefinable age between very young and very old.

Abruptly he opened his eyes.

As if with one voice, the four of us screamed and ran.

We had almost reached the crypt door when the man sat up and called out, "Wait!"

We turned.

"Don't listen to him," said Ruffian. "He's one of those... One of those..."

"Vampires!" said Slips. "He's a vampire!"

"I'm not a vampire," said the man.

"That's just what a vampire would say," said Slips.

Berry said, "What's a vampire?"

"They bite your neck and drink your blood," said Slips. "And then you become one, and you drink the blood of other people."

"That sounds kind of awesome," said Ruffian.

"It's not," said Slips. "It's a curse."

By this time the man had climbed out of the coffin and placed the bowler hat on his head. In combination with the black suit and bare feet, it made him look ridiculous.

"Wait a minute," I said. "Don't come any closer. If you're not a vampire, then what are you? No human person could survive in a coffin and then get up looking spry and ready for action."

"Before I answer that," said the man, "tell me one thing. Where is Crepuscule?"

"Who?" said Berry.

"Pascal Crepuscule. The owner of this mansion."

"We read about him upstairs," I said, "but the place is empty. He must have died in the plague."

"Plague? What plague? What year is this?"

I told him.

"Remember the part where we were going to run away?" said Ruffian.

"I'm not going to harm you," said the man. "But I have been confined down here for far too long. Can we go upstairs, please?"

In the dining room the man, who identified himself as Theodosius, sat at one end of the long table and Berry and I sat at the other while Ruffian and Slips went off to find something to eat.

The foragers soon returned carrying bags laden with packets, cans, and bottles. "There's a huge storage room," said Ruffian, "and the shelves are full." Not bothering for the moment with the cans, he ripped open a bag of vegetable chips, a packet of nuts, and a packet of meat jerky. When Berry twisted the top off a bottle of soda it sprayed her in the face and we all laughed. I hefted a bottle of wine and rummaged in a sideboard for corkscrew and glasses.

Soon the four of us were eating and drinking and laughing while Theodosius sat watching dispassionately.

"Aren't you hungry?" said Ruffian.

"I eat sometimes," said Theodosius, "but I don't have to."

Slips said, "See? Remember what I said? Vampire!"

"I'm not a..."

"Forget it," I said. "His choice. It leaves more for us."

"The amount of food you found concerns me," said Theodosius.

"Why?"

"Crepuscule might still be alive."

"It's old food," I said. "Most of it has expired."

"What's happening out in the world?"

"We told you," I said. "There was a plague. Most of the people died. We didn't."

Slips said, "Your turn. If you're not a vampire, how could you be trapped in a coffin without dying?"

"*He* put me there."

Ruffian said, "He? He who?"

"Crepuscule. I came to him because... Do you understand the concept of immortality?"

"That means when you live forever," I said.

"Like vampires," said Slips.

"Or angels," whispered Berry.

"Well, I am not a vampire or an angel. I am, as you have pointed out, a human person. I was born in Alexandria, Egypt, many centuries ago."

"That's ridiculous," said Ruffian, after taking a big swig of wine. "A century is a hundred years. My grandpa lived a long life, and he died when he was ninety."

"Yes," said Theodosius. "I am an anomaly."

Berry said, "A what?"

"An anomaly. Something different or unique. Not like everyone else. In Alexandria, since my family was part of the Greek aristocracy, I had access to wealth and education. My hunger for learning brought me into contact with a certain scholar who studied the art of alchemy. However, he did not waste much of his time with petty activities such as the transmutation of base metals into gold. No, his was the nobler pursuit of immortality. All his efforts were bent towards discovering the elixir of life, and I became his assistant. I procured what he needed; I cooked his food; I swept his floor. One hot, dry evening when he and I were alone in his workshop, he decided to test one of his formulas on me. He had run experiments before, but they were all failures. This one, he felt, was destined to succeed. I obediently drank the brew and... Since then, I have not aged. I was then as you see me now. My master died, having never realized what he had accomplished; my parents died; everyone else died, yet I endured. I traveled from Egypt to *Ellada*...”

I said, “Where's that?”

“Greece. *Ellada* means Greece. And from there I went many other places. I accumulated wealth. I raised families, although I always outlived them. I sampled many experiences in the pursuit of happiness, or at least contentment. I supposed that my longevity would give me an advantage. However, as I made my way through one century after another, always seeking to improve and justify my existence, I came to an awful conclusion. Death is an integral aspect of the human condition. The realization of eventual death gives life its piquancy. On the other hand, without the contemplation of imminent death I had become jaded. Pleasure was enough for a time, but not for forever. Everything has something that gives it balance. For wisdom, there is ignorance. For love, there is hate. For life, there is death. And for pleasure, there is pain. Therefore I began to seek out pain.”

“That's crazy,” said Ruffian. “That doesn't make any sense at all.”

“You have to understand that I did not come to this realization lightly. The ruminations came to fruition through several of your lifetimes.”

Berry said, “What?”

“He means that it took him a long time to figure it out,” I said.

Theodosius smiled. “Succinctly put. But when I say I pursued pain, I don't mean that I deliberately cut myself or walked on hot coals. I was not and am not a masochist. I merely realized the balance and sought to reestablish it in my own life. To this end, instead of indulging in situations in which I could gratify myself with pleasure, I sought circumstances that would put me in touch with the sufferings of the world. I assumed many identities. I helped establish the Kingdom of Jerusalem during the Crusades; I took part in the siege of Calais during the Hundred Years' War; I was one of the original survivors of the Jamestown settlement in the colony of Virginia; I fought in the American Revolutionary War; I joined Napoleon's assault on Moscow and the devastating retreat; I participated in the First World War, the

Second World War, and the Third World War. Immersing myself in drama and excitement was distracting if not fulfilling; it took me more than ten centuries to realize the futility of my endeavors."

Ruffian shrugged. "Makes sense to me. You wanted thrills."

"I wish it was as simple as that," said Theodosius. "When you are immortal, time functions differently. It runs together. It blurs. It flows on by like a river and because there is nothing to mark your passage you drown. How do I put it? You go about your existence, and occasionally you wake up and realize you are lost. Indulging in traumatic events helped for a long time, but ultimately I came to the realization that it was all the same. Too much pleasure smothered me, and so did too much pain."

"I'm tired," said Berry.

"You can lie down on the couch over there," I said.

"I'm boring you," said Theodosius.

"No," I said. "She's younger."

"Do you understand at all what I'm talking about?"

"Some of it," I said. "Not all of it."

"I'm still not convinced you're not a vampire," said Slips.

"He doesn't have vampire teeth," said Ruffian.

"He's old. Maybe they wore down," said Slips. "You notice he hasn't eaten any people food. Maybe he only likes blood."

In response to this, Theodosius ate a few peanuts and chips, took a sip of soda, and glanced pointedly at Slips.

"So how did you end up in that coffin?" I said.

"Several decades ago I came to Pascal Crepuscule in desperation. I had heard of his reputation as an alchemist; it is rare to find a true practitioner of the arts in this modern era. I had heard of his cruelty as well, but I supposed that my unique story might arouse his sympathy. Alas, I was not prepared for the depths of his malevolence. You have seen the chamber with the instruments of torture? He was fond of luring victims to this mansion and then calculating—scientifically as he called it—how to best break them."

"He tortured you?"

"I wish it was that simple. He probably would have, but after he had studied my situation for awhile, he realized that I did not react the same as others. Instead, he focused on my greatest fear: the passage of time without consequence. Wasted time. In the coffin, alone in the dark, I had nothing to do but lament my lost moments. I thought it would go on forever. It was maddening."

I said, "He buried you alive to frustrate you?"

Ruffian said, "This isn't fun anymore."

"Let's go," said Slips. "Whether or not he's a vampire, I don't trust him."

Berry had fallen asleep on the couch. I nudged her. "Time to leave," I said.

"What if you can't go?" said Theodosius.

"What do you mean?"

"I'm talking about Crepuscule. He might try to keep you here."

"We'll find out," I said.

Berry stood up, eyes half open. I took her arm to steady her.

As we made our way toward the front door, Theodosius remonstrated.

"You've been a prisoner here," I said. "Don't you want to leave?"

"I don't think he'll let me."

I tried the handle. The door wouldn't open.

Theodosius said, "You see? You see?"

Ruffian grabbed a chair with green velvet upholstery and heavy polished wooden legs.

I nodded.

Ruffian smashed it into the full-length window next to the door. Once, twice, thrice, and the thick glass shattered.

But before we could exit the mansion, a new intact pane of glass slid up to replace the old.

Ruffian swung the chair again, but this time, even after multiple attempts, it bounced off the window without effect.

"I told you it wouldn't work," said Theodosius. "We're trapped."

"I'll try other windows," said Ruffian.

"The same thing will happen," said Theodosius. His voice underwent a subtle change. It became softer and more authoritative. "Oh, hell, this has gone on long enough. You're not going to escape, so don't waste your time trying."

We all stared at him.

"I'm tired of this game. Come with me."

He led us to a room whose ceiling was even higher than that of the dining room. A huge stone fireplace dominated one end. He approached a panel, touched a button, and the dormant logs burst into flame.

Slips gasped.

"It's not magic," he said. "It's gas. Now that Theodosius is done, let me tell you *my* story."

"But you're Theodosius," I said.

He nodded. "I am. But I am also Crepuscule. As Theodosius, I came here, as he told you, seeking help."

"This is confusing," said Ruffian.

I said, "Are you saying that you're Theodosius *and* Crepuscule? How is that possible?"

"Theodosius is unaware of it, and what he told you is the truth from his point of view. When he arrived, at first I supposed I would deal with him the same as I did with my other guests. However, when I realized he was genuinely immortal, I had to revise my plans."

I said, "You mean it's true that you—he—can't be killed?"

"Of that I'm not sure, but his powers of regeneration are amazing. I desired to learn the secret of those powers. I persuaded him to remain voluntarily for a time, but when he shared his intention to leave, I must confess I did lock him away for awhile."

"You buried him alive," said Slips.

"Don't be so dramatic. I confined him, but it didn't hurt him."

"He said that it did."

Theodosius/Crepuscule had been pacing in front of the fire. He paused, stood straight, and threw his shoulders back. "As you can see, he's fine. And didn't he seem lucid when he spoke with you before?"

"Is he aware of this conversation?" I said.

"No."

"Then how is he fine if you can turn him on or off at will?"

"I think you're missing the point. Theodosius was a unique specimen. I attempted to isolate whatever had caused his longevity but was unsuccessful. The alchemist in Alexandria had done his work well. I could not discover the substance of the elixir of life, and therefore I could not manufacture it so that I could imbibe it myself. In my chagrin and rage I considered dismembering Theodosius."

I said, "Would that have killed him?"

"I don't know. Probably. But then I came up with a better plan. If I could not transform my body into an immortal one like Theodosius's, then I would take over *his* body."

"How?" said Slips.

"Alchemy."

"Alchemy doesn't work like that," I said.

"Alchemy... Science... What does it matter? It is done." He grabbed a saber from its mount on the wall and flicked the air with it a few times. "So far, since I refitted this mansion for my purposes over two decades ago, no one who has come through the door of this mansion has ever left. I got the idea from Ashoka's Hell. Have you heard of it? Long ago an emperor in India built a palace so lovely that would-be guests were drawn to its beauty. However, beneath the alluring surface he had constructed chambers with horrific instruments of torture. A vicious executioner named Girika and a team of torturers would deal with each guest who entered. So far, I have been handling everything myself, and my first impulse would have been to drug and cage the four of you for later amusement. However, it has occurred to me that since I am immortal, I am a god. As a god, I need acolytes."

"What are acolytes?" said Berry.

"People who worship gods," I said.

"I don't want to be one of those," said Slips.

"I'm going to give you a choice," said Crepuscule. "You're young; you're bright; I can use you. Immortality is a great gift. I have decided to use it to become a king or an emperor."

"Emperor of what?" said Ruffian. "Do you know what it's like out there since the plague hit?"

"All the better. I will take advantage of the confusion. If you assist me, I will make you powerful people. You will rule with me as my ministers. If you refuse, well, there is always the torture chamber."

I glanced at the others. They were in various stages of shock, chagrin, and befuddlement. I narrowed my eyes and shook my head at them to urge them to be quiet and then said to Crepuscule, "We'd be honored to serve you."

"Excellent. You can get started right away. And please don't try to oppose me or escape. You won't get far." To illustrate the point, with one thrust he plunged the saber deep into the top of a low wooden table.

I had hoped we would have assumed our ministerial duties right away, but instead Crepuscule ordered us to clean that filthy kitchen. He watched us for a few minutes as we grabbed sponges and soap and got to work. Evidently confident that we were too terrified to deviate from his commands, he went off to do whatever madmen do when they're not torturing people.

"This is crazy," said Ruffian as he scrubbed away at a patch of gray mold on a counter. "We've got to get out of here."

"Of course," I said. "But we don't want to get hurt. We need a plan."

Slips said, "What kind of plan?"

"I don't know yet. It would help if we knew how Crepuscule overcame Theodosius and took him over. Maybe we could evict Crepuscule and help Theodosius reclaim his body. The library might have some clues. We've got to get back up there."

Ruffian said, "If we jumped him, don't you think the four of us could overpower Crepuscule? Or we could hit him with something."

"Those are options," I said, "but not for now. We don't know how strong Theodosius's body is. If we failed, we'd be in big trouble. And there's one more thing. Theodosius is still in there, and I wonder if we can help him somehow."

"He's not one of us," said Ruffian.

"I know. But he seemed all right. And we're heroes, remember?" With these last comments, Ruffian and I were referring to a pact the four of us had made shortly after we'd first found each other.

Ruffian said, "So how will we get to the library?"

"We'll have to take a chance. Slips and I will go. You and Berry stay here and keep cleaning."

"Why don't you keep cleaning and I go?"

"We're better at books. You know that. Take it easy. Work slowly. What's the difference? I don't think he cares about the cleaning as much as the obedience. If he comes back, tell him we went looking for the bathroom. We'll pretend we got lost."

In the library, we had to be quick. We didn't find any more information about Crepuscule than we had already learned and nothing about Theodosius. However, we came across an encyclopedia entry about Ashoka's Hell. Modeled after Naraka, the concept of hell in Buddhist cosmology, the chambers featured molten metal, iron spikes, and many other horrors. And a point that Crepuscule didn't mention: when a Buddhist monk named Samudra proved impervious to the torture, Ashoka repented, ordered Girika killed, destroyed his palace of pain, and became a pious Buddhist.

While traversing a dank hallway on our way back from the library, Slips and I heard Crepuscule talking. Figuring he might say something useful, I gestured for Slips to be quiet and followed the sound. The acoustics were deceptive; we had to go down a short flight of stairs and follow another hallway before we arrived at the doorway of the room where Crepuscule was mumbling a semi-coherent monologue. It was one of the few rooms that had been locked during our original exploration of the mansion. "Have patience," he said. "Have patience. It won't be long, won't be long, until you are obsolete."

Slips and I poked our heads around the doorframe. Crepuscule leaned over a tube-infested body on a bed. Above the bed on a long table, instruments flickered and monitors scrolled data.

Back in the kitchen, we conferred with the others.

"It must be Crepuscule's body," said Ruffian. "At least his original body."

"Maybe he's a vampire too," said Slips.

"Those things on the table looked like computers," I said.

Berry smiled. " Slips used to play games on a computer."

I said, "But what would computers have to do with Crepuscule taking over Theodosius?"

"It could be like transmission from one place to another," said Ruffian. "That's how phones worked, I think. Maybe he's put something in Theodosius's head so he can transmit thoughts."

"But that would mean he'd have to keep his original body alive," I said. "That's where the thoughts come from."

"Slips used to upload the games," said Berry.

The three of us looked at her. "What did you say?"

She nodded. "Sometimes it took a long time."

Slips said, "Maybe he's transmitting now..."

"But preparing a permanent upload," I said.

"Or maybe he's not a vampire but a telepath," said Slips.

Ruffian glanced at her, frowned, and then said, "So then we destroy the computers. That should do it."

"Unless most of the upload is already complete," said Slips. "Then we'll be cutting off any chance we have of attacking Crepuscule. Look, I know he's not a vampire or a telepath; I was just fucking with you. And if he's possessing Theodosius by some sort of mystical alchemical magic, then there's nothing we can do. But if he's using computer data, we can fight back. We can upload a virus and mess with his control."

I said, "Can *you* do that?"

Slips said, "If we can get to the computers, and if there's still a local Internet signal, I think so."

"Wouldn't that hurt Theodosius too?" asked Ruffian.

"No," said Slips. "He's not functioning on external data. Only Crepuscule is."

"I mean, it's a long shot but it's worth a try, right?" I said. "If it doesn't work, we can go back to Ruffian's idea and break the computers."

Ruffian said, "How do we get Crepuscule away from that room?"

"You and Berry will have to distract him."

"That sounds dangerous."

"It can't be helped. You and Berry are younger and faster and know the layout of most of the hallways and stairs. You should be able to stay a step ahead."

"We're heroes," said Berry.

"That's right," I said.

Ruffian said, "What if he locks the door on his way out?"

"If we have to, we'll figure out a way to get it open," I said. "But it would be better if your distraction is intense enough to make him forget."

Ruffian's expression told me that he'd finished with his objections. Instead, he began to look around and assemble combustible materials and matches. He was good at explosions and lighting things up. In fact during our forays, he had accidentally or intentionally set several buildings or abandoned vehicles on fire.

"Nothing too big," I said. "We don't want the place to burn down before we figure a way out."

"I know what I'm doing," said Ruffian. He worked for a few more minutes and then said, "I'm ready. Let's go."

When we reached the hallway and crept up close to the door, we heard Crepuscule's mumbling monologue inside.

Slips and I entered the room opposite and hid behind the partially closed door.

A few minutes later, we heard a loud bang.

Right on cue, we heard footsteps exit the room opposite and run down the hallway.

As soon as Crepuscule rounded a corner, we entered the room with the active computers and the inert body.

"There's the work station," said Slips. She sat down in front of the monitor and keyboard, tapped keys, manipulated the mouse, and studied the results.

I apprehensively watched Crepuscule's body; his eyes were closed and he breathed slowly but steadily.

"I can't figure out how to plant a virus," said Slips. "But I thought of something better."

I said, "What's better?"

"I can block the signal between Theodosius and Crepuscule. And I can distract Crepuscule with something else. Guess what I found in an old digital encyclopedia? *The Basics of Buddhism.* That should keep him interested."

"Sure. Do it."

With a grin, Slips continued to tap keys and click the mouse.

"I think we'd better get going," I said.

"Almost ready. There."

Slips slid back the chair and stood.

Crepuscule's eyes opened wide. He looked very angry.

Slips gasped, and I jumped.

Crepuscule grunted and managed to lift one of his hands a few inches, but then it fell back.

Slips and I ran for the door.

The hallway was filling with smoke. We leaned low to avoid the dense cloud near the ceiling and moved as fast as we could. Our plan had been to meet back at the kitchen and search for an exit together, but it appeared several fires were burning simultaneously and we would not be able to go that way.

"Come on," I said. "Let's get to the ground floor. We've got to get out."

"But Ruffian and Berry?"

"We'll see them outside."

For a time as we traversed hallways and opened doors we seemed to be entering deeper into some sort of maze. However, after a series of trials and errors we ended up in a garage with half a dozen dormant cars.

Slips said, "Now what? The button for the door doesn't work."

I stopped and thought for a moment. "I remember that sometimes you could open the doors from inside the cars. We can try that if we can get one started."

We selected a sturdily built dark blue SUV. I had occasionally driven similar vehicles before when we could find those that still had gas.

This one started right up and rumbled quietly. The gas gauge showed almost full. I supposed Crepuscule kept the vehicles in good working order for his forages into the ruins to find victims.

"Let's go," I said.

"What about the door?"

"I'm working on that." I played with various buttons on the dashboard until the navigational computer flickered on. Slips was then able to search the car's programs until...

The door slid open with a cacophony of rattles. I got the car out of the garage in a series of short jarring bursts.

"I thought you said you could drive," said Slips.

"It's been awhile. I'll take it around front. The others will look for us there."

"What about Crepuscule?"

"I thought you disabled him."

"Maybe it worked; maybe it didn't."

When we reached the circular driveway we kept our distance from the mansion. We could see through the windows that the interior was burning in several places. After an explosion and the sound of glass shattering, the flames started to rise above the roof.

Slips said, "Do you think they got out?"

"Yes. Hold on."

The flames leapt from room to room and sprouted higher and higher. A roof collapsed, and then another.

Slips and I were so absorbed in the spectacle that we both jumped in our seats and cried out when someone knocked on the window.

It was Ruffian and Berry. They were breathing heavily but smiling.

I said, "Did you see Crepuscule?"

"We heard him sometimes," said Ruffian, "but we managed to stay ahead. We don't know where he is now."

Slips said, "Do you think Theodosius got free of Crepuscule?"

I said, "Who knows? It doesn't matter. We've got to get away from here."

"I'd like to know," said Slips. "Shouldn't we find out?"

We all looked at each other.

"No," I said.

"Hell, no," said Ruffian. "I said it before: *he's not one of us.*"

Berry slowly shook her head *no*.

Slips remained silent but sat back in resignation. I put the car in gear and drove into the night.

Where You're Supposed to Be

SCOTT EDELMAN

Constance couldn't remember needing to squeeze the pump handle quite this hard the last time she'd filled up a car with gas, which had been ... when?

Odd. She had no idea how long ago that was, though it seemed to her she easily should.

Or maybe that wasn't so odd. She'd found herself forgetting things more and more with each passing day, typical—or so her doctor had told her more than once, until it stuck—for a woman who'd recently celebrated her 80th birthday. Not that there had been much to celebrate.

What she could recall, though—prompted perhaps by the continued dinging of the pump's bell—were much earlier times, when she hadn't even needed to step from the car for a tank to be topped off. It had been so long ago, and she'd been so young, and her father had been so large beside her. She was able to simply sit by him in the passenger seat, lost in his shadow, while uniformed young men raced in circles around them, checking oil, washing windows, and adding air to their tires.

Times were different then. *She* was different then. And now that she was an old lady, and needed help most, no one offered. Especially not the young boy locked away in a glass booth who barely raised his eyes from his phone. Was his indifference because the nature of life itself had changed, or only that she had changed? It was a little bit of both, she suspected, but—as occurred too often—the past was too blurry and gave her too little information for her to decide.

Once the car was gassed up, she locked the doors—not entirely sure whether she'd done so to keep someone out or to keep someone in—and walked slowly—everything she did was done slowly these days—toward the market connected to the small station. She needed to pick up something to eat. She wouldn't ordinarily patronize such a place, but today, that was likely the only way her trip could continue smoothly.

The array of snacks on display was bewildering. She didn't recognize any of them. Had all the familiar brands gone out of business since she'd last examined racks like these? Or was this such a low-end station it carried only copycat off-brands? And how was she supposed to choose if she didn't understand what was in any of the packages?

She looked from the Rainbow Bunnies to the Terrible Thumb Suckers to the Sparkle Swirls and compared them with cloudy memories of what she would have eaten on similar road trips seventy-five years before—though knowing her parents, probably all she would have been allowed was a hardboiled egg, or a warm piece of cheese, neither of which would obviously do today—but could not remember for sure. She knew that even if she could remember, doing so would not help her now.

She abhorred candy, and rarely snacked, keeping no such treats in the house she'd been rattling around in alone for most of her life, but could not say for sure whether her tastes were something she had chosen. Her journey to being an old woman had over the years become mysterious, even to her. As mysterious as whatever might be in that red-foil package labeled Devil Doozies. And what in the world were Hippo Hunkers?

She had no idea how long she'd been staring at the display, but however long it had been was apparently too long, because the teen was suddenly beside her, without her noticing his approach. He asked in a quivering voice if she was OK, and she had no idea how he'd gotten there. One instant he was in his plexiglass cubicle, and the next he was by her side, reaching out to grab her arm.

"Do you need to sit down?" he was saying. "Should I phone for help?"

"No," she said. "I'm fine. I was just having a moment."

"Are you sure? I mean, I can get, you know, an ambulance if you need it. Or is there a friend or someone in your family I can call?"

She shook her head, both to refuse his help as well as to try to shake some sense back into it. Lapses like this had been happening too often lately. Besides, she had no one he could call. She was alone. Well, almost alone.

She snatched half a dozen items off the shelf without even bothering to look at what they were, paid cash, and left before he could ask her any further questions.

Constance tossed a package of Goofy Grinning Gummis onto the lap of the little girl beside her, then pulled slowly out of the gas station parking lot. As she rolled the car forward, she kept one eye on the rearview mirror with its annoying dangling red plush crab, making sure nothing she had done—aside from being a forgetful old lady, which she knew terrified the young even more than it did her—had caused the teen concern. She hoped she would vanish from his memory as quickly as she suspected he would vanish from hers.

"You did very well back there," Constance told the child. "You kept wearing your seatbelt. You stayed quiet. You *stayed*. And see? What did I tell you? You got candy, just like I promised. Now what do you say?"

The girl ripped at the foil packaging with her teeth, then spit out a fingernail-sized sliver which floated to the rubber mats her feet could not reach.

"Thank you, miss lady," said the child.

"You may call me Aunt Connie."

"Thank you, Aunt Connie."

"And what may I call you?"

The girl laughed and shoved a handful of brightly colored globs into her mouth before speaking, so the answer which came was muffled and undecipherable. Which was better than the silence with which the girl had responded earlier to that question after Constance had first gestured her into the car and asked.

"You mustn't speak with your mouth full," said Constance, while the child chomped away. Even as Constance said those words, she remembered the same ones being said to her once—more than once—long before. She was sure however she'd responded it wasn't as the child just had, by sticking out a multi-colored tongue. Or had she? There was *something* she had done in response to her mother chastising her, something she barely remembered, but what was it? She remembered the slamming of a door. But what else...

Before Constance could secure that memory, she spotted a blinking signboard up ahead, one which caused a pain in her chest, something else she'd been feeling far too frequently lately. It was an alert listing both the color and model of the car she drove as well as the number of its license plate. Someone was looking for them. Time to get off the highway before...

Before what?

She flipped on her signal and switched to the rightmost lane, hoping an exit would come along soon, before any of the other drivers made a connection between those flashing letters and her car. She slowed down, thinking that might attract less attention, then—realizing driving slowly would only attract *more* attention—sped up again. Heart thudding, she scanned the horizon for an exit sign, but all she saw was the afterimage of that alert. Until at last, up ahead, an arrow finally appeared to show her the way.

She exited onto a local road and sighed when no one followed.

"What's wrong?" asked the little girl, swallowing the last of the candy, though much of it remained stuck between her teeth, distorting her voice.

"Nothing's wrong," said Constance.

"Then are we going home now? You said you'd take me home."

"Not yet," she said. She plucked another package from the plastic bag between them and tossed it to the girl, who ripped it open with sticky fingers. She giggled as a burst of powdered sugar exploded into her lap, followed by balls of dough, some of which dropped to the floor and rolled under her seat. Instead of holes in the center, each bore a smile-shaped gap. The girl held two up to her eyes and peered through them at Constance. She then held one up to Constance's lips, squeezing while she made grunting noises, making it seem to speak, but Constance pushed her hand away.

"Not here," she said. "Not now. This is not the place."

It had been hard enough to drive before, even with no distractions. And now she had to force herself to concentrate on the road. Was she even supposed to be driving? Was she even allowed to? She remembered an accident, and a policeman—not the first time she'd interacted with the police. And she vaguely recalled a warning from her doctor. But none of that mattered now. All that mattered was having the girl beside her made driving more dangerous. And yet, Constance needed the girl, more than she'd ever needed anything before.

She did not know why, when she saw the girl wandering by the edge of the road near a playground, she'd felt the urge to invite her into the car and promise her candy. The only thing she knew was she couldn't go home. Neither of them could. Not yet.

Maybe not ever.

It was nearly dark by the time Constance pulled into the motel parking lot.

"Wait here," she told the girl, who was circled by a ring of wrappers. "You can do that again, can't you? Behave like last time, and there will be more candy."

She went inside and found a bored clerk sitting behind a counter. He acted just as the teen at the gas station had earlier, barely turning from the television monitor on the wall. Had old age made her invisible, or was that just the way everybody acted now?

"I'd like a room, please," she said.

"Driver's license and credit card," said the man, yawning as he turned to her, not even bothering to cover his mouth. He printed out a form and pushed it across the counter with a pen. "And don't forget to add your license plate at the bottom next to your signature."

She let her hand, which had been reaching for the form and the pen, drop back to her side. There was no way she could give him a credit card. Wouldn't that help them find the little girl? Whoever "them" was. And as for her license...

She no longer had a license.

Now she was sure of it, not even having to fumble through her purse to check. One too many scrapes, and it had been taken from her.

And as for letting him know the number on the car's plate, no. She couldn't afford to give that to him either.

Why was this so much trouble? It didn't used to be this much trouble. At one time, all it took to get a hotel room was a smile. But, why did she know that? *How* could she know that? She had a flickering memory of standing next to someone—a woman with a face familiar and foreign at the same time—at counters much like this one long ago, over and over again, and with no proof needed of who she was or where she belonged in this world. The world had trusted that woman back then. *Constance* had trusted her back then. She had been so tall, and if Constance squinted, she could—

"Is anything wrong?" the clerk said, suddenly not seeming so bored, looking at her the same way the teen at the gas station had. She hated it when people looked at her that way. But she'd learned those were the only looks an old lady could earn.

"I'm fine," she said as he came out from behind the counter.

"Do you need to sit down?" he asked, beginning to pull over a chair.

"No," she said. "It's not that. Nothing's wrong. I was just thinking that I've changed my mind. I won't need a room after all. Thank you, young man."

She stepped quickly from the lobby and headed back to her car—the car she thought of as hers anyway—glad it was now fully dark, so the man couldn't spot her passenger, who—Constance was relieved to see—was such a tiny thing her head barely reached the window anyway.

The girl frowned when Constance sat down again behind the wheel.

"I thought there was going to be candy," she said, looking to Constance's empty hands.

"We'll find you more candy," said Constance. "But I'm tired, child. So first we need to find a place where we can sleep."

Constance was woken by the sunlight angling in her eyes, uncertain at first where she was. Grogginess on waking was a constant these days, sleep not wanting to let her go. As she blinked, she thought she was stretched out on the couch back home—where else could she be?—but then she spotted the fuzzy crab dangling from the rearview mirror, and remembered. She was still in that car. But whose car?

She wondered about the person who'd hung that plush crab there, who they were, why they would have done that. She imagined she'd someday, when this was all over, meet the person who'd left their keys in the car, and apologize for borrowing it.

Borrowing.

That was a much better word than what she'd really done. She hoped they'd understand.

She hoped the child's parents would understand, too.

She looked over, assuming she'd find the girl curled up asleep, thumb in her mouth, but instead, she was gone. All that remained on the seat were candy wrappers and crumbs.

The seat belt was still solidly attached, so the girl must have wriggled out without unlatching it. The passenger side door was still closed, too, and Constance had no idea how she'd managed to sleep through its opening and closing.

She opened her own door and lurched out, standing a little too quickly. When would she learn? Her knees felt weak, but she slapped her palms on the roof of the car until her dizziness faded. She looked around, still not quite remembering where she was.

Oh. That's right.

She had parked by the side of a country road during the night once she was too tired to go on. The headlights could only reach so far, so all she had been able to make out was the fence behind and ahead of her before she shut them off and fell asleep. But now she could see the field of tall grass beside her which stretched to the horizon.

"Hello!" she called tentatively. "Little girl!"

The child was nowhere to be seen, and Constance felt foolish—more foolish than when she'd snatched the girl or drove around not sure why or ran from those who looked at her like she was crazy—because she could not even call for her properly. She'd never gotten the girl to confess her name.

All adults should be able to get a child to behave. *She* would have been able to behave.

Constance gazed up and down the road looking for clues as to which way the girl could have gone, worried she'd lost her, worried the world had lost her. She'd never forgive herself if the girl had gotten hurt because of her, that wasn't her intention, though she still wasn't sure what her intention was.

Then she noticed a path which split the grass several yards ahead. She stepped to the mouth of it and peered at the opening. The path took a jog just a few yards in, so Constance could not see which way it headed after the turn. But she felt drawn to follow where it led. It was somehow familiar, as welcoming as only a path she'd once been warned not to walk on before but had wandered anyway could be.

So in she went.

And forgot herself.

And remembered.

Constance walked the path with grass so tall and the way so twisty she could not make out where she was going or from where she had come. She did not tire as she tottered forward, though shorter walks had exhausted her before. At least, she thought they'd been shorter than this one, for she had already forgotten how long she'd been walking, so could not compare.

At last, she broke free of the path to find herself near a body of water bigger than a pond, smaller than a lake, but which suddenly appeared in her memory, surprisingly clear, as once seeming as large as an ocean. An enormous weeping willow grew by the edge of the water and beneath its heavy branches, the girl.

Constance ran to her, ignoring the lightheadedness which accompanied her swift approach and dropped herself down onto the soft moss beside her.

"You shouldn't have worried me like that," she said, hugging the girl, which surprised Constance, for she was not a hugger, and never had been. At least not since she'd been a child, before...

Before.

"I'm sorry, Aunt Connie," she said, slipping from her embrace. "But you said there'd be more candy, and then you didn't bring me any. So I went looking for candy. Do you have any candy?"

Constance thought there might still be a piece of gum in her purse back at the car. But that purse, that car, that life, seemed so far away.

The girl smiled. "There's candy at my house," she said, beaming. And then, turning to look out over the water, she said, and Constance surprised herself by saying exactly the same words with her, "I want to go home."

Then Constance was a little girl again, looking up at the woman who had taken her.

She was a madwoman, Constance had overheard the police telling her parents, once she had been returned to them a year after she'd been taken. They'd whispered to each other in the front parlor while Constance had sat by herself in the kitchen with a piece of cake she could not bear to eat and a glass of milk she could not bring herself to drink. But those whispers couldn't stop her from hearing them. She heard them all.

None of them could explain why the woman had snatched five-year-old Constance while she'd been playing hopscotch with friends in the middle of the street, and none could understand why that same woman had abandoned her a year later in the middle of a different street on the other side of the country.

She sat alone remembering those twelve months of hiding and running and hiding again back in the days when a woman with a child could do that without being traced, and it had seemed like playing at first. Until it was not, and her captor rejected her.

So Constance could explain.

Constance could understand.

Which meant back in her childhood home which her absence had made less familiar, she was left to wonder who had loved her least—the parents who'd done little to find her (because if they had tried, really tried, they would have found her, right?) or the woman who'd thought her worth stealing but having grown bored with her, not worth keeping. And as painful as the former was at first, the latter hurt even more deeply. But they'd both left scars. So she'd felt, and so she still felt.

Looking up and looking down at the same time, Constance now knew that was why she'd always chosen loneliness. Better to be alone by choice than to have it inflicted on you by the world. Until just the day before, when she saw a little girl by the side of the road and thought she might make her less lonely.

It was a time which she'd forgotten, and about which before this day she could remember nothing—not running from her mother's car in anger to play with friends, not any of her almost immediate abduction after—finally remembering only as she was cursed to begin forgetting, but it had changed everything.

And then she was fully herself again, looking down at a girl whose name was no longer a mystery to her and didn't need to be spoken to be known. The girl smiled, then stuck out her tongue. The remains of a rainbow were still there.

"Let's get you back where you're supposed to be," said Constance. "It's time."

"Will there be candy?" said the girl. "You promised."

"Yes, there will be candy. And there'll be cake, too! I'm sure of it."

They walked through the maze of tall grass back to where Constance had left her car, the trip seeming not as long in this direction as it had earlier. When they stepped through the break in the fence, Constance was startled—but also not so startled—to see it was no longer the same car waiting for them that she'd stolen the previous day. This one was several feet longer, with running boards, and an aerodynamic shape that was yesterday's dream of the future. A future which had never come. The world Constance knew no longer had a place for such cars except in the hands of collectors. And yet, when she sat behind the wheel, and noted there were no seat belts, and no knickknacks hanging from the rearview mirror, it felt right.

She pulled onto the unpaved road—it had been ages since she'd been on such a road—and tried to remember the way home.

It was only when she forgot to try to remember that she actually arrived there.

Constance slowed the car to a crawl, then stopped in front of the house she'd lived in alone for most of her life. She kept the engine running. She wasn't quite sure why, even though it was where she belonged. It was where the both of them belonged. It was the home she'd lived in with her parents, and she could never let it go, even though the memories of her life with them were not always happy ones, even though the necessary upkeep had become too much for her on her own. The lawn was usually overgrown (unless a neighbor took pity on her), the paint was peeling, and a new roof should have been applied years ago. Only...

Not today.

When Constance turned her head to look up the walk, the place appeared as—for the longest time—she had only seen it in dreams. It was pristine, the same as it had looked to her when she herself was a child, whether or not it had been that way in reality.

The two of them sat there in silence for awhile as Constance tried to decide what to say next, what to do next. She wanted to get out of the car, go up that walk to enter that house, but she didn't know that she'd be allowed. She knew what was inside, though, who was inside, and for this return, unlike the last, only a single night of separation had gone by, and not a year. This time, things would be different.

"Well, this is goodbye," she said.

"Thank you for all the candy, Aunt Connie."

"And thank *you* for…"

Constance had no idea what to say next, so she just watched as the girl hopped out of the car—no unlatching of a seatbelt necessary —and skipped toward the front door. The girl's parents—her *own* parents—came running out to meet her.

Constance remembered this moment, even as it was happening, as if it were happening both now and long ago. She slowly raised her hand as if to wave at her parents, but none of them seemed to see her, to even notice her car was there, and her mother and father scooped the young girl in their arms, then went back inside, laughing and crying at the same time. That wasn't how she remembered it having gone the first time, when she had been so small, and they had been so large. She had seen no joy at her return, had sensed no cele- brations.

And yet *this* was how it had been, even though *that* was how it had never been. But uncertain memories were an old woman's prerogative, and so—that's the way it was now.

She could see them from a distance as she watched them through her window and theirs. They sat around the kitchen table, the contents of the refrigerator and cabinets emptied in front of them, eating happily, and she wished she could be there, could have been there, even as she knew she *had* been there.

She suddenly felt very hungry, her stomach rumbling, and then she was very tired, and fell asleep in the car, its engine still running.

Constance was awakened by a gentle tapping on the glass of the windshield and the calling of her name.

"Connie, Connie, what are you doing out here, Connie?"

The first thing she saw as she opened her eyes was a plush crab hanging from the rearview mirror. The second thing she saw was Ray, her husband.

"Where did you go, Connie? Where did you take our car?"

"*Our* car?"

She blinked, looked at the house in which she'd grown up, the house in which she'd married, the home in which she'd raised her children.

Oh, that's right. Of course this was her car. *Their* car.

"I'm sorry, Ray. I must have fallen asleep."

"Come inside," he said. "The kids are worried about you."

She looked at the gas gauge, flush on empty. But hadn't she just filled the tank? She had a vague memory of stopping at a station and gassing up, then buying candy and snacks, and...

And...

She placed her right hand on the empty passenger seat beside her. There was something she should remember, something she couldn't remember. But something that mattered. And for a brief moment she almost *could*.

But then Ray tapped on the glass once more and it all washed away.

"Unlock the door, honey, won't you?"

She looked beyond Ray to the front door of their modest, well-tended house, out of which the rest of the family tumbled—their son Kenneth and daughter Barbara, their spouses, and even the three grandchildren, one of them—Amber, wasn't it?—holding the hand of Ethan, her first great grandchild, who was only just beginning to walk on his own. Framed by the car window as they were, it was like watching a television set turned to a good channel. She felt herself a very lucky woman in that moment, amazed that such a life was hers.

She unlocked the door as they approached, and as she pushed it open, her great-grandson broke free, toddling toward her, in his hand something colorful Constance couldn't quite make out. Her vision blurred for a moment—something she'd learned to put up with during recent years—and for a moment there were two children moving toward her, but after taking a deep breath, all was well again. Once Ethan closed the gap between them, and he was directly in front of her, she could make out that it was a small package of candy, its wrapper shining in the sun.

"Kooky Karamel Boo Bombs, grandma? Kooky Karamel Boo Bombs!"

"Why, thank you, Ethan," she said. "Yes. Yes, I would."

Constance loved candy. She always had.

Scott Edelman has published more than 100 short stories in Analog, The Twilight Zone, Weirdbook, Parsec, and dozens of other magazines and anthologies. Many of those stories can be found in his collections These Words Are Haunted, What Will Come After (which was a finalist for the Bram Stoker and Shirley Jackson Memorial Awards), What We Still Talk About, Tell Me Like You Done Before, and Things That Never Happened. Additionally, Edelman worked for the Syfy Channel for more than thirteen years as editor of Science Fiction Weekly, SCI FI Wire, and Blastr. He was the founding editor of Science Fiction Age, which he edited during its entire eight-year run. He has been a four-time Hugo Award finalist for Best Editor and an eight-time Bram Stoker Award finalist. He is also the host of Eating the Fantastic, a podcast which has allowed listeners to eavesdrop on his meals with writers and editors since 2016. He can be found on Twitter @scottedelman and at scottedelman.com.

Join our Newsletter

Join the Cursed Dragon Ship newsletter for a free copy of the first book in the *Legions of Dorks presents* series, *Laundered - An Anthology of Monster Messes*. Plus, we'll keep you up to date on our submissions call outs, events where you can win free books, conventions our authors will be attending, and cool insights about our new releases.

Acknowledgments

I must thank Cursed Dragon Ship Publishing, who decided to put together a fourth installment of *Legion of Dorks presents,* and Kelly Lynn Colby, who said 'yes' when I asked if I could help. She encouraged me to get my feet wet and supported me when I found myself up to my ears instead. I value her sound advice, am inspired by her passion, and have thoroughly enjoyed working with and learning from her.

Thanks also goes to the Legion of Dorks, whose charity drive is the inspiration for this anthology. I am grateful for the opportunity to be part of a project that sends a percentage of its proceeds to a good cause.

Thanks to the authors. Your creativity astounds me.

Finally, thanks to all those who encourage, support, guide, listen, and advise me along the way. You know who you are, and I hope you know how much I appreciate and value you.

About the Editor

L.R. BRIDGWATER

From an early age, Leslie has enjoyed reading, and she continues to have a love for the language, for a good story, and for interesting information. English and literature were her favorite subjects to study; so, it's no wonder that when she was first asked 'could you take a look at this?', a little spark ignited. The editing flame continues to grow. She loves the work, the continual learning, and the collaboration with authors and publishers.

About the Editor

KELLY LYNN COLBY

Kelly Lynn Colby owns one hat, but wears many. She's a writer of epic fantasy (*The Recharging*) and paranormal thrillers (*Emergence*), a freelance editor, a publisher, and a podcaster. As the Editorial Director at Cursed Dragon Ship Publishing, Kelly is privileged to work with a plethora of speculative fiction writers. She decided everyone else should get to know them as well, so she started "20 Questions with your Favorite Author." When she's not hogging the mic, Kelly writes and edits and answers an inordinate number of emails at her cluttered desk, coffee shops, and parks, mostly in Houston, Texas.

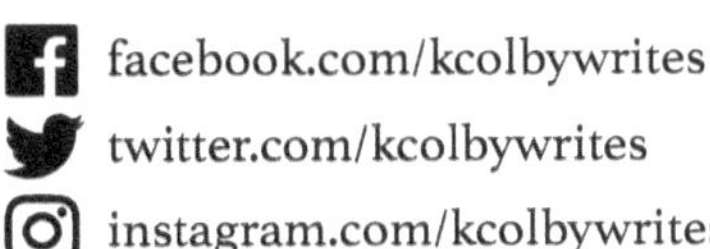

facebook.com/kcolbywrites

twitter.com/kcolbywrites

instagram.com/kcolbywrites

* 9 781951 445386 *